D0065579

O4#3

THE BARONESS
OF BOW STREET

By the same author

DULCIE BLIGH

THE
BARONESS
OF BOW STREET

By
Gail Clark

G. P. Putnam's Sons, New York

Library of Congress Cataloging in Publication Data

Clark, Gail.
The baroness of Bow Street.

I. Title.
PZ4.C5926Bar 1979   [PR6053.L298]   823'.9'14
ISBN 0-399-12334-2   78-22609

THE BARONESS
OF BOW STREET

Prologue

Night had fallen upon London. A hackney coach clattered over the damp cobblestones, its lights dim in the thick, wet fog. The hard-faced coachman flogged his beast. There was an eerie stillness in the streets, an absence of the raucous noises that usually issued from gambling hells and dilapidated tenements that housed thieves, whores and murderers. The emaciated horse stumbled, almost fell. Cursing, the coachman leaped down from his high seat.

He heard, then, countless angry shouts, a scant distance away. Bow Street, he thought, and scowled. Grasping the bridle of his unhappy horse, he forced it over the slippery cobblestones. If there was to be violent protest against the law, the coachman meant to have his say.

They stepped into a wider street, where shops, a tavern and substantial houses sat back a neat distance from the road. Outside Bow Street Public Office massed a milling, sleazy mob, their voices raised now to deafening pitch. Here were Covent Garden's denizens, prostitutes and pickpockets, dollymops and cracksmen, every example of London's seething underworld. Lit by linksmen's torches, it was a gathering as festive as any hanging. Through the crowd shuffled hawkers of hot chestnuts and oranges, beer and gin.

"What's about?" asked the coachman of a dull-eyed slattern. She held a baby sucking a gin-soaked rag.

"They've nicked Leda Langtry again." The woman spat on the cobblestones. Even the coachman knew of Leda. He swore.

Inside the stuffy courtroom, the oaths of Bow Street's Chief Magistrate went unvoiced. Sir John glanced around the chamber, filled to overflowing with rowdy spectators, and thought with a flash of humor that it looked as if sixteen hundred persons had been invited to a house incapable of holding more than sixteen. But it was not a matter to amuse him for long. Already the Chief Magistrate had read the Riot Act to disperse the angry mob, and he wondered if next he would be forced to call in the dragoons.

"Leda Langtry," he said, his eyes tired beneath the powdered wig. She stood before him, her wrists crossed and bound, a gentle-faced elderly woman with white hair. "You will cease to enliven my court with further burlesque incidents, or suffer the penalty."

A cozy, plump figure clad in black, she grinned unrepentantly. "Will I?" she murmured, so quietly that none but he could hear. "Don't lay odds on it, Sir John! You may read in the *Apocalypse* tomorrow the afflicting details of my suffering."

Though Sir John's expression did not change, his annoyance grew. Leda might look like one's notion of the perfect grand-mother, but he knew from past experience that she could be vicious indeed. He picked up his gavel. He had known, of course, that a bench warrant had been issued for Leda's arrest, but he could not have foreseen that she would be brought to Bow Street. Sir John would have much preferred to have before him culprits taken into custody on charges of theft. London had been, in the past few weeks, plagued by an outbreak of daring robberies, and the most rigid and searching inquiries had brought forth not the slightest clue.

"Do you mean to keep me standing here forever while you air-dream?" demanded Leda irritably. "By all that's holy, this is a *most* infamous proceeding." She smiled sweetly. "And so I shall tell the world, Sir John!"

"Quiet!" he roared, and brought down the gavel with such force that it cracked like a thunderclap through the room, briefly silencing the noisy spectators. "Leda Langtry," he said sternly, "you have been brought before me on very grave charges. What say you in your defense?"

"You grow lax, Sir John!" She dared reprove him as if he were an errant schoolboy. "You have not yet warned me that any statement I make may be used as evidence against me." The audience tittered, delighted as always to see a facer delivered to the law.

The Chief Magistrate repressed an urge to retaliate in kind. Had he the freedom to follow his own inclination, he would dismiss Leda with nothing more than a severe admonition and a caution to reform her conduct. But Sir John dared not defy his Regent.

"Be damned to your impudence!" he said softly, then raised his voice. "Leda Langtry, it is my duty to tell you that on the evidence presented before me, I must remand you for trial."

"No!" gasped Leda, and fell back a step, looking more dead than alive. Angry jeers filled the room

Sir John rose, his weary features impassive. "In the interim you will be lodged at Newgate Prison. I leave you, madam, to reflect on your coming fate."

Chapter One

"Well-a-day!" said Lady Bligh, peering intently at the morning newspaper. "Yet another robbery has been committed and I'm sure—considering the paltry efforts of Bow Street to apprehend the culprits!—that it isn't to be wondered at."

Mignon glanced curiously at her aunt. Her prior acquaintance with this one of her relatives was slight, though the Baron and Baroness Bligh were a matter of no small discussion, most of it censorious, within the family circle. Dulcie was as notorious for her eccentricity and flamboyance as her husband was for his adventurousness—and for other attributes as well, which unfortunately, were never discussed in Mignon's hearing. "Oh?" said she.

Lady Bligh screwed up her patrician features and sneezed. The Baroness had, as a result of attending a Vauxhall masquerade, taken a lingering cold. The Baron had precipitously embarked, shortly thereafter, upon an excursion to the Continent, there to witness for himself the ravages left in the wake of Napoleon. All the world

was traveling that fall, now that the Emperor had been over-
thrown: elegant ladies fared forth, watering at the mouth in anticipation of fashionable new wardrobes; gourmets and libertines
threaded a path to Paris, gorging themselves in transit on French
food and wine and feasting their eyes on a panorama of feminine
beauty unequalled anywhere.

Mignon glanced at the portrait of her uncle that hung above the
fireplace. Maximilian Bonaventure Bligh, rover and rogue, was one
of the most spectacular figures of his day. A swarthy man with
gray-streaked raven hair, heavy-lidded dark eyes and an aquiline
nose, he was both dashing and unpredictable, a great traveler, a
collector of rare and curious objects. He was also an impenitent and
incurable rake and credited with more conquests than Don Juan.

"People hoped," said Lady Bligh with the uncanny accuracy of
thought that was one of her less lovable traits, "that Bat would
stop sowing his wild oats when he came of age." Her smile was
more than a little wicked. "They were disappointed, of course!"

Mignon did not wish to discuss her absent uncle, who rendered
her acutely uncomfortable by the knowing quality of even his
painted gaze. "You were saying?" she murmured politely. "Something about another robbery?"

"Indeed I was." Dulcie waved her newspaper as if it were a flag.
"Lady Coates has been relieved of a faro bank of five hundred
guineas, and two of her footmen have been discharged on suspicion
of the theft. Fools! This is only the latest in a rash of robberies, all
of which I'll vow have been perpetrated by the same clever gang of
criminals."

Mignon did not know quite how to respond. Lady Bligh's
involvement in the recent Arbuthnot scandals had been highly
deprecated by her family, but the Baroness was far from being
prostrated by the resultant notoriety.

"Lady Coates?" Mignon inquired cautiously.

"Yes, and I'm sure it's no more than she deserves, having fleeced
countless ensigns and French émigrés." Lady Bligh drained her
teacup and Mignon leaned forward to refill it. "Some women of

fashion, my dear, keep faro tables as a source of income—the holder of the bank is bound to win." She fell silent, absently stroking the huge orange-striped cat, Casanova by name, that sprawled across her lap. Perched on the back of her massive carved chair was a huge hyacinth macaw. "Hang him from the yardarm!" muttered Bluebeard irritably.

Mignon covertly studied her aunt, wondering for perhaps the hundredth time why Dulcie had commanded her presence in London. Had Lady Bligh but known it, her timing was admirable. Mignon's family had been only too happy to send her off to London and out of temptation's way, for Mignon had blotted her copybook in a manner that not only sent her long-suffering mother very nearly into convulsions but that made her chances of forming an eligible connection remote indeed. An eligible connection! thought Mignon resentfully. She would wed the man of her choice, no matter how grave a *mésalliance* it might be, or she would wed no one. She might be in London, she might rub shoulders with the *ton*, but she would derive no pleasure from the experience.

"Foolish child!" said Lady Bligh, apropos of nothing at all. "You are a veritable innocent." Before Mignon could protest, her aunt had lapsed once more into reverie.

Dulcie Bligh was a stunning creature, tall and voluptuous, with elegantly sculpted cheekbones, an arrogantly aristocratic nose, a generous mouth and a determined chin; her age had to be one of the best-kept secrets of the century, and her looks would never betray her. The Baroness that morning wore a purple velvet gown with lace yoke and sleeves, an exquisitely embroidered shawl, satin slippers with ribbon lacings, and a fortune in amethysts. She could have sat for a painting, thought Mignon, and wondered what the artist would have made of Lady Bligh's orchid hair.

Dulcie frowned. "These impudent robberies," she said abruptly, "have affected everyone, from the Secretary of State to the beadle of St. Brides, with a severe case of nerves. Thus far assaults have been made on the Guildhall and the Royal College of Physicians, the Post Office and the Royal Exchange, as well as on various

private establishments in Mayfair and Marylebone." She picked up
a biscuit and idly crushed it in one hand. "It is obvious that the
authorities need assistance, dear Mignon! How fortunate for them
that we have elected to remain in Town."

"We?" said Mignon faintly. She was more than a little in awe of
her aunt, whose erratic thought processes were, to a mere damsel of
two-and-twenty, nigh incomprehensible. Dulcie had an uncanny
knack of knowing things that, logically, she could not.

"We," replied Lady Bligh firmly, dividing the biscuit equally
between her pets and gazing expectantly at the doorway. "The
investigation of crime will prove an excellent antidote to your
unhappy romance." Mignon stared speechless at her aunt, for there
was no way Dulcie could have known of that *débâcle*. She was
saved a reply by Lady Bligh's butler, who appeared like an appari-
tion in the doorway.

Gibbon was a cadaverous individual with a shock of white hair
and a death's-head face, and his voice had all the *joie de vivre* of a
funeral bell. On this occasion, however, he was given no opportunity to speak. "Show him in!" said Lady Bligh, and sneezed
emphatically. Her lively black eyes fixed Mignon. "A young man
occupied entirely by his own pleasures," she remarked, "as are so
many young men, and none the worse for it! Pay attention to him,
my dear. Your opinion may be of no small importance by-and-
by."

Mignon shook her head in perplexity. "Are you speaking of
Gibbon?" she asked incredulously. And then their visitor stepped
across the threshold and drove all other considerations from Mignon's head.

He was as handsome as Adonis, a tall and well-made man in a
brown jacket and cream unmentionables, worn beneath a topcoat
of tan broadcloth. His shirt collar was high and crisp, his cravat
faultless, and his waistcoat boasted smartly-shaped, smoothly-roll-
ing collar and lapels. The hair that curled slightly over his collar
was a burnished reddish-gold. His features were emotionless and
aloof, lending him a haughty air. "Shiver my timbers!" croaked

Bluebeard. Mignon looked away and firmly reminded herself that she was the unhappy victim of love gone wrong.

The gentleman in turn scrutinized the room and its occupants. Talk about this house was unceasing. The Bligh town mansion was the repository of the Baron's more concrete flights of fancy, and this particular chamber, octagonal in design and furnished in shades of black, white and gray, boasted not only a domed ceiling with fan design but walls enlivened with dancing nymphs, gryphons and other fantastic beasts. Full-bosomed caryatids supported the fireplace's mantelpiece.

"Overwhelming, is it not?" inquired Lady Bligh, briskly shoving the cat from her lap and rising to her feet, thus revealing herself as even more well-endowed than the ladies who adorned the fireplace. "But you have not come here to gawk, surely! Get on with it, young man."

It was generally conceded that the Baron Bligh's most bizarre and incomparable treasure was the fascinating, imperious Amazon who was his wife. Despite himself, the caller's lips twitched, and a hint of warmth appeared in his brown eyes. "Forgive the intrusion," he said, his gaze lingering on Lady Bligh's orchid curls. "I would not have rudely broken into your privacy had it not been a matter of some import." His slight bow was the epitome of elegance. "I am Ivor Jessop, ma'am." Mignon, watching with amusement the stranger's reaction to her aunt, thought his husky voice one of the most pleasant she had ever heard, one to charm canaries down from their perches, or send ladybirds flying into the boughs.

"Of course you are!" retorted Lady Bligh, simultaneously fluttering her long lashes and shoving her visitor into an ornately carved chair upholstered in silver-gray Italian velvet that matched the window hangings. She then picked up the orange tomcat and resumed her own seat.

"Ivor Jessop, Viscount Jeffries, thirty years of age. Your parents are both presumed dead; from the time of their divorce you were raised by your uncle, Lord Calvert—quite worthy, I'm sure, but a dreadful bore!—whose heir you are. You are a trifle wild, possess only a rudimentary sense of humor, and have the *entrée* everywhere; you also have all you could wish for, or so you think, including wealth, breeding, and an avaricious little opera· dancer named Zoe!" Having nicely astonished her guest, Dulcie smiled. "You also have a look of your mother, young man!"

Mignon, who had been idly picturing their guest's *petite amie*, a damsel doubtless frail and tiny and exquisitely fashioned, was intrigued by his lack of ease. It did not appear a sensation with which he was familiar, or one for which he cared. "I am here on a matter of some delicacy," he said coolly, with an unreadable glance at Mignon. "One of which I would prefer to speak with you privately."

"Privately?" repeated Lady Bligh, propping her feet inelegantly on a stool and crossing her slender ankles. "Ah, you refer to my niece! You may ignore Mignon. In truth, she may prove of no small service to you."

Mignon, with no desire at all to play benefactress to a man who so strongly resembled the carved satyr masks of the chair in which he sat, had risen to her feet. "If you will excuse me," she said politely, seeking ineffectually to mask the resentment that the Viscount's attitude had aroused, "I'm sure I can find something to occupy me elsewhere."

"Poppycock!" replied Lady Bligh. "Sit down, my dear, and overlook our guest's boorish manner. The gentleman has a great deal on his mind." Her inscrutable gaze flicked from Mignon's startled face to Ivor's darkening countenance. "Proceed, if you will! We are wasting time."

"Very well." Already regretting the impulse that had brought him there, the Viscount regarded his hands. "I have come in behalf of a friend of yours, Lady Bligh, one whom you have not seen in a number of years, and who is now in serious difficulties." He paused, obviously wondering how he might proceed. The Baroness offered him no assistance, but gazed in a visionary manner upon the portrait of her spouse. "In short, Lady Bligh," Ivor said, "your friend is presently lodged in the Newgate Prison prior to her appearance at the bar of the Old Bailey."

"Ah," murmured Dulcie, "the freedom of the written word! One who dares come out in support of the Luddite rioters and their machine smashing, and then compounds her offense by traducing Prinny, is not likely to long escape meditation in a prison cell." *the Prince Regent - george, Prince of Wales 1811-1820*

"May I ask," inquired the Viscount, his brow furrowed, "how you knew of that?"

"You may not!" snapped Dulcie, and Mignon stifled an impulse to applaud. Lord Jeffries' self-possession would not remain intact through many encounters with the Baroness!

"The London *Apocalypse,* most radical of the city's news sheets, and Leda's *tour de force!*" The Baroness picked up a newspaper from the stack beside her chair and waved it. "How I knew of Leda's arrest is not important; it is a matter of far more curiosity that a gentleman of your vast superiority would consort with a female whose pen works untiringly for the laboring classes, especially those small farmers who are being displaced by the Enclosure Acts!"

"Consort!" The Viscount struggled with strong emotion, then threw back his head and laughed aloud. "Leda is more than two decades older than I—almost, I believe, your own age, Lady Bligh!" Dulcie's fine eyes narrowed and he smiled. It was, Mignon decided, a facial exercise in which Ivor Jessop seldom indulged and one that became him mightily. "I made her acquaintance recently and quite by accident," he continued, "and although I do not agree with Leda's political extremism, I am fascinated by her eccentricity. She spoke to me of you during the Arbuthnot matter: hence my awareness of your one-time friendship."

Lady Bligh rose and paced the floor with considerable grace. The orange cat, left in sole possession of the chair, looked cautiously up at the blue parrot before settling himself comfortably. "You wish me to use my influence on Leda's behalf." Dulcie paused to contemplate a chess set carved in jasper. "Why? Leda is merely following in the footsteps of her fellow journalists. Leigh Hunt went the same route a couple of years past, receiving a £500 fine and a sentence of two years' imprisonment in Surrey Gaol. He called Prinny 'a corpulent Adonis,' as I recall."

"This is a somewhat different case," the Viscount replied, following Dulcie's movements with his eyes. Definitely one for the ladies, thought Mignon. "I would apply to my uncle in Leda's behalf, but he is a very sick man."

"Nor," said the Baroness dryly, deserting the chessmen to prop one elbow on the marble mantelpiece, "would he approve of your concern. Consider! This is not Leda's first sojourn within Newgate's bleak walls. She indulged in a piece of satire against the House of Lords some years back and was treated to a three-month imprisonment."

The Viscount also rose, treating Mignon to a rare view of a superb masculine physique. She hastily averted her gaze, applying it instead to the volume of verse she'd been reading some time before. "Leda is an elderly lady," Ivor said, his voice hard, "and hardly of a constitution to happily suffer prison life. I had hoped your friendship might prompt you to act in her behalf, but I see I misjudged you. Forgive me for disturbing your no doubt important pursuits!"

"You sound like your uncle," the Baroness remarked irritably, then paused to sneeze again. Mignon suspected her aunt did not care for the Viscount's choice of terms, and little wonder. Lady Bligh and the unfortunate Leda might have been much of an age, but Dulcie looked so far from elderly that she could have been Lord Jeffries' peer.

"And," added Lady Bligh, waving her lace handkerchief for emphasis, "a more pompous windbag than Lord Calvert I have yet to see!" She appeared not to notice that the Viscount drew himself up indignantly in his uncle's defense. "I haven't said I wouldn't help you, young man, although your concern is misplaced. You would do much better to leave Leda where she is!"

"Nonsense!" Ivor looked as if he strongly wished himself elsewhere, as indeed he did, having come to consider Bligh House as little better than a raree-show and the Baroness the prize exhibit. "I cannot imagine what you're thinking of!"

"Naturally not, and fortunate it is." Lady Bligh smiled roguishly. "So I am to go to Prinny and ask his forgiveness on Leda's behalf? A pity that our Regent is as ridiculous as he is thin-skinned, or it wouldn't matter a whit that Leda informed the world that he enjoys his vices and leaves politics to his ministers; that he entertains shapely tightrope dancers in his private rooms at Carlton House while leaving Lord Castlereagh to represent England at the Congress of Vienna!" Mignon, no peruser of newspaper accounts, giggled. Jeffries glanced at her, but she was once more studiously buried in her book.

"Or," mused Dulcie, running her fingers through her orchid-colored curls, rather to their detriment, "do you prefer that I apply to Lord Warwick, who acts as Prinny's emissary in such matters, and who is a thoroughly detestable man?" She squinted contemplatively. "Warwick it shall be! He cherishes a violent antipathy to my husband, considering Bat a despoiler of innocent English womanhood."

"And is he?" queried the Viscount, diverted.

Lady Bligh laughed huskily, but her amusement quickly fled. "I will ask you once more to reconsider," she said, moving from the fireplace to stand beside Mignon's chair, "and leave Leda where she is. I will secure her release if you are set on it, but only because if I do not you will find someone else who will."

"Precisely," said Ivor. Mignon, eyes glued unseeing to the printed page, thought it would be a hellish life to act as servant to this haughty man.

"Very well." The Baroness shrugged. "The consequences are on your head. You will remember that I warned you."

Lord Jeffries' expression was wry. "Lady Bligh," he said, with patent sincerity, "you may be assured that I will forget no detail of this encounter!" Mignon felt his gaze on her. "I trust your niece is as discreet as you say. I do not care to have my association with Leda made public knowledge."

Mignon raised her eyes and in them was an expression that made the Viscount arch one sandy brow. Dulcie's hand dropped to her niece's shoulder. "You may trust Mignon," she said calmly. "That is something else you may have reason to recall."

Ivor suspected if he remained much longer in the presence of this exasperating woman he would forget his gentlemanly precepts and say something unforgivable. "I will take my leave of you, then." He made an exit as graceful as it was abrupt.

"The toad!" erupted Mignon, rubbing her bruised shoulder. What had Dulcie been afraid she'd say? "He didn't even thank you."

"Young Jessop will have ample opportunity to express his gratitude." Again Dulcie wore that odd little frown. "I fear we will be seeing a great deal more of him."

"We will?" Mignon was studiously nonchalant. Lady Bligh regarded her niece, and her mobile mouth twisted into a secretive little smile.

"Rhymed tales of corsairs and exotic slave girls and lovesick Eastern princes," murmured the Baroness. "I think you will find, my dear, that Wordsworth reads much better when not held upside down!"

"The devil!" muttered Mignon and tossed aside the book. Sure that the Viscount's brown eyes missed little, for all their owner's unreadable hauteur, she rose to inspect herself in the silvered looking glass that was topped by an eagle motif. Staring back at her was a very ordinary damsel, taller than average, with bright red hair and freckles, whose only claim to beauty was a pair of large sea-green eyes. Then, in the mirror, she saw the huge blue parrot lean forward and apply his sharp beak to a particularly tempting patch of orange fur. The cat shrieked and leaped straight into the air.

"Poor Casanova!" The Baroness rapped her knuckles sharply

against Bluebeard's beak, then cradled the tomcat, who looked as though he'd like to make a meal of his tormentor. "As to that, poor Leda, too. The dashing Viscount would have saved us a great deal of trouble if he'd only listened to me."

But Mignon, stricken by the realization that she hadn't spared even a single thought to her lost love for over an hour, made no reply. "Silly chit!" said Dulcie, depositing herself and her bristling burden once more in the carved chair. "*You* do not mean to cooperate either, I see!"

Mignon abandoned the looking glass, her spirits further oppressed by its familiar message that she would never be other than plain. "Cooperate in what manner?" she asked bluntly. "It is good of you to have me here, and I am grateful, but I think I should be informed if you mean to involve me in some scheme."

Lady Bligh was as devious as she was lovely, and not given to explanations. "My smelling salts!" she gasped, suddenly stricken as feeble as if she were twice her actual age. Imitating his mistress perfectly, Bluebeard sneezed.

Chapter Two

The Chief Magistrate of Bow Street sat at a scarred desk in the small and stuffy office that had originally been tenanted by Colonel Thomas de Veil, magistrate for Westminster and Middlesex, who had been both corrupt and energetic, and who had hounded criminals with a vigor that quite astounded them. There had been many occupants of the shabby Bow Street quarters since then, among them the Fieldings and Sampson Wright and Sir Richard Ford; but Sir John could not see that the conditions they battled had noticeably improved.

"Dulcie," he said, inspecting his visitor. She wore a purple velvet gown and a hooded cape of purple-blue taffeta lined with rose. "What brings you here?"

Lady Bligh opened wide her bright dark eyes and grinned impudently. "Why, you, my dear. Since you won't do the pretty and call on me, I have come to you." She paused to sneeze. "Bat is off jaunting about the Continent, surveying dead horses and shattered homes and the crippled remnants of Napoleon's *Grande Armée.* He will then proceed to Vienna, where the Allied Sovereigns and ministers have assembled to rearrange the map of Europe according to their various ambitions. What gaiety that sad city shall see! Vienna is thronged with crowned heads and ambassadors and ministers, all engaged with hunting and shooting, drives and promenades and vast dinners, evening assemblies and balls and *petits soupers,* plays and operas." She threw back the hood of her cape. "Though to tell truth, John, I cannot envision Bat promenading in the Prater and watching the Danube passing idly by."

Nor could the Chief Magistrate, who had no high opinion of the fifth Baron Bligh, considering him an unconscionable rake as well as the most untrustworthy of men, and he ventured to say as much. Had Sir John been fortunate enough to win Dulcie's hand in marriage, *he* would not spend the greater portion of the year away from her side. He glanced once more at Lady Bligh, who at that moment, and despite her orchid curls, appeared the most demure creature in existence, and repressed a smile. It was perhaps fortunate that Fate had not thus favored him. Life with Dulcie would doubtless have resulted in his early demise from an apoplexy.

"Tsk, John!" reproved the Baroness. "A most uncharitable attitude! At last report, Bat was administering the last rites to a dying British soldier whom he found in a church at Champagne. But I have not come to talk of Bat!" Dulcie settled herself more comfortably on her hard wooden chair. "Dear John, if you have a moment to spare, I wish to speak to you."

The Chief Magistrate rubbed his forehead, which was deeply lined. Bow Street was exceptionally busy just then, due not only to the robberies but to a complicated case of fraud in which a certain Member of Parliament was implicated. But he could no more refuse Dulcie than he could hold back the tide. "What is it, then?"

"I shan't tell you," retorted his heartless tormentor, "until you have offered me some tea. It is no wonder that you are sulky as a bear! I vow, your entire existence is dedicated to dispensing justice. What of pleasure and amusement, pray? Dear John, if you keep up at this pace you will be old before your time!"

If Lady Bligh was up to further shenanigans, as appeared very likely, Sir John thought he would turn her over his knee. He had not yet forgotten the cursed Arbuthnot business, when her ladyship's damnable meddling had brought her into grave danger and had him fretting his guts to fiddlestrings. He put down his pen and rose to bellow down the hallway for her ladyship's tea.

"Much better," said Lady Bligh, in a tone that made the Chief Magistrate temporarily forget both crime and miscreants. "I flatter myself that I am precisely the diversion that you need." A gangling underling appeared with the refreshments.

"You," Sir John retorted, when they were once more alone, "are a cursed nuisance, Dulcie!" His expression belied his words; the weary face wore a smile.

"Am I not?" agreed the Baroness cheerfully, balancing the teacup in one hand as with the other she sought ineffectually to repair an unpinned orchid curl. Sir John struggled with a wish to take that heavy hair in his hands and to bury his face in its perfume. Lady Bligh blushed. "You are also," he said wryly, "a great deal too intuitive."

"Poppycock, John!" Dulcie abandoned her efforts and fished in her reticule for her handkerchief. "You might recall that my intuition has in the past been of no small service to you."

Sir John wisely skirted this topic. God forbid he should encourage Lady Bligh's crime-detecting efforts! Her assistance in the Arbuthnot case, based on a combination of shrewd conjecture·and feminine illogic and what could only be divine revelation, had nearly driven him into a fever of the brain.

"Play off your cajolery elsewhere, Dulcie," he said gruffly. "Tell me why you are here."

Lady Bligh surveyed him speculatively over the frivolous square of lace, then briskly blew her nose. "First," she announced, "we shall engage in a little polite conversation, for it is an art in which you are sadly deficient."

"Oh?" Sir John lifed his heavy brows.

"I have a niece staying with me. A good-tempered friendly little creature who is perfectly contented if you tell her that her teeth are pearls and her eyes emeralds." The Baroness frowned. "I have great hopes of Mignon! She is, thankfully, not as dull as she sounds, having fallen fathoms deep in love with a man most unsuitable to her rank and barely being stopped in the very nick of time from totally ruining herself. Mignon is very wealthy, did I say?"

Sir John, watching the various expressions that played across her bewitching face, was thoroughly bemused. "No," he replied, somewhat wistfully.

Lady Bligh leaned forward and rapped his knuckles with her saucer. "Stop woolgathering, John! It is a matter of no small consequence that Mignon made so unfortunate a choice."

"Very well!" he snapped, miffed. "What have your niece's indiscretions to do with me?"

"Nothing, as yet." The Baroness set aside her teacup and moved to stand beside his desk, looking down at him solemnly. "Matters draw fast to a crisis, and it weighs on my heart most heavily."

Sir John gazed up at her with equal gravity, taking in every detail of that extraordinary beauty from her disheveled hair to her inquisitive little nose. "Tell me what troubles you," he said, and took her hand.

Dulcie leaned back against his desk. "I had a caller this morning, Ivor Jessop, with a boon to beg." A faint smile hovered around her mouth. "Begging, I might add, is something the Viscount is quite unaccustomed to! He is a very haughty young man, though I know nothing worse of him than that he once threw an inkwell at a waiter's head."

"What has Jeffries to do with your niece?" asked Sir John. The Chief Magistrate, though he did not deign to waste his time in the frivolous pursuits of the *ton*, was by birth a member of the aristocracy.

"Again, very little, as yet." Dulcie, dark eyes knowing, sat back further on the desk and gracefully crossed her legs. "The Viscount came to see me in behalf of Leda Langtry. You recall the lady, I'm sure."

Sir John gave up the struggle and abandoned himself to enjoyment of the interview. He knew full well that he was being manipulated most adroitly. "I remember her," he said. Sir John had little love for members of the Press, who had a nasty habit of heaping odium on Bow Street, particularly in the matter of blood money, bounty paid to informers and thieftakers for denouncing culprits. Payments of blood money threatened to reach the awesome sum of £80,000 that year alone, and as a result Sir John's Bow Street Runners were often accused of sending men and women to their deaths for the sake of a reward. Sometimes the Press accused his Runners of succumbing to bribery and sometimes accused them of worse. In the previous century one Jonathan Wild, a thieftaker, had built up a huge criminal organization, employing the very robbers that he was paid to apprehend, and his efforts were well remembered down to the present day, kept alive partly by an unsympathetic Press.

"Leda was imprisoned for a libel that she wrote and will stand trial at the next session."

"Libel!" snorted Lady Bligh, with an emphasis that sent hairpins flying across the room. Sir John wondered what his subordinates would think upon discovering them. "I sympathize with the Luddites myself, for the poor men believe that the machinery they smash has done them out of their jobs."

"Perhaps," agreed Sir John, "but Leda did not present her arguments logically. It was not her sympathy with the rioters that landed her in Newgate, you know, but the fact that she chose to write of our Regent with a pen dipped in bile."

"Ah, Prinny," mused the Baroness, in a knowing tone that inspired Sir John with unreasoning jealousy. All London knew that the Prince Regent nourished a long-standing *tendresse* for Lady Bligh. "These robberies," she added, so suddenly that the Chief Magistrate started guiltily. "What do you propose to do about them, John?"

"There's very little we *can* do," he retorted sharply, for this was an extremely sore point, "with neither description nor trace of the culprit to follow." Lady Bligh's avid expression caused his flesh to crawl on his bones. "I've had my best men on the case and they've learned nothing, Dulcie. Don't think that you may be better! I forbid you to interfere."

"Interfere?" The Baroness was wounded. "Unfair, John, to think such a thing of me! I *never* interfere."

"No, you merely follow your nose where it may lead you, and that's generally into trouble." Her innocent expression, and low-cut neckline, inspired him to further confidences. "We have had recourse to our Criminal Record Office, but without result."

"Your best men." Lady Bligh thoughtfully tugged one of her delicate earlobes. "Who, pray?"

That there was a purpose to this conversation Sir John never took leave to doubt. Heaven forbid that he ever encountered the crafty Baroness in the witness-box! "Townsend and Sayer," he replied, "though to do so I had to interfere with their duties concerning the Regent. Neither discovered anything. Ruthven had no better luck, though he's my leading expert on bank robberies and forgery. Nor did Vickery, for all his expertise in tracking down and recapturing escaped prisoners of war."

"Bank robberies," mused Dulcie. "I do not believe your culprit, as you call him, has yet committed a bank robbery."

"As yet?" Sir John was suddenly alert. Lady Bligh might be exasperating and capricious, but there was no denying that her foresight was formidable. "What are you trying to tell me?"

The Baroness slid off his desk, sending his senses pleasantly reeling with her heady perfume. "If I meant to tell you something, John, I would do so without roundaboutation." She turned to look out the window and the Chief Magistrate remembered belatedly to exhale. "I conclude you have not seen fit to utilize Crump's talents in this affair?"

"Crump!" Sir John scowled. "Crump is a clever enough rascal, and has managed to do well for himself in reward money, but I suspect this scoundrel would easily outwit him. To my mind, Crump's most outstanding achievement has been the apprehension of an enterprising couple who fought a duel in two balloons."

"You refer to the criminal in the singular." Lady Bligh stared somberly into the street below. "I suspect you are mistaken. I suspect also that you undervalue your enterprising little Crump. He may arrive at the truth via circuitous routes, but arrive at it he does."

Sir John remained briefly silent, drinking in the sight of Dulcie bathed in sunlight like a lissome purple-haired nymph. "Very well," he said, going to stand beside her at the window. "If it matters so much to you, I will put Crump on the case—not that I anticipate he will achieve any better result than his predecessors!"

"Dear John!" Dulcie touched his arm. "It is so *good* of you to indulge my whims! Crump will discover a budget of wonders, I vow! Now, we have had a good deal of joking, but it is time to get down to business. There is an errand that you may execute."

Sir John had been too long acquainted with the Baroness to be startled by her abrupt changes of mood. Who but Lady Bligh would dare order the Chief Magistrate of Bow Street Public Office to execute her commissions as if he were a footman? Succumbing to temptation, he lifted his hands to straighten her coiffure. "What errand?"

Dulcie drew back to look up at him, her lively countenance alight with mischief. "Why, to conduct Leda home from Newgate, of course. Your wits are sluggish today! What else would I ask?"

The Chief Magistrate glowered at her. "Take care, Dulcie!" he growled. "You fancy yourself battling injustice, but the Regent's wishes cannot be denied."

Lady Bligh opened wide her eyes and drew forth from the bosom of her gown an official-looking document. "Why, John, of course not! Here is the order for her release. I think you will find it all it should be."

Sir John held the paper, still warm from contact with her body, as if it might momentarily burst into flame. "Where did you get this?" he demanded.

"From Warwick," responded the blithe Baroness. "I did not think it wise to apply to Prinny, poor man! He is very nearly dying of a disgraceful debauch, you know, having sent for George Coleman to come from the King's Bench Prison to entertain him. A pity, is it not, that a dramatist and theatrical manager should be imprisoned for debt! They sat up all night carousing until Prinny was literally dead drunk and had to be carried to bed. Sir Walter Farquar has saved his life, but at the cost of twenty-seven ounces of blood." She shrugged. "To further poor Prinny's distress, he is being dunned in the streets for his debts and the *most* discreditable stories about him are going the rounds of society."

"I would appreciate it," said Sir John, "if you would stop trying to humbug me! *How* did you persuade Warwick to give you this release?"

"Warwick was not in the least anxious to be of assistance, as you can imagine, but he soon saw the advantage of cooperating with me. In short, dear John, I have certain information in my possession, the publication of which would make life most uncomfortable for him."

"You would," retorted the Chief Magistrate wryly. "This mania of yours for collecting damning information will land you in serious difficulties one day." It was an unhappy thought, and one that haunted him.

"Piffle!" Dulcie brushed idle fingers along the windowsill. "Life would be very dull indeed, did I leave other people's business to them and confine myself to my own!" She looked at him thoughtfully, head cocked to one side. "Are you thinking I should have applied to you for assistance? I could not so compromise you, John! It was you who committed Leda to Newgate, after all."

"So it was." For a man who deprecated Lady Bligh's involvement in what might be logically considered his affairs, Sir John was unaccountably relieved. "Save me further blandishments! I will see Leda safely home. In return you might tell me what Ivor Jessop has to do with her, and why you are so prodigiously interested in this recent outbreak of robberies."

"So I might." Lady Bligh adapted an attitude every bit as provocative as those employed by the lightskirts who plied their trade in Covent Garden's narrow streets and winked at him. "Much as it distresses me to refuse you, in this case I think I must. But you are very kind to oblige me about Leda and I am very, very grateful to you."

"All the same," Sir John said ruefully, "I would vastly prefer to see that particular troublemaker remain behind bars."

"Leda?" Dulcie stepped back, drawing the hood of her cloak over her again unruly curls. "Oddly enough, John," she murmured somberly, "so would I." By the time the Chief Magistrate thought to question this startling intelligence, the Baroness had gone.

Chapter Three

Crump sauntered along the busy streets of the West End, passing by the fencing rooms in St. James's Street and Gentleman Jackson's Bond Street boxing saloon, as well as shops and smart hotels dedicated to serving the aristocracy. The haunts of the *ton* roused not envy but anger in Crump. While walking in Mayfair he would call to mind the filthy slums and unlit streets of Westminster and Lambeth, those mazes of tumbledown houses and fever-ridden alleys where half-naked children played in open sewers and well-dressed gentlemen dared not venture even in daylight.

Crump was a rotund, jovial-looking man with observant blue eyes and a balding skull adorned by a scant fringe of black hair. He was also one of that select group known commonly as the Bow Street Runners. And a good one, he thought, despite Sir John's current annoyance with him, an annoyance inspired wholly by the fact that Lady Bligh, during the wretched Arbuthnot business, had not only placed herself in danger but had outwitted him. Crump twirled his gilt-headed baton. A race apart were the aristocracy, with blue blood flowing in their veins, and the Baroness Bligh was even further removed from the commonplace. She was as silly as she was lovely, deplorably frivolous, conspicuously crazy, and she furthermore possessed a happy knack of falling on her feet. It was to Lady Bligh that he owed his present engagement; due to her influence with the Chief Magistrate, Crump was at last to try his hand at solving these daring robberies, the most recent of which had taken place at White's Club. Crump thought he would call at Bligh House later on to express his gratitude, there to be regaled by the Baroness with tidbits of tittle-tattle from high society, and just possibly to learn what had prompted her intervention in his behalf.

He had been in the tavern across from Bow Street headquarters, sipping geneva and making the acquaintance of pickpockets, housebreakers and others of their ilk, when Sir John summoned him. The Runners were condemned for their practice of frequenting flash houses, for keeping company with thieves, but there were no few advantages in acting the part of a spy. In such places, where careless tongues were rendered further incautious by libations of gin and ale, an enterprising thieftaker could gather a wealth of information and locate criminals, earning himself a comfortable share of government reward money.

It was not an easy living, Crump reflected gloomily. Government rewards were usually divided between the prosecutor, witnesses and the arresting officer. Parliamentary rewards, paid by the government to anyone who brought a criminal to justice, were on a sliding scale of £10 for a shoplifter to £40 for a highwayman. Little wonder that some constables and watchmen ignored minor misdeeds in hope that the felons would become sufficiently emboldened to commit more serious felonies! Crump agreed with Sir John that the system was both inadequate and unfair.

His purpose, however, was not to lament injustice but to investigate a crime. Crump peered up at White's handsome and well-proportioned narrow brick facade, at the Corinthian pilasters be-

yond which wealthy lords gambled deeply night and day. It would
be a sharp set-down for his fellow Runners, mused Crump, if *he*
solved this perplexing series of crimes. Townsend in particular
needed taking down a peg or two; the man who had left a career
as a costermonger to serve under Sir John Fielding had now gained
fame for his habit of dressing in the same manner as the Regent.
Crump glanced once more at the building before him, noting the
unusual absence of the bow window set, the most prominent of
whom was the irreverent Beau Brummell, and approached the
front door.

Crump's entrance into this particular bastion of the aristocracy
was one that he would long remember, and not for the warmth of
the welcome he received. The doorman gazed upon him with
raised eyebrows, apparently stricken dumb; the hall porter, of a
more timid disposition, gasped and looked ready to swoon; while
the turbaned Negro page, whose duty was to collect hats and coats,
grinned maliciously. "I believe," said the doorman, having re-
covered his voice, "that you wish the tradesmen's entrance, sir! If
you will proceed around the building —" His words ended in an
abrupt expulsion of breath, occasioned by the application of
Crump's gilt-headed baton to his midriff.

"Aye, so you'd like to think, laddie!" retorted Crump genially,
and stepped across the threshold. "Lord love you, *I* know I'm not
elevated enough in rank to be admitted into such high company!"
The doorman wore a face of perfect horror as Crump flourished a
card identifying him as a peace officer on the staff of the Chief
Magistrate, Bow Street. "Set your mind at ease!" advised the
thieftaker. "I've been engaged through the usual channels, the
owner of this establishment having applied to the Chief Magistrate
for the services of a Runner, promising to pay a fee and also
handsomely promising a reward. So kindly conduct me to Mr.
Raggett immediately!"

"I am afraid," said the doorman, recovering sufficiently to close
the door, "that I cannot, Mr. Raggett being prostrated by the theft

of his silver plate. Instead you will have to deal with Mr. Throckmorton, Mr. Raggett's man of business."

"Very well." Crump's tone brooked no argument. "But first you will conduct me through these premises and acquaint me with the various means of access." His smile was jovial. "Before we set about investigating a robbery, my lad, we must ascertain whether entrance was effected by some outside agency, or whether it was committed from within." His bright eyes alighted on the hall porter, who was quaking in his shoes. "Which happens more often than you might think, servants being every bit as susceptible to temptation as the criminal class!" The porter blanched and leaned for support on the grinning page. A bright lad, thought Crump, and filed away the observation for future reference.

Thus it was that plain Mr. Crump of Bow Street was conducted on a tour of White's select club, founded over a century earlier as a chocolate house, and now famed as a gambling establishment where fortunes were made and lost and family estates abruptly changed hands. There were few club members in evidence, perhaps due to the inconveniences that resulted from the robbery, perhaps because gentlemen who gambled until dawn could hardly be expected to rise before noon. Crump studied the notice board in the lobby where prostitutes posted cards; he passed the green baize tables where gentlemen, hats tilted over their eyes, played whist until their pockets were emptied or exhaustion overtook them; he visited the kitchens where were prepared the somewhat dull dinners for which the club was known; he inspected every avenue of entrance and egress. At length he was conducted into the Visitors Room, where awaiting him was a ludicrously fat gentleman with a dignified air.

"Well?" demanded the individual, in irascible tones, his eye fixed on Crump's waistcoat. This was a fanciful creation of pale pink silk with an allover pattern in rose, worn over a second waistcoat of plain rose. "Have you found our missing plate? Damned if I know why Raggett called in Bow Street! It's nothing but a wretched waste of time. While you saunter about poking and prying into corners, the thieves will be halfway to France!"

"That's not likely, guv'nor." Though Crump remained affable, he was inspired by this belligerent attitude to draw forth his battered pipe. "Why should your thieves travel all the way with stolen plate when all they have to do is melt it down in an iron ladle held over a fire?"

"No!" moaned Mr. Throckmorton, and sank into a chair. "The silver plate melted? Unthinkable!"

Crump thoughtfully threw open a window and lit his pipe, the smell of which was atrocious in the extreme. Mr. Throckmorton's agitation had not escaped Crump's bright eye. "Suppose," he said, through a smoky haze, "that you tell me what you know about the robbery."

"Suppose," snapped Mr. Throckmorton, grimacing at the tobacco smell, "I don't!" Crump merely puffed harder on his pipe and Mr. Throckmorton threw up his hands. "Oh, very well! About the hour of 10 o'clock this morning the butler, as is his habit, proceeded to the plate closet to remove the supply of silver necessary to ready the dining tables for the members' reception. He discovered that the double doors had been forced open and a large quantity of silver removed, including the massive silver candlesticks that he'd deposited there the previous night."

"Pardon me, guv'nor," said Crump, thumbs hooked in his waistcoat as he rocked gently to and fro on his neat little feet. "Does the butler recall if he locked the plate closet at that time?"

"Of course he did!" Mr. Throckmorton's glance was decidedly hostile. "What's more, the hall porter will vouch for it, having seen him do so."

"Ah." Crump's eyes narrowed. "The hall porter and the butler, you say? And just how much do you know about those two men, guv'nor?"

"They've worked for this establishment for a great many years!" Mr. Throckmorton's cheeks had turned a bright red. "You can't think *they* were involved in this! Why, 'tis obvious our robbery was carried out by desperate and dangerous characters!" He shuddered. "And fortunate it is no one caught them red-handed, or we'd have seen bloodshed."

"Aye," said Crump, "doubtless you would. Did anyone see your dangerous ruffians? Or anyone suspicious lurking about the premises?"

Mr. Throckmorton opened his mouth, then paused, a crafty look on his face. "*I* did!" he announced. "As suspicious looking a person as one would hope to see, and skulking about the club the very afternoon before the robbery. No doubt he was looking for a means by which he might get in."

"Did you mention this sinister character to anyone?" asked Crump, puffing on his pipe even more energetically.

"No," said Mr. Throckmorton. "But I can describe him to you! He was thin and dark, brown-haired and furtive. Quite evil looking, in fact! And he had no notion of how to dress. No doubt he forced his way into the building after everyone was asleep and made his exit by the same means."

"Uncommonly promising," mused Crump, earning Mr. Throckmorton's first smile. "And a tissue of falsehoods from end to end! I warn you, guv'nor, that it's a serious offense to trifle with the law."

"Do you accuse *me* of lying?" Mr. Throckmorton's bulbous nose was mottled with outrage. "A gentleman, sir, does not tell a lie! Nor does he cheat, go back on his word or flinch from the consequences of his actions! Did I not consider you beneath my notice, Mr. Whatever-your-name-is, I would call you out for this insult."

"Would you, guv'nor?" Crump was enjoying himself. "Apparently you've forgotten that dueling is against the law. I suggest you give me the rest of the story without circumlocution! You've already given me ample ground for suspicion of yourself, you know."

"Preposterous!" cried Mr. Throckmorton, gasping for air like a dying carp.

"Not at all." Crump began to despair of learning anything useful from this man. "I have an expert's knowledge of locks, you see, and it is quite obvious that entrance was not forced. Nor were any of the windows tampered with. Therefore, if thieves entered this house, they either were admitted by someone already within, or they had access to a key." He radiated goodwill. "Do *you* have a key, Throckmorton?"

"No!" The gentleman looked fit to leap out of his skin. "I do not. What are you saying, man? You can't think that anyone here would admit robbers to the premises?"

"Can I not?" inquired Crump. "Despite the Banbury tale you've spun me, no one else noted any strangers near this building at any time approaching the robbery, and there is no evidence of forced entry. Since you dislike the notion that the thieves were admitted into the house, perhaps you would prefer to think the robbery an inside job."

"No, no!" wailed Mr. Throckmorton, wringing his chubby hands. "Think of the scandal were suspicion to fall on one of our members!" Crump, who'd never entertained such a notion, nearly choked on his tobacco smoke. "The club would never survive such infamy! Raggett would be forced to close his doors!"

"And you," said Crump, "would lose your most profitable business. Mr. Throckmorton, I begin to understand your concern." Abruptly he raised one plump hand, for the gentleman looked ready to hang round his neck in tears. "Never mind! With your cooperation—which I might say I've seen precious little of!—we may be able to forestall that particular disaster."

"I fling myself on your mercy," said Mr. Throckmorton meekly.

"I thought you might! Go on, then. What happened after the butler discovered the theft?"

"Chaos, sir, chaos!" replied Throckmorton gloomily. "He informed the housekeeper and the rest of the staff, the idiot! They were immediately all up in arms, alternately accusing each other of the misdeed and speculating upon how it might have been done. By the time Raggett heard of the theft, the house was in an uproar. He, of course, immediately notified me, then apparently called in Bow Street."

By which time, mused Crump, any clue that pointed to the thief's identity had been destroyed. "It is my opinion," he said aloud, "that the guilty party entered through the front hallway and departed the same way, which argues that he was not an uncommon enough caller to excite either comment or interest."

"My conclusions exactly," said Mr. Throckmorton, so preoccupied with gloom that he didn't even flinch when Crump emptied his pipe against the windowsill. "Although in a household of so many people, a stranger might conceivably go unobserved."

"I have spoken to the butler." Crump placed the pipe in his pocket. "He recalls admitting no one to the house except club members. Nor did anyone appear at the tradesmen's entrance other than people who may be logically accounted for. The hall porter verifies his account, and swears that on one could enter or leave the club during the hours it was closed without his knowledge, since he locked and bolted the door and placed the key in his pocket."

"True." Mr. Throckmorton spoke from the depths of despondency. "Except for the chimney sweeps, who by rights should have gone to the back door."

"Chimney sweeps!" In his excitement, Crump rose on his tiptoes. "What chimney sweeps, guv'nor?"

"Why, the usual chimney sweeps, I suppose!" replied Mr. Throckmorton, who was greatly astonished at the Runner's tone. "How should I know? The butler admitted them early this morning—as I said, they came to the front door—and they left some time later with a bag half full of soot. Why the devil are you suddenly interested in chimney sweeps?"

"A bag of soot," mused Crump, eyes half closed. A pity Throckmorton, gazing at him in pop-eyed perplexity, lacked sufficient wit to appreciate his brilliant reasoning. "Damned clever, if I say so as shouldn't. Fetch the butler, if you will. I'd like to learn more of those lads. It's as plain as the nose on your face, guv'nor. In that bag they carried not soot but silver plate."

Mr. Throckmorton was not convinced, having never encountered a particularly clever chimney sweep, but he was happy to accept any explanation that did not implicate the club's members. He scurried to fetch the butler before Crump could change his mind.

Chapter Four

Lady Bligh, clad in a rich and simply cut gold silk gown with a drawstring neck, lounged upon the yellow satin couch in a charming state of indolence. Her heavy hair, that day pale blue, was drawn high upon her head, with flirtatious curls escaping to caress her temples. The Baroness had only recently returned from a breakfast given to two thousand people in the Horticultural Gardens. She brought with her a prize-winning Providence pine, weighing eleven pounds, which she had filched from beneath the owner's proud nose. Beside Dulcie on the couch was her orange cat. The parrot was not in evidence, having been confined to his cage in the Baroness's bedroom following an audacious invasion of the kitchens of Bligh House, where he startled the cook into hysterics.

They were in the Grand Saloon, an exquisite chamber with tall velvet-draped windows, a gay rococo ceiling and a marble fireplace topped with Sicilian jasper. Seated near Mignon's straw-colored French chair was her most persistent admirer, Lord Barrymore, a gentleman of medium height and neat figure, with brown hair and blue eyes. The most courteous of cavaliers, thought Mignon, and one of whom even her mother would have to approve. Unfortunately, Mignon did not, and was even so ungrateful as to wonder what there was in her appearance or manner to inspire such devotion. Whatever his reasons, Tolly had positively dogged her footsteps ever since their first meeting, shortly after she had come to Town. She turned away from Tolly, whose unfailing cheerfulness never failed to grate on her nerves, and studied the fourth occupant of the room, a plump and cozy matron with well-groomed white hair and warm brown eyes who was clad in unrelieved black. Leda Langtry looked far more like a cozy gossip than the author of radical and libelous prose, and she reminded Mignon strongly of someone. Try as she might, Mignon could not think who.

"Don't thank me yet!" said Lady Bligh, her long and slender fingers, heavily laden with topaz rings, tapping against the sofa's arm. "I only obliged Jessop because I knew that if I did not, someone else would." She studied her guest and sneezed. "I must say, Leda, that you do not appear to have taken any great harm from your experience!"

Leda cackled, dispelling her air of gentle unworldliness. "I suppose I should have uttered deep groans and fainted over the rails of the dock? It's no great distance from Fleet Street to Newgate, and many a journalist has walked there by way of Ludgate Hill to see prisoners hanged, or to attend trials in the Old Bailey next door, or to stand trial himself!" She sipped greedily at her ratafia, a drink made of apricots and cherries and other fruits, their kernels bruised and steeped in brandy. "Residence in Newgate has been a hazard of the profession ever since the first news sheets were produced in the Stuarts' time. *Then* the risks were even greater! One might suffer the loss of an ear, or be hanged and drawn and quartered." She grinned. "Which, I daresay, is exactly what Prinny would like to do to me."

"You are very foolish, Leda," Lady Bligh interrupted reprovingly. "What purpose can it serve to make the Regent your enemy?"

"None at all!" retorted Leda gaily. "I've simply no time for a man who has himself bled to a suitably pastel complexion so that he may persuade the lady of the moment that he suffers a broken heart. To give you the word with no bark on it, Prinny is a popinjay!"

"I take it," Dulcie said wryly, through her handkerchief, "that your reprieve has not inspired you to mend your ways. This is not America, where you can gain an interview with the President by ambushing him while he bathes nude in the Potomac. Although I *will* admit that was enterprising of you, Leda!"

"God in heaven!" Leda hiccupped, then scowled. "You sound just like Ivor! *He* thinks I should sit by the fire knitting and composing my memoirs. Stuff! Someone needs to keep our politicians on their toes. *You* wouldn't know anything of that, having no thought in your frivolous head but for your everlasting balls and dinners and promenades!"

"I see," retorted the Baroness, sitting erect, "that time has not taught you to curb your unpleasant tongue. A fine way, Leda, to speak to your rescuer! But I am far more interested in the Viscount that in your opinion of myself."

"Ivor?" Leda looked faintly shocked. "Dash it, Dulcie, you're nearly twice his age!" Mignon immediately regretted her giggle, for it brought Lord Barrymore's attention back to her.

"Shocking," he murmured, with the phlegm indispensable to the man of fashion that his affected manner proclaimed him to be. He waved the beaver hat and bamboo walking stick in his hands demonstratively. "I fear this conversation is hardly fit for your ears."

"Nonetheless," snapped Mignon, loud enough to draw Leda's inquisitive eye, "I mean to enjoy it!" She thought regretfully of her lost love, whose numerous sins had not included placing her on a pedestal.

"Good girl!" said Leda. "Enjoyment is all, at least at your age, and so Dulcie will tell you, even though at *her* age she should know better!"

"Surely," retorted Lady Bligh waspishly, "we can carry on this conversation without these continual references to my age! I grow more and more convinced, Leda, that I should have left you to rot in Newgate!"

"And so you should have," agreed Leda, draining her glass. "The life in Newgate would have provided me with enough sordid information to incriminate the entire justice system in England and enough shameless sin to titillate me until the grave."

"Your tastes certainly have not changed since our last meeting," remarked Lady Bligh.

"Not a bit! I merely indulge them now." Leda looked wickedly at her hostess. "You might try out prison life yourself, Dulcie! 'Twould make a break in your life of uniform dissipation. And one a great deal more enlightening than dallying with the Viscount!"

"Ladies!" Lord Barrymore was driven by the low tone of this exchange to outright protest. "I vow, you go too far! May I remind you that a young lady is present?"

Mignon was far too well bred to tell her suitor precisely what she thought of his untimely intervention. "Hush, Tolly, do!" she said. "I'm sure I'm not so easily shocked."

"Your niece, you say?" Leda inquired of Lady Bligh. The Baroness nodded. "Then you don't need to worry about *her* tender sensibilities, my lad! Exposure to Dulcie would inure even a woman of very low condition to shame!" The ratafia had apparently gone straight to Leda's head, for she squinted in a most vulgar manner at Tolly. "What'd you say his name was, Dulcie?"

"Barrymore," Lady Bligh was conscienceless; she rose and refilled Leda's glass. Tolly sat stiffly at attention and Mignon gloated most uncharitably at his discomfort.

"Barrymore, Barrymore," mused Leda, and appreciatively lifted her glass. "Cripplegate, Hellgate and Newgate and their foul-mouthed sister, Billingsgate! Elegant and spendthrift Irish rakes! An illuminating ancestry, to be sure!"

An angry muscle twitched in Tolly's cheek. "I claim no relation to that particular family, madam." His composure was admirable, but Mignon noted that his fingers tightened on the bamboo cane.

"Ah, more's the pity!" retorted Leda, obviously in high fettle. "A little debauchery might do you the world of good, my lad!"

"Leda, do behave!" Lady Bligh's tone was extremely disapproving, a thing so unusual in her aunt that Mignon stared. "We were speaking of the Viscount! An admirable young man, if a trifle too concerned with his consequence."

"Were we?" said Leda vaguely, her brown eyes fixed thoughtfully on Mignon. "It is his upbringing, no doubt. If only—but there's no use crying over spilt milk! Come here, girl."

Mignon obeyed, more than a little amused. It crossed her mind that, for a lady crossed in love, she was finding London a source of no small entertainment. "She'd pay back dressing," Leda said, eyeing without approval Mignon's plain muslin gown. "Well, young woman, how're you enjoying your aunt's house?"

"Tolerably well, ma'am," Mignon replied sedately, but could not repress her smile. "Though Dulcie's dissipations leave her little time for me!"

Leda hooted. "I might've known Dulcie wouldn't waste her time with a miss as prim as you seemed! Has she told you yet what she means to do with you?"

"Do with me?" Mignon bent and lifted Casanova to her shoulder, where he purred with remarkable violence into her ear. "I'm afraid I do not take your meaning." She looked not at Leda but at Dulcie's frown.

"Then I'll warn you only that your aunt is an incurable busybody!" Leda retorted. "Far be it from me to throw a spanner in the works." She looked at the Baroness, who stared enigmatically into space, and abruptly dropped her bantering attitude. "In truth, you are an excellent creature, Dulcie Bligh, and it was monstrous good of you to take up the cudgels on my behalf. Did you know that the debtors' prison at Newgate is a hotbed of vice, run by gaolers who torture the prisoners at will? Have you heard of the

Press Room beneath the Old Bailey where the *peine forte et dure* is still carried out? Prisoners are spreadeagled on the floor and heavy weights put on their bodies until confessions are literally crushed out of them!"

The Baroness had held up a frail hand for silence. "You will not make a reformer out of me," she responded, "for all your zeal! I know your invective is both feared and admired, Leda, but this crusading spirit of yours fills me with considerable uneasiness. In short, I very much suspect you will find yourself in the devil of a fix!"

"The devil," retorted her guest, "fly away with you! I'm not so easily done for as all that. And when did you become so cow-hearted, Dulcie?" Feeling her presence no longer necessary, or even particularly desired, Mignon retreated to her chair. Lord Barrymore looked with displeasure at the battle-scarred tomcat that she still held. So Tolly was no admirer of animals, mused Mignon, and resolved that thenceforth she would take Casanova with her everywhere.

"*Not* cow-hearted," protested the Baroness, watching with every evidence of displeasure as Leda adjusted her rusty black bonnet, "but prudent. There is such a thing as Fate, my friend! I see you are going to persist in your wrongheadedness and ignore my advice. Where do you go next? You'd do much better to stay here and dine."

"Pah, that's hours away and I've not the stomach for your rich fare." Leda tied her bonnet strings into a lopsided bow. "Anyway, it would ruin my digestion to sit at table and look at your blue hair. Hussy!"

"Ingrate!" responded Lady Bligh promptly, touching those lush curls. "It is not indigestion my fashions inspire in you, but nostalgia and regret!"

"You're obviously as perceptive as ever, and as provoking." Grimacing, Leda rose. "It's oysters and champagne for me, and then I must go and grovel before Warwick—hell and the devil confound the man! I hope I may express myself in a suitably subdued and penitent fashion, though I'd advise no one to make book on it." As she spoke, she moved toward the door. "But first I shall visit a certain firm of soap boilers, where the body of a clerk was found with his blood and brains strewn all about the floor. Are you sure you won't accompany me, Dulcie?"

"Yes." Lady Bligh looked positively glum. "But I will see you to the door."

"You may read about it tomorrow then, in my *Apocalypse.*" Leda's voice echoed back as the ladies proceeded down the hall. "I shall print all the horrid details, with revolting particulars of the mutilated corpse. A pity it wasn't a woman. Which reminds me, Dulcie, I must congratulate you on your handling of the Arbuthnot matter. A pity more details weren't released to the Press." They rounded a corner then, and the Baroness's reply was lost.

"What an odd creature!" said Tolly, moving at last as if he'd come to life from stone. "Unthinkable, that you should have been exposed to her!" His gaze was warm. "Your aunt is a delightful woman, my dear Miss Montague, but I cannot think her influence is of the best. You will think it presumptuous, I suppose, if I say she is not precisely the person I would have chosen to look after you."

"You are correct," Mignon replied, musing that no one had elected Lady Bligh to act as chaperone. Rather, the Baroness had chosen Mignon, and for a purpose that remained unknown. "I *do* think you presumptuous!" His face fell and, being kindhearted, she hastened to make amends. "You have my best interests in mind, I know."

"Dear Mignon!" So overcome was Lord Barrymore that she feared he might fall to his knees at her feet. "If I may call you so? Would that your safekeeping was in my hands! But I speak too precipitately, I know. Forgive me. I will mention *that* matter no more until our acquaintance has had an opportunity to blossom, until you have seen for yourself the depth and durability of my devotion to you."

"I think you forget, Lord Barrymore," said Mignon, wishing

ardently that Dulcie had not seen fit to leave them alone together, "that I am two-and-twenty years of age, and hardly in need of either a keeper or a chaperone."

"Lord Barrymore?" He arched a brow. "Tolly, surely. And you are the merest child."

Mignon cast frantically about in her mind for a means of distraction and hit upon a brilliant ploy that, if it did not give Lord Barrymore a positive disgust for her duplicity, would put his tedious devotion to good use. "There *is* something you can do for me, if you will," she murmured, "but it requires the utmost secrecy. You must speak of it to no one, not even my aunt. Nor must you question me."

"Anything!" Lord Barrymore was fervent. "Ask for the moon, the stars, and I will fetch them for you!"

"It's nothing so difficult as that." Mignon drew forth a letter from her sleeve. The posting of this item had proven no small challenge. She dared entrust it to none of Lady Bligh's servants, not wishing to tax her aunt's tolerance by means of a forbidden correspondence with an ineligible *parti*. "Merely see this safely posted for me."

"As you wish." Without even glancing at the address, Lord Barrymore tucked the letter away. "Tell me more of your aunt's strange caller. Just who *is* Leda Langtry?"

"A childhood friend of Dulcie's," Mignon replied, relieved that he had temporarily abandoned his courtship. "And the publisher of a weekly news sheet. Dulcie, as you may have gathered, was instrumental in securing Leda's release from Newgate." She shrugged, then caught the slumbering cat as it slid from her lap. "I know little more."

"A degrading situation," observed Tolly dispassionately, "for a female of apparently gentle birth. I'll wager she has an interesting tale to tell! What is her connection with Warwick?"

"If Warwick had his way," said Lady Bligh, appearing as if by magic in the doorway, "all journalists would be either transported or hanged." In her wake trailed a maidservant burdened with a teapot and two cups. "Charity!" protested the Baroness. "Have you not learned to count? I said *three* teacups!"

The maid, an extremely timid creature with homely nondescript features and straggling mouse-colored hair, looked ready to cry. "I'm sorry!" she stammered. "I thought you said two."

"No matter!" said Lord Barrymore. "I was just preparing to take my leave." The maid fled, sniffling dolefully.

"Odd," remarked Mignon, staring after the girl, "but I can't rid myself of the feeling that Charity dislikes me."

"Nonsense, my dear Miss Montague!" Again she had earned Lord Barrymore's approval, it seemed. "You are a great deal too imaginative, though that is no great fault in a young girl. The wench is doubtless just envious of one who is her superior in so many ways."

"*Is* it nonsense?" murmured Lady Bligh, her remark almost unnoticed in the flowery effusions with which Tolly presented them as he took leave of them. "I'm not so sure." At last he was gone and her dark eyes moved to her niece, who with a sigh of relief sank back into her chair. "My dear, such a *worthy* young man!"

Mignon met her aunt's twinkling gaze. "Dull as ditchwater, you mean!"

Lady Bligh poured the tea, presented her niece with a cup, then seated herself once more on the sofa, propping up her feet on a circular table inlaid with double rows of brass. "I've a notion," she said thoughtfully, "that there's more to your young Romeo than meets the eye."

Chapter Five

Simpkin was a most superior valet, a seeker after perfection who could truthfully claim that he had never forgotten a single bag or portmanteau, and who prided himself that his master never set foot outside his lodgings in clothing improperly pressed or boots that lacked a mirrorlike perfection. But Simpkin, for all his virtues, possessed one unadmirable trait: he eavesdropped.

It was purely a matter of expediency, of course, and one for which Simpkin was nicely rewarded by his master's wife, who liked to be kept informed of her spouse's peccadilloes. Lord Warwick was not required to live in this elegant hotel at the West End of Town; he had a home of his own, a perfectly suitable establishment which had been graced by a long succession of his eminent ancestors. That fine structure, however, was currently occupied by Lord Warwick's wife, a lady so lost to the precepts of good taste that she had lately attended a ball so covered with jewels that she could not long remain standing and had to be followed around with a chair. While accepting her largess, Simpkin deplored a lady so lacking in discrimination that she had most recently announced to the world that her husband kept by his bedside little books of nursery rhymes. All in all, thought Simpkin judiciously, it was as well Lord and Lady Warwick had chosen to live apart. He stopped and applied his eye to the keyhole.

Lord Warwick stood by his writing desk, his features mottled with rage. Confronting him was a small and white-haired woman clad in black. As the valet watched, she brandished a fist beneath his master's nose. "You needn't threaten *me!*" she said vehemently. "I promise I'll publish an entire series of scurrilous articles about people in high places, yourself included, you damned humbug!" In the hallway Simpkin, having come to a belated recognition of Leda Langtry, moaned.

"You exhibit boundless effrontery, and in the most revolting manner, madam!" retorted Lord Warwick. He was a tall, stooped man with gray hair, a hooked nose, and features that could have been pleasant but were instead always sour, perhaps due to the tenor of both his disposition and his thoughts, which at that particular moment concerned his visitor's decapitation by the ancient Sword of Justice that hung on the Old Bailey's wall. "Come, be reasonable! I will admit that I can hardly blame you for holding no high opinion of a Prince who excels at nothing more regal than shooting chimney pots and riding horses upstairs, but I can and do blame you for publishing your opinion to the world!"

Leda promptly demonstrated the recklessness only to be expected from a female who had visited the insane in an American asylum, invaded a convent and interrogated the nuns, and smoked a peace pipe with heathen redskins. "Thus requiring public punishment," she commented, "and adding to the not inconsiderable matters which you must, as your Regent's right hand, personally oversee!" Her tone contained little appreciation of his exalted position. "Poor man! You would much rather deal with Princess Caroline, would you not? I understand she is currently conducting herself indiscreetly with an Italian of humble origin, so we must conclude that she does not return your regard."

Lord Warwick looked distinctly discomfited, and Leda grinned. "Then there is the shocking lack of decorum in the Lower House! I myself have seen the chosen representatives of the people sprawling on the benches with their hats on, talking of insignificant trifles while serious discussions went on! *That* would make an excellent topic for a newspaper article, would it not?"

"I see it is no use," he said grimly, "to discuss the matter with you. If you have finished with your recriminations and your idle threats, I ask that you vacate these premises. The intervention of Lady Bligh will not protect you a second time. Your moments of liberty are limited; I suggest you make good use of them."

"Oh, I shall!" Leda's eyes sparkled in a most unsettling way. "Fancy, *you* and Princess Caroline! I hadn't suspected—but there it is! My readership will be delighted!"

With an angry oath, Warwick moved forward. "Print one word of *that*," he promised, "and I'll not only see you in Newgate, I'll see to it you hang!"

"Oh, you'll see me," Leda replied, scurrying prudently toward the exit. "And before you think, Warwick!" Simpkin, crouched enthralled in the hallway, was not quick enough to escape the opening door. "Shame!" reproved Leda as the valet clutched his bruised forehead. "Have you forgotten that curiosity killed the cat? Don't trouble yourself, I'll find my own way to the door."

"Simpkin!" his master roared. On reluctant feet, the valet entered the room.

"Simpkin!" said Lord Warwick, again with loathing. "Is it not enough that you remove the hot coals from the bedroom fireplace while I sleep and deposit them in a lacquered coal scuttle, thus filling the room with stench and smoke? How *dare* you admit that pestilent female to my private quarters? Damned if I shouldn't dismiss you!"

A fine way to talk, thought Simpkin indignantly, to one who

looked after his master's interests in a fatherly way, even delivering to tearful ladies their *congés!* "Yes, your grace," he murmured meekly.

Lord Warwick pulled forth a handkerchief and mopped his brow, then hefted a bottle of port. "I don't mind telling you, Simpkin," he said, after drinking deeply, "that it was a damned unpleasant interview, and one for which I hold you responsible! That repulsive female writes the most depraved newspaper articles lamenting the increase in crimes of violence, the ineptitude of Bow Street, and the corruption of Parliament. Now she promises to write one about me! God's bones, I'd like to see the entire newspaper world that stretches between Temple Bar and St. Paul's decimated by a plague!"

"Very good, your grace," said Simpkin, wondering if he was meant to personally undertake this awesome task.

"You're a fool, Simpkin!" said his master. "I wonder why I put up with you. If you ever admit that creature to these rooms again, you'll be dismissed, and without a reference, understand?" The valet nodded mutely, "Very well, then, prepare my bath!"

Simpkin set about this task with great efficiency, demonstrating his noiseless step and politeness of manner, his good temper and subserviency, all the time trembling lest he rouse his master to further wrath. Simpkin wouldn't repeat his error; he'd slam the door in Leda's face if she ever dared show it there again. It wasn't unlikely that she would, Simpkin reflected gloomily. From what he'd seen of Leda Langtry, she was as feisty and imprudent as a fighting cock.

Lord Warwick sat down at his desk and stared at an excellent bust of Cromwell that sat thereupon. If he was slightly truculent, it was not without reason! He raised to his thin lips another glass of port, a refreshment of which he stood in much need after the fatigues of such a long and trying day. He heartily regretted that he had ever encountered Leda Langtry.

Her arrest on the charge of intention to traduce and vilify

Prinny had caused widespread indignation and made the Regent even more unpopular. As if matters had not been bad enough, thought Warwick somberly. The usual attacks on Prinny for his immoral character and his abominable treatment of the Princess of Wales had increased a hundredfold during the visit to London of the Allied Sovereigns. Relations between the Prince Regent and the Tsar of Russia had at best been strained, and the Tsar had not improved matters by waltzing energetically around Lady Chalmondely's ballroom with Lady Jersey, one of the Prince's earlier conquests, and Lady Bligh, whom the world knew he wished to make his next, while treating Lady Hertford, the current favorite, with a marked lack of interest. Now Prinny was drinking even more heavily than usual, and that was a prodigious amount indeed.

Poor Simpkin, emptying hot water into a metal bath, dropped a can. Lord Warwick turned to glower at his valet, an exercise somewhat difficult to execute due to the high shirt collar which brushed his earlobes and framed his chin. "Another female you will not admit to these premises," said Warwick severely, "is Lady Bligh. You *do* recall Lady Bligh, Simpkin?" .

"Yes, your grace." The wretched valet retrieved the can. An interesting interview *that* had been, and one which had earned Simpkin a handsome remuneration from Lord Warwick's spouse. A few more similarly enlightening encounters and Simpkin would be able to retire.

"Your bath is ready, your grace," said Simpkin hesitantly, prepared to either help his master to disrobe or, if it seemed wise, to flee. Lord Warwick emptied his glass and rose.

There was yet another interview to be conducted that evening, and the anticipation of it was almost more than Lord Warwick could bear. He unlocked a drawer of his desk and drew forth a sheaf of banknotes. This night would see him vindicated of a great many past slights! thought Warwick. Even Prinny would be forced to admit the cleverness of a mind that had outthought the experts at Bow Street. But he had long since learned to be cautious. He touched the banknotes almost lovingly. Before he presented his conclusions to higher authorities, his suspicions would be confirmed.

Simpkin goggled at the banknotes, of which there was an awesome pile, as he helped his master to disrobe. Briefly he wondered if his master, having finally come to an appreciation of his invaluable services, meant to render a reward. But Lord Warwick remained silent. "That will be all, Simpkin," he said at last, lowering himself into the bath.

"Very good, your grace." Correct as ever, the valet left the room. He did not, however, set about the many tasks with which he normally filled his time, such as washing the glass and silver used at luncheon or attending the sitting room fire. Instead he shut himself in the pantry, there to count the banknotes that he'd palmed from the stack on his master's desk. Simpkin had his own ways of dealing with ingratitude.

Lord Warwick sank into his steaming bath with a deep sigh. He had no complaint of his hotel, which made every concession to his comfort, including a goose-feather bed large enough to contain two or three people, and a half dozen wide towels. Indeed, thought Lord Warwick, the only fly in his domestic ointment was his moronic valet! No matter. After this next interview he would repair to his club, there to mingle with congenial souls and celebrate his cleverness by winning a few rubbers at whist. So lost was Lord Warwick in reverie that he jumped, splashing water all about the floor, when the door opened. Surely the wretched fellow hadn't come so soon!

It wasn't the expected visitor who stepped into Lord Warwick's room, nor his valet, but a familiar black-clad woman, heavily veiled. The ugly bonnet afforded a glimpse of her white hair. "You!" he said, with annoyed embarrassment, sinking down to his chin in soapsuds. "Why the deuce have you returned?"

The invasion had not gone unnoticed in the butler's pantry. Simpkin scampered hastily to the door of his master's room and bent once again to the keyhole. The sight of Lord Warwick interrupted ignobly in his ablutions made Simpkin nearly swoon. A knocking on the outer door recalled him to his senses and the valet hurried to answer it, wondering frantically if there was any way out of the damnable dilemma he found himself in. Lord Warwick would have his head on a platter for this carelessness.

Simpkin was incorrect; Lord Warwick was not considering beheading his valet, but boiling him in hot oil. "Answer me!" he demanded of the female, whose shoulders were shaking with silent mirth. "How dare you burst in here?"

"I'd dare a lot for this," she said, moving closer. Lord Warwick had no time to do more than stare at the pistol that she held.

The shot, heard throughout the hotel, was loud as thunder in Lord Warwick's vestibule. Simpkin, who had just opened the front door to admit another caller, gasped and turned white with alarm. As one, the men hurried down the hallway. The valet threw open the door and stared. The room was empty of anyone but Lord Warwick, in his bloody tub. "My lord!" gasped the valet and fell against the desk. "My lord, speak to me!"

"I think," offered Lord Barrymore, surveying his host with a practiced eye, "that you'd best fetch a doctor."

Simpkin gaped, noticing for the first time that the bath was shaped like a vast metal coffin, and tore his gaze away from its grisly contents. He moved away from Lord Warwick's desk, bare now of banknotes, then stared pointedly at the open window "Oh, sir!" he moaned. "I very much fear that we've been robbed."

"Yes," said Lord Barrymore thoughtfully.

Chapter Six

Crump, having fortified himself with a bobstick of rum slim, moved cautiously among the crowds who bustled along Fleet Street. Once this had been a sanctuary for debtors and duelists, thieves and murderers, as well as imprudent poets anxious to escape the pillory. Nor had the situation greatly changed, thought Crump, gazing with interest at timber-fronted shops with swinging signs above their entrances. Those who cast slurs upon the King's majesty were still in need of refuge. His wistful eye alighted upon one of the ancient taverns that were so common there. He would need more than a shilling's worth of punch to fortify him for *this* task.

He passed up the tavern. There was no time to waste, though Crump more than half suspected that his pigeon had already flown. He touched the paper in his pocket, a writ granted by Sir John for the apprehension of a murderer. The papers were full of the astonishing details of Lord Warwick's death, and the London

Apocalypse had gone so far as to poke fun at what it termed the plodding efforts of Bow Street. Clever, thought Crump. The Chief Magistrate heartily rued the day that the great Fielding had broken with tradition and admitted journalists into his court, a precedent that many of his predecessors had ample cause to regret.

Even allowing for Sir John's natural disgust with the backhanded blow Fate had dealt him—for Lord Warwick's murderer could be none other than a woman whom the Chief Magistrate had personally escorted from Newgate only days before, a fact that was recalled with grave displeasure by Sir John's superior, the Home Secretary—Crump felt that his own treatment had been grossly unfair. After hearing Simpkin's tale of a violent quarrel between his master and Leda Langtry, and the valet's further assertions that Leda herself had shot Warwick, Sir John had delivered himself of a scathing denunciation of Crump's intelligence and demanded that the Runner make an immediate arrest.

The thieftaker reached his destination, the shop that housed the *Apocalypse*, above which Leda had her home. It was not a bad neighborhood, thought Crump. These coffeehouses were far different from those he frequented, catering not to unwashed criminals and their whores but to wits and scholars, journalists and writers, who exchanged information no more damning than a clever *bon mot*. Adjusting his waistcoat, buff satin with an open pattern in black velvet, Crump stepped into the shop.

The scene that greeted him was one of considerable chaos. Bustling about the small front room were at least five people, all of them engaged in conversation. Leda sat on the dirty floor, sorting busily through a pile of wrapped newspapers, while a dark young man, his clothes an appalling mishmash of styles, bent over a large, odd-looking piece of machinery.

"Egad!" he cried and swooped down upon the startled Runner. "You've come at last, and high time! As I have told Koenig, his steam press is of little use to us without an understanding of how the wretched thing works!" Crump's arm was seized and he was dragged across the room. "Proceed!" cried the dark stranger, whose eyes were so pale they were almost colorless. "We shall watch in wide-eyed wonder as you perform a modern-day miracle!"

Crump stared at the monstrous chunk of machinery and thought he was more likely to pull a rabbit from his hat. Indeed, this strange young man with his narrow twitching nose and watery eyes looked like that small beast. "Peace, my lad!" said Crump, holding up his hand. "You've made a mistake."

"A mistake!" shrieked the young man, in tones so shrill he attracted the attention of everyone in the room. "A mistake, you say! We have a paper to get out—four full pages with advertising, local news, political comment and vigorous leaders written by the editors! Embellished, of course, by the sapient observations of that brilliant commentator upon human folly, the Bystander! A mistake, you call it! Men, sirrah, have died for less!"

"Cut line, Willie," said Leda calmly, from her ignoble spot upon the floor.

"Leda!" cried Willie, eyebrows dancing frantically up and down. Crump felt as if he'd stepped into a madhouse. "Koenig swore his steam press could print in an hour eleven hundred copies of a single four-page sheet! Now this fellow claims we have been taken in! Bubbled, in fact!"

It was obvious that Crump must make a move to silence this extremely vocal young man. He did so with reluctance, aware that every person in that tiny chamber would regard him as the enemy. "Lord love you," he said genially, touching the brace of pistols resting round his plump waist. "I don't know anything about your steam presses, being here on an entirely different matter." He pulled forth his identity card. "The name is Crump, and the address is Bow Street!"

"A Runner!" cried Willie, clasping his hands to his chest. "You brave, brave man! Leda, why didn't you tell me you'd seen fit to notify Bow Street?"

With an ink-stained hand, Leda pushed straggling white hair off her forehead. "Because," she said wryly, "I didn't. Begone, the lot of you!" Her fellow workers filed into the printing room, where a man and a boy were busy at the press, but Willie remained behind. A sudden silence descended. The ill-fitting windows rattled with the beat of passing horses' hooves, the cries of peddlers, the shouts of the news vendors.

"Notify Bow Street of what?" asked Crump. Now that Leda was safely in his clutches, he could afford to take his time. There was much in the present situation that aroused his curiosity.

"Of robbery!" said Willie, almost hopping up and down. "We have been violated, Mr. Crump! Yesterday afternoon I returned to the office to find our priceless prose scattered about the floor, trampled on, our most stunning bursts of rhetoric burnt to ashes in the grate!"

Crump peered around the cluttered room and wondered how anyone could detect, amid such muddle, that robbery had taken place. "Was anything stolen?" he asked, though with little interest. Crump had sufficient experience to smell a red herring when one was dangled under his nose.

"Nothing to signify," replied Leda, rising to her feet and wiping her hands against her skirt. "Some personal papers, my pistol, a pair of my shoes."

"Ah, now," said Crump smoothly, "you'll be pulling my leg!" Though he appeared bland, the Runner's senses had come to attention at mention of that pistol. Well they might claim it was stolen, he thought, since that item had caused a man's death.

"Mr. Crump!" tittered Willie, with an unmistakable leer. "We wouldn't think of doing such a thing!" He sidled closer to the Runner. "Highly improper it would be, though a delightful way to pass one's time!"

"Willie!" interjected Leda, before Crump could verbalize his indignation. "Do behave yourself." Her brown eyes rested on the Runner, and in them was perplexity. "I did not call in Bow Street, considering our little burglary much too inconsequential to engage such great minds. Why are you here? I hope you will not take it

personally, Mr. Crump, if I tell you your presence inspires me with
an ugly presentiment!"

Well it should, thought Crump, for the weapon found by
Warwick's body had been identified as Leda's pistol, and she was
furthermore known to be a crack shot, as attested by a miserable
wretch who, intent on breaking and entering her shop, had had an
unfortunate confrontation with the business end of that pistol. He
looked at Willie, capering about the room like a performing
monkey. Why did Willie strike a chord of recognition when
Crump had never set eyes on him before? "Just who is *he?*" the
Runner asked Leda, with a jerk of his head.

Willie had heard. "*I,*" he announced, drawing himself up dramatically, "am the one and only William Fitzwilliam, my dear
Mr. Crump!" The Runner glowered unappreciatively and Willie
held up one slender and none too clean finger. "Ah, I see you do
not recognize the name! Very well, I shall elucidate." He took a
deep breath. " 'Through the galleries of Windsor rambles the old
mad king, wild of hair and eye, in his violet dressing gown, here
playing a harpsichord for a heavenly chorus that only he can hear,
there lecturing an equally invisible senate!' "

"Willie," interrupted Leda, to Crump's relief, "writes a column
for my newspaper. He calls himself the Bystander."

"I am at your service, Mr. Crump!" Willie executed an inept
bow. "Only tell me how I may assist you!"

"You might," snapped Crump, fast reaching the end of his
patience, "cease pitching me gammon! Else I'll see *you* in gaol!"

"Gaol!" shrieked Willie, ashen. "Witness me atremble with the
palpitations in my heart! But it is the curse of the journalist to
suffer punishment for the expression of his views. Witness the great
John Walter who founded the *Times! He* went to Newgate for
criticizing the Duke of York and while there had his sentence
increased because, while incarcerated, he further censored the Prince
of Wales, the Duke of Clarence, and the Duke of York again. I
shall bear my punishment manfully if only *I* may write my column behind bars!"

"Devil take you, make an end!" bellowed Leda, and Willie paused midspeech. She turned wearily to Crump. "Out with it! Why are you here?"

"Leda, Leda," chided Willie, crooking an admonishing fore-finger. "This is Mr. Crump's opportunity to learn more of the newspaper world. Would you deny it to him? Think what benefit a knowledge of journalism might be in the pursuit of his trade!" His pale eyes gleamed. "And think what benefit Mr. Crump might prove to us, being as it were on the inside! We might, with his assistance, publish detailed accounts of atrocious crimes before our competitors even knew they had occurred."

"An excellent notion!" said Leda thoughtfully. "What do you say, Crump?"

The Runner impatiently reached into his coat pocket. This nonsense had taken up some considerable time. "I hold a warrant for your apprehension, Leda Langtry, on the charge of murdering Lord Warwick. You must consider yourself in custody."

"*Now* I remember!" Willie screwed a tarnished monocle into one eyesocket and triumphantly regarded Crump. "I thought, old fellow, that you looked damned familiar! It was you who took Leda into custody before. I saw you, having prudently taken refuge in the printing room. Gad, but we must soon consider you quite one of the family."

"Warwick's murder?" repeated Leda, doing what Crump con-sidered a creditable impersonation of one stunned. "Good God, you must be mad."

"Tell that to the Chief Magistrate!" Crump drew forth a pair of handcuffs, which closed with a snap and a spring. "The evidence against you is so overwhelming that the jury probably won't even retire."

"Infamous beyond all description!" wailed Willie, staring at the cuffs. "Do you mean to lead poor Leda shackled through the streets? Mr. Crump, for shame!"

"For shame to you!" retorted Crump, fastening the cuffs around Leda's wrists. "Interfering with the law is a serious offense, and I'm not unaware that you've been treating me to a rare mare's nest. To what purpose, I might ask? Can it be you're in this thing up to your own neck?"

"Mr. Crump!" Willie clasped his throat, a picture of dismay. "And I liked you, upon my soul! But I fear that in the pursuit of this particular friendship, your choice of occupation will prove an insuperable obstacle."

"So the jury won't go out?" asked Leda, gazing unhappily upon her shackled wrists. "You seem damned sure of yourself, Mr. Crump!"

Crump was not to be goaded into mention of Lord Warwick's valet, who professed himself willing to swear to Leda's guilt in the witness-box. "Aye," he said somberly. "That I am."

"Despair not, Leda!" Willie danced enthusiastically about the room. "We shalk make it a *cause célèbre*. The world will rise up in arms to protest that Leda Langtry is confined to Newgate, there to mingle with thieves and murderers and other unmentionable scum, and will clamor for your release." He smiled smugly. "Meanwhile you shall take notes as the scoundrels practice their dying speeches and smuggle those notes to me. We shall have their last words in print before the wretches ever mount the scaffold!"

"It's more likely you'll be there yourself, my lad!" growled Crump, inexorably guiding Leda toward the door. "I warn you I mean to look most particularly into *your* activities!"

"Mine!" Willie looked like a startled hare. "I vow you are quite mistaken in me, Mr. Crump, but in my eyes it is a very amiable fault for you to overvalue me so." He glanced at Leda. "Never fear! I'll see you don't hang, dear one, even if you *did* dispatch Warwick to his final rest, which I doubt!" He raised his head and looked down his nose at Crump. "Your innocence must be apparent to any right-thinking man."

"Right-thinking!" sputtered Crump, whose progress had been so impeded by the dawdling, silent Leda that he had barely reached the doorway. "You think it right and proper that you should interfere with the apprehension of a murderer?" Willie's smile, a gesture of singular sweetness, only intensified the Runner's wrath. "A pretty scoundrel *you* are, my lad!"

"Thank you, Mr. Crump!" said Willie, his grin even broader. "I, in my turn, might call you a proper bastard!" Having reduced the Runner to apoplectic silence, he turned to Leda. "I'll notify our solicitor of this abominable development. *He'll* know what to do! Do you wish me to send word to anyone else?" His voice was a wicked, sly whisper, and his pale features wore a look of great anticipation. "The Viscount, perhaps?"

"Yes, tell Ivor," Leda said abruptly, rousing from her trance. "You'll like that, won't you, Willie? Fool! Ivor has as little liking for you as *you* have for the frail sisterhood! And you might tell him to inform Lady Bligh." She jingled her handcuffs and glared irritably at Crump. "Well, why do you dawdle, man? If I must go to Newgate, then let us proceed!"

"The poor Viscount," murmured Willie, "will be *quite* enraged. I fear, Mr. Crump, that this day's proceedings will bring you a number of enemies."

Crump clapped his hat upon his head, not trusting himself to reply, and practically shoved Leda into the street. He had forgotten that she was numbered among Dulcie's *protegées*. Even the thought of the substantial reward offered by the government for capture of a murderer could not reconcile him to another set-to with Lady Bligh.

Chapter Seven

"You are positive, Culpepper?" asked Dulcie, so deep in concentration that her eyes were nearly crossed. "Although I don't know why I should doubt you when I anticipated as much!"

"Nor do I!" retorted the dour and disapproving Culpepper, whose expression was as severe as her mistress's. "*You'll* be dragged off to Newgate next, and *then* think what the Baron will say!"

"Culpepper, Culpepper!" The Baroness adjusted her cashmere shawl, embroidered in gold and silks of all colors, ten ells long and worth a thousand pounds. "You will give Mignon the impression that you are a positive stick-in-the-mud! And all because I insisted that you treat yourself to beefsteak and oyster sauce and a rendezvous with your adoring night watchman."

The abigail vouchsafed no reply, but shuddered eloquently. It seemed odd to Mignon that Dulcie's gaunt and sour-faced dresser should have a beau but love was blind, she supposed, and in this instance love must also be both undiscriminating and fearless.

"Is there anything else?" asked Culpepper, for Lady Bligh had fallen into a reverie. Culpepper was a confirmed spinster, but such was her devotion to her mistress that she would even encourage the watchman who was besotted with her, to serve Dulcie's ends. Culpepper only hoped that she wouldn't be requested to marry the whiskey-swilling fool.

The Baroness sneezed and, handkerchief in hand, waved her abigail away. Culpepper hovered in the doorway, concerned. Dulcie regarded her, then smiled. "Thank you, Culpepper!" she said gently. "You are a great comfort to me."

Mignon, watching from a comfortable plump chair, puzzled over the exchange after Culpepper took her leave. Mignon had fast come to understand that there was little rhyme or reason in the goings-on at Bligh House. She studied Dulcie, whose hair was now lime green. The Baroness wore a cream muslin gown with elbow sleeves and an open center over an exquisite slip and countless strands of pearls. She looked as fetching, if not as innocent, as a mere girl.

"Ah, to be truly young again!" said Lady Bligh, so aptly that Mignon started. "Alas, I am not, my dear." Feebly, she drew her shawl closer about her. "The frailties of age have crept into these weary bones. Now I find myself no longer capable of the things I wish to do."

Had Mignon been longer acquainted with Lady Bligh, she might have derived no small amusement from this pathetic speech, but Mignon was a girl with a great deal of compassion, and the thought of her aunt so stricken with years filled her with remorse. "Dulcie!" she cried, and hurried across the room. "Are you unwell? Pray tell me what I can do to help you!"

"Dear Mignon!" The Baroness languished artfully. "It is good of you to offer, child! But you are much too young to bother with an old wretch like me." She raised a trembling hand to her brow. "You should be attending balls and routs, gaily breaking hearts without thought for tomorrow, not running errands for an ancient crone. I would not think of spoiling your pleasure, Mignon."

Mignon sank to her knees by the couch and took her aunt's hand. "I did not come to Town in search of pleasure," she said quietly, "as I think you know. Only tell me what I may do to help you, Dulcie! I'm yours to command."

The Baroness opened her eyes and smiled vaguely. Mignon wondered if she imagined the mischievous twinkle that danced in those dark eyes before the lids drooped again "Dear, *dear* child!" said Lady Bligh faintly. "You are so kind."

Thus it was that when Viscount Jeffries called again at Bligh House, he found that the Baron Bligh's incomparable Drawing Room had become the setting for a moving tableau—the Baroness, posed most aesthetically on a blue striped couch with an orange cat slumbering at her feet; her niece, kneeling beside her, looking worried indeed.

"What's this?" inquired Ivor of Lady Bligh's butler, who stood at his side, feet shuffling nervously. "Is your mistress ill?"

"Maybe, and maybe not," replied Gibbon in hollow tones. A muscle twitched at the corner of his mouth. "I wouldn't dare to say."

"Gibbon!" announced the Baroness, without opening her eyes. "Give Viscount Jeffries back his snuffbox immediately, or I shall never speak to you again!" To Ivor's amazement the butler extended his hand, on which reposed an exquisite porcelain-inlaid piece, then beat a hasty, shambling retreat. "Nor," called Lady Bligh after him, "will you pick the pockets of this particular caller again. Jessop, do come in!"

Ivor, suspecting this errand was a grievous waste of time, stepped almost reluctantly into the room. "Close the door," said Dulcie in tones that were decidely grim. "Not that I imagine it will do much good!"

Mignon sank back on a stool and regarded their visitor. He might be handsome as Apollo with the sunlight glinting off his red-gold curls, and possess a figure that needed aid from neither buckram nor corseting; he might be elegant and wild and the acknowledged heir to a peerage and a long rent roll; but she, or so she told herself sternly, could find nothing to admire in him.

Ivor had been briefly distracted from his mission by the grandeur of his surroundings, awesome even to one who had been born sucking the proverbial silver spoon. He was particularly struck by a marble fireplace so huge that a man could stand in it upright or, if he were so inexplicably inclined, sit in the antique iron grate. Before the fireplace stood a massive gold fire screen framing a plate of glass so transparent that it was scarcely distinguishable from air. A splendid place to toast one's toes in wintertime, thought Ivor, then smiled at his whimsey. He turned then, and the smile clashed violently with Mignon's glare.

"Children!" said the Baroness briskly, swinging her feet to the ground as she sat upright. "I vow I do not know which of you is the more absurd." She patted Mignon's curls. "Come, Jessop, and sit down. We have much to do and in a very short time."

Ivor crossed the stone floor, his brown eyes fixed on Mignon. In them was a puzzled expression. The Viscount, being both wealthy and personable, and consequently long pursued by marriageable damsels and their hopeful mamas, was not accustomed to young ladies who regarded him as if he were the fiend incarnate, particularly rather unprepossessing young ladies with freckles and bright red hair. Mignon, following his thoughts with fair accuracy, scowled even more dreadfully.

"Wrinkles, my child!" said Lady Bligh, and smartly pinched her niece. "Now, Jessop! I sympathize with your feelings, and confess that my own spirits are of a somewhat melancholy cast. But it will not do to sit back and lament poor Leda's fate! She is a creature of wit and influence, after all, and could if she chose be courted by the great for her company." The Baroness sighed, then sneezed. "A pity that she does *not* choose! Leda sees and hears much that does not make its way to the printed page."

"You know then," Ivor inquired cautiously, trying to make sense of this speech, "that Leda has again been taken into custody?"

"I do," Dulcie retorted, and Mignon stared. So *that* was the information that Culpepper had brought! "In connection," the

Baroness added, "with Warwick's murder, of course. The fool! I told her to avoid him. If ever a man was ripe for murder it was Warwick, and Leda makes a perfect scapegoat."

Lord Jeffries frowned, an act which made him look very young and vulnerable. Mignon quickly dropped her eyes to her hands and reminded herself sternly that she was mourning the lover who'd been so cruelly torn from her arms. "I tend to agree with you," he said. "I cannot see Leda provoked to murder. If only we knew the details!"

"We shall," promised the Baroness, smoothing her startling green curls. "You may trust me for that."

"I think I must," replied the Viscount ruefully. "Never have I felt so helpless! Even my uncle, who might have been induced to come to Leda's aid, though not without strenuous protest, is unapproachable." His mouth twisted wryly. "Percy is suffering from a severe case of the gout, brought on by the consumption of a turkey stuffed with chestnuts."

"Percy," said Lady Bligh absently, "is an idiot."

"I don't suppose," ventured the Viscount, "that you'd care to tell me how you learned of Leda's arrest? I do not believe the matter is publicly known."

"It will be," the Baroness prophesied. "Mignon, fetch our visitor some claret!" Reluctantly, Mignon rose to obey. So confusing and unwelcome were the emotions roused in her by sight of Viscount Jeffries that she would have preferred to empty the decanter's contents over his damnably handsome head. Their hands touched as he took the glass from her. Mignon flushed and turned quickly away, resenting mightily the amusement in his eyes.

"There is something I must confess," Ivor said, and dropped his gaze to his claret glass. "Perhaps you have wondered at my concern with Leda's predicament."

"Believe me," Lady Bligh interrupted, in an extremely repressive manner, "explanations are unnecessary. Indeed, I beg that you refrain!"

Ivor looked inquiringly at his hostess, who was frowning at the closed door. "But I must!" he replied. "Believe me, it is important that you know."

"I don't suppose," said Dulcie gloomily, "that you'd take my word for it that I already know?"

"How could you?" inquired Ivor gently, and set down his glass on a table inlaid with brass. "When you have no idea of what I mean to say?"

Lady Bligh sighed and pulled the orange cat onto her lap, where it purred gustily. "Remember Mignon!" she advised. "You will not wish to make her privy to your secrets. You would do much better to postpone your confessions until another day."

Ivor glanced at that young lady, who paused in her restless pacing of the room—an exercise that revealed to the discerning observer a pleasing grace and an even more pleasing physique—to stare at her aunt indignantly.

"If I could help it I would not tell, but it must come out." As Ivor searched for words, he surveyed his gleaming boots. "As you must know," he said, "my family traces its line back to Osbert, Duke of Calvert, who founded the Abbey of Coventry, married the famous Lady Godiva, and died in 1087." Lady Bligh yawned and he frowned. "Succeeding generations were brought up with a strong sense of duty and family—too much so, I sometimes think— and my uncle Percy must be the highest stickler of them all. My father, on the other hand, was something of a loose screw, or so I'm led to understand. When my parents were divorced, Percy insisted my mother resume use of her maiden name."

"What an extraordinary affair!" Briskly, the Baroness dumped the cat onto the floor and rose to her feet. "You need more claret, young man! Divorce is shocking, to be sure, but you need not let it trouble you. Some of the best people have been divorced, even members of my own family!" Despite his protest, she refilled his glass. "I'm sure Mignon does not mind."

"Dulcie!" gasped that damsel, who was leaning in an unladylike manner on the back of a settee.

"You misunderstand," said Ivor firmly. "I am not acquainting you with my family history merely to pass the time." Lady Bligh opened her mouth but he continued inexorably. "I had been accustomed to thinking my mother dead until I made Leda's acquaintance, which was quite by accident. Even then, she did not tell me, but she has a co-worker who is not so scrupulous." He smiled. "I'll swear Willie knows every secret in the world."

"That's the resemblance I couldn't pinpoint!" cried Mignon. "It has puzzled me ever since I met Leda." She felt the Viscount's gaze and flushed. "You have your mother's eyes."

"Hell and the devil confound it!" muttered Dulcie, and kicked a table leg. "Addlepates, the pair of you, and so you will learn." She turned on Ivor. "Enough confidences for one day, I beg! You are a noted pugilist, young man. In atonement for going against my wishes, you will demonstrate for me various of those noble methods of self-defense."

And thus it was that Mr. Crump, paying a call to Bligh House, was ushered into the Drawing Room, there to witness the Baroness, green hair tumbling down her back, deliver to Viscount Jeffries a decided facer, which resulted in an ignoble bloodied nose.

"Bravo, Dulcie!" cried Mignon, clapping her hands. Crump and Gibbon stared.

"Dear Mr. Crump!" said Lady Bligh, leading her victim to a chair and pressing upon him her handkerchief. "Gibbon, some ice! You witness my latest interest, Crump, and I vow I shall enter the ring. Do come in! Have you come to enliven our spirits with your unpretending good nature and joyous temper? Sit down, Crump, sit down!"

Stark mad in white muslin, concluded Crump gloomily, and sank into a chair. "I'm afraid this isn't a social call, Baroness."

"No?" Dulcie opened wide innocent eyes. "What then, Crump? Do you wish me to help you solve another little mystery?" She perched on the edge of the sofa, seemingly intent. "I shall be delighted, of course! What will you have me do?"

Crump had thoroughly filled himself with salt beef and carrots, washed down with three pints of beer, before attempting this very dangerous and unsafe undertaking, and still he wished Sir John had seen fit to send another man. "No mystery," he said, eyeing the huge orange cat that gazed at him so malevolently. "We have our miscreant already, and she'll hear the Condemned Sermon preached at Newgate."

"Crump!" gasped Dulcie, as Gibbon reentered the room. "Do you mean to touch my heart and endanger my peace of mind?"

Gibbon thrust the ice at Mignon, then stalked across the room to tower over the Runner. "Bridle your tongue!" he demanded, white hair standing out at angles from his head. "Or I'll tell Sir John myself that you've been plaguing the Baroness!"

"Oh, no, you won't, laddie!" retorted Crump, who was after all no stranger to Lady Bligh's queer flights. Enthralled, Mignon applied the ice to Ivor's neck with a force that made him wince. "Have you forgotten," added the Runner, "Sir John's pocket watch? If he so much as sets eyes on you again, Sir John is likely to clap *you* in gaol."

"It might be worth it," Gibbon retorted, twitching, "to boot you out the front door!"

"My butler," explained the Baroness to the room at large, "was once a Runner himself, but his natural proclivities toward petty theft ended what might have been a remarkable career." Pulling the exquisite shawl up over her head, she waved a feeble hand. "You may go, Gibbon! See that we are not disturbed."

Crump wondered, apropos of disturbances, if he should mention that his arrival had startled an extremely homely female who was eavesdropping outside the Drawing Room door, but a baleful hiss from the orange cat sent the thought from his mind. He gazed about the room, overwhelming in its opulence, and his curious eye alit on the huge blue parrot. "Bloody landlubber," remarked Bluebeard conversationally.

"Let me make you known to my companions," murmured

Dulcie, in dying tones. "The somewhat battered gentleman is Viscount Jeffries, and his ministering angel is my niece, Miss Montague." Flushing, Mignon snatched her hand from the Viscount's neck. He caught it in his own before she could move away.

"Considering that it was your aunt," he murmured around the bloody handkerchief, "who so maltreated me, don't you think you might at least offer me your sympathy?" Mignon only scowled. "What an unfriendly creature you are," he added quietly. "Do you dislike me so much? If so, I am sorry for it."

Mignon looked at the firm fingers that grasped her wrist and experienced an odd feeling along her spine. A thrill of pure terror, she told herself; the Viscount was obviously a cold-hearted sensual blackguard. Nonetheless, such was Mignon's nature that she could only reply honestly. "You are mistaken," she said, raising her eyes. "I don't dislike you."

Crump paid very little attention to the two of them, beyond noting that Viscount Jeffries was bang up to the mark in a cloth coat with clawhammer tails and tasselled hussar boots, and that Dulcie's niece wore a pleated dotted lingerie dress with several frills. He focused his not inconsiderable intellect upon Lady Bligh. "I must ask you a few questions, Baroness, about Leda Langtry."

At least this, reflected Mignon, had the effect of diverting the Viscount's attention from herself, though he still grasped her hand. She wondered at herself, for she was more regretful than relieved.

"Leda?" repeated Dulcie vaguely. "Ah, yes, the *Apocalypse*. I recently did her a favor, I believe, though it is difficult to recall. Was it yesterday or the day before? Why I did it, I cannot say."

"You arranged for her release," retorted Crump woodenly, his cautious eyes returning to the crouching cat, "from Newgate. There's no use denying it, Baroness."

"Deny it?" cried Lady Bligh. "Of course not. I deny nothing, my dear Crump. There, does that make you happy?"

Crump stared sadly at his hostess who, with only her elegant nose in evidence, looked like nothing more than an animated shawl. The Runner's mood was not the most sanguine; his efforts to trace the chimney sweeps who had been at White's Club had resulted in the discovery that these, alas, had been sweeps after all, sent by the firm responsible for White's noble chimneys. But Crump was tenacious, and he knew well the smell of a rat. Crump would eat his hat if those two sweeps didn't bear watching.

"Leda Langtry," he said, trying another line of attack, "has been committed to Newgate to await her trial for the murder of Lord Warwick. The evidence against her is overwhelming. If you have possession of any information that may help Mrs. Langtry, Baroness, I urge you to reveal it to me now."

"*Miss* Langtry, to be precise," murmured the Baroness, and sneezed so emphatically that the shawl fell further forward, completely covering her face. "And I don't believe a word of it!"

Crump wiped his sweaty palms on his waistcoat. "There's no question whatsoever of her guilt," he said curtly. "The murder weapon has been positively identified as hers, and Warwick's valet admitted her to the apartments." He stared uncordially at his shawl-covered hostess. "Come, come, Lady Bligh! You don't want me to tell Sir John you've been uncooperative!"

"To threaten an old woman!" shrieked the Baroness, tumbling sideways in a heap, which unnerved Crump so greatly that he belched. He cast a nervous look at Mignon.

"Senility," helpfully observed that damsel, who was, with a dampened cloth and a perverse pleasure, wiping the Viscount's battered face. "I'm afraid that neither Lord Jeffries nor I can help you, both of us being all at sea."

Crump doubted the truth of this, having had prior and unpleasant experience with Lady Bligh's duplicitious relations, but a moan from the Baroness recalled his attention to her prone figure. "Murder!" she uttered, in doomlike cadences. "Leda? Unthinkable! You might as well tell me the world is coming to an end."

The Runner had an impulse to thwack the sofa's inert burden with his baton, but the parrot chose that moment to swoop through the air. Crump ducked, knocking his chin smartly against the chair's wooden arm.

"I begin to think," murmured Ivor to Mignon, "that your aunt is totally unprincipled."

"*That* is an opinion," she replied, suppressing her laughter, "with which I can only agree." She did not meet his gaze, leaning forward instead to drop the damp cloth over Casanova, engaged in battling the handsome tassels that swung from Ivor's boots. The cat streaked across the room, up the side of Crump's chair and over his bent back, before escaping his unwelcome shroud. Mignon could not help herself; she dissolved into giggles, which brought from her companion an answering and thoroughly enchanting smile.

"The devil!" spat the Runner, thoroughly unnerved. "We know your friend called on you here that day, Baroness. Kindly tell me what she wished to speak to you about."

"Mignon!" moaned Lady Bligh, feeble and still prone. "Memory fails me. Kindly tell dear Crump what Leda had to say."

"She said," promptly replied Mignon, "that you were both frivolous and dissipated, that I would repay dressing, and that the Regent is a popinjay." The Viscount's thoughtful gaze was fixed on her face.

"Did she mention Warwick, miss?" asked Crump, ever hopeful.

"I believe she did." Mignon frowned. "But it was Dulcie who said Warwick wished to see Leda transported or hanged." She smiled brightly. "Is that what you wished to know, Mr. Crump?"

It was not. Crump gazed unhappily at the nearest window, hung with golden Norwich damask. If only he might retire to a peaceable country village, there to deal with nothing more vexing than smugglers and highwaymen! "I suppose you all wish to see Leda discharged and paid for her inconvenience and expense," he growled. "Well, it won't wash! She's as guilty as bedamned, for all she may claim she has an alibi! There isn't a juryman alive who'll believe she was visiting with an old friend at the time of Warwick's death." He leaped to his feet as the parrot murmured in his ear.

"An alibi." The Baroness righted herself and threw back the shawl, revealing tousled green hair and a cunning grin. "Dear Crump, you are *so* informative!"

The Runner swore an awesome oath, and placed his hat so forcefully upon his head that it slid down over his ears. "You're leaving us so soon?" cried Lady Bligh as he strode wrathfully toward the door. "But you have not told us how we may assist you!" He turned on his heel and glared at her. Dulcie smiled seraphically. "For instance, I don't believe you know that Warwick himself spent some time in the Fleet Prison, a not uncommon address for Prinny's friends."

If Crump could only have had his way, Lady Bligh would have joined that illustrious group behind bars, there to remain for a very long time. Apparently this uncharitable wish didn't show on his face, for the Baroness swiftly moved to his side and took his arm in a manner, Crump thought dazedly, as abandoned as any street-walker.

"I will see you out!" she said, and guided him toward the door.

Mignon reflected that her aunt had a positive genius for leaving her alone with eligible young men. She looked at the Viscount, undeniably considered a fine catch for any miss. "Well," she said weakly. "It looks as if your mother has landed herself in the devil of a mess."

"Doesn't it?" agreed Ivor cordially. "It also looks as if we may trust your aunt to get her out again! But you must not refer to Leda in that manner. As far as the world is concerned, my mother is dead, and Leda prefers that the matter be left there."

"Does she, indeed?" inquired Mignon, who not only loathed injustice in any form but was grateful for an excuse to think the worst of this disturbing man. "She prefers to go about her business unhindered by wealth and luxury, I suppose! And so you leave your mother's rescue to my aunt, so that you may remain unbesmirched by scandal? It gives me no high opinion of you, Lord Jeffries."

Ivor rose to his feet and looked down upon her from his not inconsiderable height. "How fortunate," he remarked, with an amusement that made Mignon grind her teeth, "that your opinion is of so little concern to me, Miss Montague. But I will return the favor, since we are taking liberties. *I* consider it a pity that the girl who possesses the loveliest eyes I've ever seen possesses also the most vicious tongue." Too stunned to even deliver a scathing retort, Mignon watched speechless as he swept her a mocking bow and walked calmly from the room.

Chapter Eight

While Sir John sat long hours in judgment in the lower front room which served as the Bow Street court, persons accused of more serious crimes—treason, murder, felonies—underwent trial at the Old Bailey Session House. Eight sessions, presided over by the Lord Mayor, Recorder, and judges, were held each year.

The Old Bailey stood in the heart of London, at the corner of Newgate Street. Outside the grim building were held public hangings, executions so popular with the citizenry that the windows overlooking the gallows were filled with family parties sipping tea and well-dressed dandies who amused themselves by squirting the throng below with brandy and water.

There were no executions scheduled for this day, but there was to be a late sitting in court. Already the clock of Old St. Sepulchre's Chruch, across the street, had chimed the time, and the black-robed usher of Number One Court had recited his spiel, which concluded with a pious request to God to save the King and

the King's Justices. "From what, I wonder?" murmured Lady Bligh
irreverently, watching the entrance of the Lord Mayor, clad in his
richest robes of office and carrying his plumed cocked hat, as well
as an absurd little bouquet that was perhaps intended to battle the
stench of unwashed humanity that filled the room. Following him
across the herb-strewn floor were his sheriffs, his sword carrier and
his mace bearer.

Standing beside his mistress under the balcony and close to the
dock, Gibbon indulged himself with various dark mutterings. He
did not approve of Lady Bligh's ventures into the world of crime
and criminals. He looked about gloomily. Among so many people,
a clever pickpocket might have reaped a veritable harvest, albeit
from those with little left to steal. Gibbon himself suffered no such
compulsion, not in this place.

On a long bench in the front of the cramped and somber court
sat the Justices, robed lawyers, aldermen with their chains of office
around their necks. The body of the room was thronged with a
restless murmuring mob. On this, the last day of the sessions, all
prisoners convicted on capital charges were herded together in the
dock to receive the death sentence. Among those on the raised
platform were two gentlemen found guilty of murdering a lavender merchant and burying his body in a gravel pit. Clinging to
the rail was Tiger Tim, so called in consequence of his enormous
strength, who could take in his teeth the waistband of a man of
ordinary size and carry him about the room as a cat might a
mouse. Tiger Tim could also, as he had more than once demonstrated, commit quite efficient murder with his huge hands.

"So this," mused the Baroness, "is what Leda may look forward
to."

At least, Gibbon thought, looking down at her, the Baroness
undertook these forays in adequate disguise. In a hideous purple
gown, with a gaudy shawl around her shoulders and a garish red
wig upon her head, Dulcie looked like an abbess. As such she was
indistinguishable among the crowd.

"It is my painful duty to tell you that you have but a few more days to live," intoned the Lord Mayor. Dulcie, fine eyes narrowed to thin slits, watched him intently. "It is to be hoped that the sacrifice of your lives may induce others to abstain from embarking upon criminal careers."

"Enough!" announced the Baroness, so decisively that the Lord Mayor paused midspeech. She swept grandly from the courtroom and Gibbon followed, so embarrassed that even his ears flamed red.

Oblivious to her butler's chagrin, Lady Bligh stepped into the paved courtyard. "Vastly edifying." she remarked, adjusting the bright green bonnet that sat atop her garish curls. "Unless Leda is to come to a singularly sticky end, we must make up our minds to take the field."

Gibbon's blood turned to water at the plurality of that pronoun. "I beg that you will allow me to fetch you a carriage," he said solemnly. "This is not the sort of neighborhood that you are accustomed to, my lady."

"Nonsense!" Dulcie stepped into the street and observed her reflection in a broken shop window. "Grotesque, am I not? And most artfully done! We will walk, Gibbon. The exercise will do you good."

"Very well, my lady," said the butler hollowly, blushing to the roots of his lank white hair as his mistress took his arm. "Though it's not at all what's proper, and I don't like it above half."

"Go to blazes!" said the Baroness cheerfully. "I vow you are afraid of your own shadow, Gibbon. You'll escort me next to an actual hanging—and I pray it may not be Leda's!—if you exhibit further sulkiness." Glancing at the grand old church of St. Sepulchre's and the bell that rang out the doom of condemned prisoners, Gibbon closed his mouth. His mistress was not prone to idle threats.

They passed by slums and homes that had been mansions a century ago, their rotting walls inhabited now by vermin and vice; by the Newgate meat market; by the College of Surgeons and Surgeons' Hall to which the bodies of executed felons were taken for dissection. With each step Gibbon's spirits fell lower. At last

Lady Bligh paused outside Bart's Hospital in nearby Giltspur Street, and turned to gaze sternly at her butler.

"What are you afraid of, Gibbon?" she asked. "The denizens of the neighborhood—or the likelihood that I'll make you return Lord Barrymore's stickpin? Set your mind at rest! I daresay he'll never miss it. Though if I were you, I'd be very loath to part company with that particular piece."

"Lord Barrymore," Gibbon ventured, "was with Lord Warwick's valet when the body was discovered. I thought you might wish to know, my lady, it seeming a trifle queer."

"Perhaps." Dulcie frowned. "Warwick and Tolly would hardly seem kindred spirits, though I believe they belong to the same club. Continue, Gibbon! What else have you learned?"

Gibbon had kept up his contacts with the criminal element, including thieves, pawnbrokers and dealers in stolen goods, though not with an eye to assisting his mistress in her infernal inquiries; and though Crump was hardly approachable in regard to such things, there were other Bow Street men who were proof against neither discreet questioning nor bribery. "Warwick," he said, "had a lot of enemies. He wasn't above profiting from other people's mistakes, ferreting them out and threatening to expose them if his silence wasn't bought."

"I thought as much," murmured the Baroness.

"Warwick's inquest provided little in the way of sensation." Gibbon, at his mistress's insistence, had attended that event. "Bow Street is convinced of Miss Langtry's guilt, based primarily on the fact that the murder was committed with her pistol. There's no doubt of *that:* the gunsmith who provided her the pistol came forward and made oath that the bullet in the, er, body and the bullets remaining in the pistol were all cast in the same mold."

"They contained some distinguishing mark, I suppose?" mused Lady Bligh, skirting with delicacy a drunk snoring in the gutter. "The devil!"

"Yes, my lady," agreed Gibbon. "It gave me a nasty turn. There was a very small round pimple on all of them, produced by a tiny

hole in the mold." He cleared his throat dramatically. "Miss Langtry, however, claims that the weapon was stolen from her only
hours before the murder, and her story is corroborated by various
of her employees."

"Leda," snapped the Baroness, so emphatically that both her wig
and her plumage were knocked askew, "has made a rare mull of it!
My patience with the wretch is quite exhausted. What's this
Crump let slip about a possible alibi?"

"Pray moderate your manner, my lady!" hissed Gibbon, his
mouth twitching as he glanced nervously over his shoulder. "I am
not wishful of drawing attention to ourselves."

"We already have," retorted the Baroness, unconcerned. "In
truth, we are being followed even now." Gibbon wore a face of
perfect horror and she patted his arm. "Nothing to signify, I assure
you! Continue, Gibbon. What of Leda's alibi?"

Gibbon, reflecting that he'd lived like a duck hunted by a spaniel
ever since making the Baroness's acquaintance, replied obediently.
"Everyone thinks it's so much humbug, my lady. There *is* something else queer, and that concerns Warwick's valet."

"What?" demanded Dulcie, moving closer to her butler and
sending him all in a muck of sweat. "Relax, Gibbon! I simply do
not care to be overheard."

Gibbon was far from being reassured. He was well aware of his
station in life even if his mistress was not, and though he adored
her he thought it shocking that she should even deign to touch his
hand, let alone cling to his arm so tightly that her green plumes
tickled his nose. "Yes, my lady," he said repressively. "Simpkin—
that's the valet's name—seems to have come into money suddenly.
He's been wasting the ready in prime style ever since Warwick
died."

"Odd," mused the Baroness, "that Simpkin has not come to the
attention of Bow Street. I fancy it may also be to our advantage."
She sneezed. "And Crump is wearing a new darkish colored wig,
without powder, which becomes him, wretched man."

Crump had endured a long and arduous day, which began the

night before when he and his brother officers had been called upon
to attend a masquerade held at the Argyll Rooms, where by way
of novelty the revelers competed to pull off the head of a live goose
hanging upside down. From there the Runner had proceeded to
Ludgate where the well-known jewelers, Messrs. Rundle and
Brydges, Court silversmiths, had been relieved of £35,000 worth of
merchandise by sleight of hand. Crump had taken down the particulars of the man and woman who were involved and had
arranged for handbills to be distributed, providing descriptions of
both the culprits and the jewels and offering a reward for useful
information. No fewer than nine men had been examined that day,
and careful watch was being kept on the home of a notorious fence
who not only organized burglary on a grand scale but also had
elaborate arrangements in his house for melting down precious
metals. Crump was not confident, however, that the crime would
be so easily solved. If this latest robbery had been committed by the
same felons as the previous ones, the stolen items would not soon
resurface. Nor would the thieves be so foolish as to commit a
robbery in broad daylight without donning adequate disguise.

Crump himself was no stranger to the fine art of camouflage and
often had recourse to a makeup box procured at great expense from
a needy actor. Indeed, at that moment even Crump's own mother
would not have recognized him, for the Runner's genial features
were obscured by a shaggy wig and a hideous false beard. The
clothes he wore were filthy rags, unlivened by even one of the
waistcoats of which he was so fond. Crump was hot on the trail of
interesting quarry indeed.

Crump had not left Messrs. Rundle and Brydges empty-handed,
having in his possession a scrap of material found at the scene of
the crime. The Runner was an expert in such matters, having even
appropriated an old gown of Leda's that bore some suspicious
stains. That those odd splotches couldn't be proved to have been
caused by blood didn't deter him; Crump had a theory that
accounted for the various crimes, one in which Leda Langtry

played no small role. The robbery at Warwick's chambers nicely linked her to the other recent burglaries.

Yet even with Leda in quod the thefts continued, which indicated a criminal organization of no small size. Sir John might believe there was no connection between Warwick's murder and the robberies, but Sir John wasn't as clear thinking in some matters as a Chief Magistrate should be. Witness his fondness, thought Crump sourly, for the annoying Lady Bligh. There were seven Public Offices in the Metropolis, all of them modeled after Bow Street. Of all those guardians of the peace, Crump was the only man with ill fortune enough to encounter the Baroness.

Crump's ill will was not without foundation. He'd spent the entire afternoon trailing that lady, a pursuit which had taken him to, among other places, Gunther's, the famed pastrycook in Berkeley Square, and to the British Museum, where an appalling muddle of works of art and natural curiosities was preserved in a miserable building. There Crump had been forced to hide behind an enormous stuffed giraffe while her ladyship and Lord Barrymore waxed enthusiastic over an enormous pair of stag's antlers. Only when the pursuit led him to Sadler's Wells in north London did Crump discover that the lady in the huge, concealing white gauze bonnet adorned lavishly with tea roses was not Dulcie at all, but her niece, Mignon. Diddled, mused Crump, and royally. At least he had avoided sitting through a production of a Shakespearean play, but that was scant consolation for the grievous waste of his time.

There a further reason for Crump's annoyance. He could not imagine why Lady Bligh should wander in trollop's attire through the slums of London where even a watchman would not willingly risk his neck, instead of disporting herself more properly at the theatre or at the velvet-covered écarté table. But there she was, hanging on her butler in a manner that raised both Crump's suspicions and his spleen; and here he was, in close pursuit.

Lady Bligh leaned even closer to her companion and murmured a few words. Hoi! said Crump to himself, and edged closer. The

Runner had no doubt that the Baroness, if she so wished, as she so obviously did not, could be remarkably informative.

"Lord Byron," said Dulcie to her butler, "has said that the three greatest men of this new century are Brummell, Napoleon and himself, in that order. Silly man! He quite forgot Bat." She sneezed. "Do stop pouting, Gibbon! I suppose you wished to accompany the Baron upon his adventures. You would have been greatly shocked, you know. The male population of France has been sadly depleted, and the fields are being cultivated by women and children while the bones of their menfolk lay bleaching in godforsaken lands. Bat has taken upon himself the consolation of an entire nation of lonely, grieving women." She giggled maliciously. "No doubt he will quite exhaust himself, poor thing!"

Gibbon, long inured to the extremely liberal philosophy of his mistress, and very much aware of the stealthy approach of their tracker, squirmed uncomfortably. To keep up with the Baroness, one needed eyes in the back of one's head.

Lady Bligh, it seemed, had that facility. "Much can be forgiven a man with sufficient wit to call France's new ruler 'Louis the Gouty,' as Byron does," she said, then turned on their startled shadow a smile so wicked that it would have done justice to Lucifer. "Do come out from behind that lamp post, Crump! It is hardly of sufficient width to conceal you."

Crump stepped forward, hot with embarrassment, and fidgeted under the Baroness's amused gaze. "Dear Crump," murmured Dulcie, hand on her hip in a very provocative pose, "I would very much like to know why you have been following me! It is a sad day—or evening!—when a lady cannot go about her business without Bow Street trailing at her heels."

"Bow Street," retorted Crump, "might be very interested in that business, Baroness! It seems very much to me as if you're up to some devilment."

"Does it?" inquired Dulcie, a roguish gleam in her dark eyes. "I might say the same to you, dear Crump! You do look a complete quiz in that abominable get-up."

With difficulty, Crump refrained from retorting that Lady Bligh's own attire was hardly less grotesque. "Ah, now," he said genially, "you must see that I have a job of work to do, and it'd go a great deal forwarder if you weren't so determined to hinder it."

"Hinder you?" The Baroness was shocked. "A dire accusation, dear Crump. I see nothing will do but that I must confess, since you have caught me, as it were, in the very act." She moved forward and took his arm, leaning so heavily against him that he stumbled. "It is low life!" mourned Lady Bligh. "I have a positive lust, dear Crump, for vulgarity."

The Runner might have chosen to take exception to this clanker, had he not then lost his balance and gone sprawling in the filthy street. "Good gracious" cried Dulcie, springing back. "Gibbon, do help him to his feet."

"Never mind!" growled Crump, rescuing his wig from the gutter and clapping it onto his head. Sir John, of course, would never believe that the fragile-looking Lady Bligh had tumbled him to the ground. The Runner glared at Gibbon, whose death's-head features were split by a grin, and wondered how that worthy might be persuaded to surrender himself to Bow Street as King's evidence.

Dulcie bent over and rose with a small battered notebook in her hand. "I believe this is yours," she said, and extended it to Crump. "It must have dropped out of your pocket when you fell."

There were a great many items resting in Crump's ample pockets, but his Occurrence Book had not been among them. In fact, as he suddenly realized, he had not set eyes on that valuable little volume since he last visited Bligh House. Recalling the extreme cordiality of Dulcie's leave-taking, he eyed her suspiciously.

The bold Baroness leaned forward and ruffled his false beard. "He who eats plums with the devil," she said cheerfully, "must not be surprised if he gets the stones spat in his eye."

Chapter Nine

Lady Bligh scowled thoughtfully at a tall, black-gray building with narrow windows and an arched gateway adorned by three grim statues. Atop the castellated roof, a windmill drew some of the foul air out of the prison. Newgate was notorious for the ill usage accorded the prisoners who lived there in stinking filth, the fortunate ones fed by friends or relatives, the others by turnkeys who charged exorbitant prices for inedible food. With a ferocious little smile, the Baroness swept forward. After a brief conference with a gap-toothed gaoler, during which several coins changed hands, she vanished inside.

Newgate was a complex establishment, containing a Master Debtors and a Master Felons' side for those who could afford to buy decent accommodations; a Common Side for Debtors and Felons, for those who could not; the Press Yard, the Castle and the Gate; and cells and dungeons beside. Lady Bligh was conducted to the Press Yard.

There the air was clean and warm and fresh, suited to the wealthy men and women who purchased their own rooms and provisions and lived in relative luxury. Leda sat at a small table, gloomily contemplating a bottle of wine.

"Well, Leda!" said the Baroness, and sat down. "You are looking well. I take it you are not existing on a diet of water and thin gruel?"

Leda snorted and eyed her visitor, resplendent in a dark gray cloth coat with a white collar, and a black felt bonnet with velvet ruches, a black satin ribbon and black ostrich plumes. From beneath this bewitching confection peeked silver curls. "Hardly!" she retorted, and rapped the wine bottle with her knuckles. "I am even allowed two blankets under which to sleep. Somone has made a financial arrangement with the Head Keeper for my comfort, it seems!" She grinned. "Did I only wish it, I could obtain any comfort—or any vice."

Inexplicably, Lady Bligh frowned. "Since when are *you* so prim?" complained Leda. "God in heaven, you must know that men can even have their own servants here, and that their wives and mistresses may visit when they wish! The gaoler makes a handsome income from his fees." She sighed heavily. "I suppose I must thank Ivor for his open-handedness, but I would have preferred he did not become involved in this."

"I am afraid," said Dulcie, looking about her with great interest, "that wish may be denied you." She sneezed and the plumes on her bonnet danced. "I think, Leda, that it's time we talked seriously."

Leda's hands closed tightly on the wine bottle and she regarded her visitor with an unhappy scowl. "Do you, too, mean to ask me if I murdered Warwick?" she grunted. "I'll tell you what I told the others, that the lot of you may go hang!"

"Oddly enough," retorted the Baroness, "I am not as concerned with who killed Warwick as with why. There are a great many possibilities, and as many candidates." She ran one gloved hand along the table's edge. "You yourself can claim a great number of enemies, Leda."

"I don't deny it." Leda seemed proud rather than ashamed of the fact. "So you think I'm innocent, Dulcie Bligh? That I did not, in fact, steal back into Warwick's apartments and shoot him dead?" She chortled. "Did you see the item that Willie inserted in the *Apocalypse?* 'Peer Interrupted Fatally in his Bath!' It was masterful."

"Willie?" queried the Baroness.

"Aye!" In her enthusiasm, Leda thwacked down the bottle so forcibly that the table rocked. "Willie Fitzwilliam, my associate. The scamp went on to say that the noble efforts expended by magistrates and officers to capture the murderer have little hope of being crowned with success, and that an innocent female languishes in gaol while the actual perpetrator of the cold-blooded crime wanders around the city free." She chuckled. "I must see that you make Willie's acquaintance, Dulcie! Not that I imagine you'll find him to your taste."

"Yes." Lady Bligh remained thoughtful. "I believe I must meet your Willie. But you will not make the introduction, Leda. Even if I wished to secure your removal from this place, I could not."

"Pah!" retorted Leda. "If you *wished,* you could gain the release of every prisoner here, but I doubt even your rakehell husband would care to see you pay Prinny's price! Never mind, I shan't hold it against you, though I'd give a great deal to know what's going through your scheming little brain." The Baroness said nothing. "How *is* Max?" Leda asked. "What a handsome devil he was, with that Mephistophelian smile."

"He still is. Bat is just now in Paris, taking opium with Madame de Staël—you will recall that she was denounced on the floor of the Convention for conducting a monarchist conspiracy while cuckolding her husband? Society frowns upon a woman who thinks herself as free as a man to sample romance!—and enjoying the conversation at La Récamier's salon. She is a virtuous woman, Bat reports, and a lovely one." Dulcie pursed her lips. "Do stop trying to throw dust in my eyes, Leda! I am perfectly aware that you are willing to hang rather than implicate Viscount Jeffries in your somewhat scurrilous activities! It will not serve. With each moment of your silence, Ivor becomes more deeply involved. If you do not make an effort to help him and yourself, the pair of you will dangle from the deadly Never-Green!"

Leda leaned back in her chair, a genteel and rosy-cheeked figure in her old black gown. "We've come a long way, have we not?" she said, her brown eyes expressionless. "I remember when you first appeared in Society, to such good effect that the rest of us might have been antidotes. It wasn't long before the whole world learned that you, a green girl from the country, already had the devilish Max in tow. You must have broken half the hearts in London between the two of you!"

"Not yours, Leda," said the Baroness, her fathomless eyes fixed on her friend's face.

"No, not mine." Leda's expression was wry. "I'd already made my choice. Worse luck, I married him! But that's all water under the bridge." She folded her hands in her lap. "Who are you to help me, Dulcie Bligh? What can you know of this damnable fix I'm in, you with your jewels and your bold Baron, your excesses and your intrigues? I daresay you've never wanted for anything in your lifetime!".

"True," said Dulcie calmly. "Which is precisely why I'm here. Your predicament, Leda, is the perfect antidote to any possibility of my becoming complacent. No more high flights, I beg you! If you do not mean to cooperate, tell me so, and cease wasting precious time."

Leda twisted a loose strand of hair around one finger in a curiously girlish way. "Oh, very well! I suppose I must trust you. Ask your questions, since you're so determined. I'll tell you what you want to know."

"Excellent!" Lady Bligh propped her elbows on the table and cupped in her hands her forceful chin. "There is a rumor that you claim to have been elsewhere at the time Warwick was killed. I suggest you tell me the name of the person you were with." Leda wore an obstinate look. "Warwick's valet is prepared to go into the witness-box and give oath that it was you who killed his master, Leda! Can you imagine the repercussions were you to hang?"

"Mary Elphinstone," said Leda sourly. "I doubt you will remember her, for Mary was as timid and insignificant a chit as ever appeared in Society. However, she once rendered me a small service and I am in the habit of occasionally visiting her. She lives in greatly reduced circumstances now, in a small cottage near the Ratcliffe Highway."

"You are a wretched liar, Leda!" Frowning, Dulcie rose. "And a very silly one. Would it have been so terrible if your timid Mary revealed your secrets?"

"Yes!" snapped Leda, grasping the wine bottle as if she meant to hurl it at her visitor. "How the devil did you guess *that*, Dulcie. Just how much do you know?"

"A great deal," replied the Baroness, staring somberly into space, "and a great deal less than I should. This is a pretty kettle of fish you've landed yourself in, Leda. I don't like the appearance of things at all."

"Do you suppose *I* do?" Leda lowered the bottle to the table. "I tell you, I'm at wit's end. Each day I'm urged to make a full confession of my guilt, to be take down in writing by a clerk and by me signed. I vow I'd do it, too, if I thought the matter would then end."

The highway from Charing Cross to St. Paul's was thronged with elegant carriages, well mounted horsemen, and handsomely dressed foot passengers. Through the arch of Temple Bar rattled the Lord Mayor's coach on its way to the Guildhall. Lady Bligh, jostled by innumerable tradesmen and their customers, gawked at by all who saw her, paid as little need to the wickedness and bustle of Covent Garden as she did to the elegant shops of The Strand. She moved gracefully through the throng, applying to those who barred her way an elegant elbow or a fashionable shoe, apparently unconcerned that this solitary rambling could have easily led to social ruin.

She paused to look upon the old courts and alleys that lined Fleet Street. The vista did not seem to afford her any great pleasure. Lady Bligh's delicate nostrils flared, her lush lips thinned. She walked toward the shop that housed the London *Apocalypse*.

The front room was deserted except for one slender young man who sat on the floor before a monstrous piece of machinery which he eyed with abject gloom. His ghastly attire proclaimed him no follower of fashion. Uncombed brown hair sprang from his skull, and a monocle magnified one pale eye. "One must accept the goods that the gods provide," observed the Baroness unenthusiastically, and sneezed.

Willie sprang to his feet and stared. "Zounds!" he cried. "Lady Bligh!" Beaming, he advanced on her. "You have quite overturned me! Never did I think to see a Baroness grace these humble premises!"

Dulcie's inquisitive eyes darted around the room. She sank down onto a rickety chair.

"I would shake your hand," said Willie, extending his own, which was gloved. "A custom which is loathesome to me, but I *do* admire you, Lady Bligh! Ah, I see you wonder why I wear gloves. It is for the better preservation of my white skin, to which I, like Lord Byron, attach great importance!" He gazed upon the gloves, which were a great deal more pristine than the rest of him. "These are the hands of a genius, Baroness! They have penned a melodrama which I hope to see produced on no less than the stage at Drury Lane. I call it *A Sop To Cerberus,* and I have found a brilliant though unknown provincial actor who would be perfect in the lead role. It shall make me both famous and wealthy, and then you will be pleased to boast of how you made my acquaintance in a humble printer's shop." He paused, somewhat theatrically. "The name is William Fitzwilliam, alias the Bystander. *You* may call me Willie, Lady Bligh!"

"If I were to call you anything," responded the Baroness, crossing her ankles to reveal black slippers and white stockings, "it would be 'damned impudent.'" Willie stared at her. "So you have written a play! Not a moment too soon, considering that you have been borrowing money on nonexistent future prospects and signing post-obits at ruinous rates. I suppose that you may hope to be confined to the King's Bench Prison, which is principally for debtors, rather than to be lodged with Leda in Newgate. The Bench is not a bad place, I believe, with cookshops and circulating libraries, coffeehouses and artisans, for all they're lodged behind thrity-foot walls." With a flick of one wrist, Lady Bligh opened a dainty enameled snuffbox. "Though one may live agreeably there, one is still behind bars."

Willie, whose eyebrows had leaped wildly up and down during this speech, leaned against the edge of a rickety table. "Egad! I begin to think I've misjudged you, Lady Bligh."

"You have," agreed the Baroness, and took snuff. "I suspect we might deal fairly well together, young man, if you will refrain from treating me to any more of your infernal prose."

"Infernal prose!" gasped Willie, highly indignant. "May I remind you, madam, that the sword is less mighty than the pen? Even now I plan an *exposé* of three very high officials at Bow Street who have conspired with a gang of swindlers. It will come as a thunderclap to the City and spread over Europe the greatest alarm!" He clasped his hands and gazed raptly heavenward. "Of course Leda's release from prison might make me change my mind."

"Even now," retorted Dulcie, though with a hint of amusement, "there are those who wish to see you committed to Newgate to await trial for complicity in murder and robbery."

"You jest!" said Willie weakly, his pale eyes fixed on Lady Bligh's face. "Egad! It's that wretched Crump, of course! He has been positively hounding me, and in a manner that makes the blood boil in my veins."

"It is no more than you can expect," the Baroness replied

severely, "when you go out of your way to antagonize him! Contrary to what you may believe, Crump is a very clever man. He may reach the truth through incredibly tortuous routes, but reach it he does."

Willie was a picture of gloom. "Lady Bligh," he said, with great sincerity, "you are making a positive tangle of my heart strings. I have a very unpleasant vision of myself taken into safekeeping for a variety of crimes. Is there nothing we can do to avert this great calamity?"

"Are you a gambler, Willie?" inquired Dulcie brightly. "Among your other sins? If so, you may be of some assistance." She paused. "I don't suppose you know how to read the Tarot cards?"

"The *what?* asked Willie faintly..

"I thought not." The Baroness was wistful. "Oh, well! You are fond of Leda, I gather, and even fonder of the opportunity to publish your columns. You may render no small help through this newspaper, if you print what I tell you."

Willie crossed his arms, his nose wiggling as if he'd caught some pleasant scent. "The difficulties of newspaper publishing are great, Lady Bligh, and the rewards small. The tax on printed matter will soon reach four pence per sheet on every newspaper of one and one-half sheets. Many small businesses have already gone under." He shrugged. "Leda may have had unexpected resources at her disposal but, as you have already pointed out, I hardly have the funds to undertake such an expensive enterprise. Nor do I care to be set up in the pillory at the Old Bailey, there to be saluted with garbage from Fleet Street."

"You are sadly lacking in courage." Dulcie tugged on an earlobe. "Very well, I will supply you with the needed money."

"Are you suggesting," cried Willie indignantly, "that I can be *bought?* I am a true artist, Lady Bligh!"

"You," retorted the Baroness, "are a true scoundrel! But I shall not quibble, since everything is going as badly as possible. You shall have the money you need to produce your play, but I will expect more than ample return for my investment."

"You'll have it!" Willie slid off the table to caper maniacally about the room. "Zounds, but you're a woman after my own heart, Lady Bligh!"

The Baroness also rose to her feet and regarded her newly acquired associate ruefully. "Your heart?" she said. "No female will have access to that, I vow! Cease your capering, Willie, and listen to what I'd have you do."

"Baroness!" cried Willie, dropping to his knees at her feet. "for you I will do anything!"

"You may have cause to regret that remark," Dulcie retorted. "Do get up off the floor! First, you will not further antagonize Crump." Willie's face fell. "Secondly, you will ferret out for me the truth of those 'unexplained resources' of Leda's to which you referred. And thirdly, you will mingle freely with your theatrical connections and report to me all you may hear."

"My theatrical connections," mused Willie, who in the act of rising resembled a long-legged spider. "What link can there be between Warwick's murder and the stage? Can it be you have an urge to tread the boards, Lady Bligh?"

"What I have," retorted the Baroness waspishly, "is a damned unpleasant hunch. You need know no more."

"Tell me one thing." Abruptly abandoning his posturing, Willie revealed himself as a very worried young man. "Do you think Leda innocent?"

"As innocent as you yourself." Dulcie's fine features were drawn.

This answer did not elevate his spirits. "I'll tell you one thing," he said unhappily. "I've sometimes wondered if Warwick's death is somehow connected with these robberies." Lady Bligh opened her mouth to speak but he raised a protesting hand. "Hear me out! It's not as far fetched as it sounds. Stolen from Warwick's quarters was a considerable amount of money. It is common knowledge, though apparently not to Bow Street." He watched the Baroness, who was restlessly pacing up and down. "I vow I do not know what to make of it, Lady Bligh!"

"Willie." Dulcie paused in her perambulations to regard him.

"Are you trying to tell me that there was something smokey about those notes?"

"Smokey, indeed, Baroness." Willie's homely features were crinkled with puzzlement. "If what I hear is correct, those stolen banknotes were very clever forgeries."

"How quick-witted you are, Willie." Lady Bligh's enigmatic eyes rested on his. "And it is equally clever of you to wear those gloves! But I fear Crump will soon learn that there is more than printer's ink staining your hands."

Chapter Ten

"How dreadful for you!" gasped Mignon, fluttering her eyelashes in good imitation of her aunt. "I vow, I should never have been able to close my eyes without again seeing the horrible scene!"

"Oh, it was not so bad as that, Miss Montague!" Lord Barrymore smoothed the sleeves of his dark brown frockcoat, which he wore with a buff kerseymore waistcoat and light blue merino trousers, and smiled. "Though I am grateful that you were spared such a ghastly experience! After all, I have witnessed death before, having been a member of the Prince Regent's own regiment. But you, my dear young lady, can have had no experience with such unhappy things." His blue eyes were warm. "Which is the way it should be. For an innocent young girl to have stumbled as I did into so unpleasant a scene would have been dreadful."

"I should say so!" grumbled Culpepper, who was playing chaperone. "What would Miss Mignon be doing going to Warwick's quarters in the first place?" Her disapproving gaze rested on Lord

Barrymore's pleasant face. "Are you suggesting she's the sort of shameless chit who would visit a gentleman's lodging? Bite your tongue, Lord Barrymore!"

Tolly stared aghast at Lady Bligh's abigail. "Nonsense, Culpepper!" Mignon said, stifling an ignoble impulse to laugh at her swain's discomfort. "Lord Barrymore was speaking hypothetically. I'm sure he didn't mean that *I* am in the habit of visiting gentlemen like Warwick."

"I should hope you're in the habit of visiting no gentlemen at all!" responded Culpepper. Mignon flushed, recalling her lost love. She had not precisely visited his lodgings, but she had kept no few assignations with him. Ah, but he had been a handsome rogue.

They were in the Music Room, a large chamber with windows of Mexican onyx and rose-garlanded friezes, a Pompeiian ceiling and Persian tiles. A Roman fountain spouted water in the exact center of the room. Culpepper sat rigidly erect on an uncomfortable looking carved chair, while Lord Barrymore lounged on a satin-covered settee. Mignon, clad in a green silk tunic over a lingerie skirt with lace edging, was posed gracefully at a beautiful grand piano inlaid with ivory and tortoise shell.

"How progress your aunt's endeavors?" inquired Lord Barrymore, judging from Culpepper's remote expression that it was safe to speak again. "I have told you of the episode at Warwick's, and that the valet admitted Leda Langtry but did not see her leave. He believes she secreted herself somewhere on the premises and returned to commit the foul deed after he had left his master alone." He leaned forward, elbows on his knees. "I am sure I have the greatest sympathy for poor Miss Langtry! True, she did not impress me as a woman suitable to associate with one as young and innocent as yourself, Miss Montague, but I cannot but pity a wretch driven to such desperate lengths. It is, I fear, a sad reflection on Warwick's character."

Culpepper snorted and Mignon eyed her thoughtfully. Lord Barrymore's frankness, she reflected, had not extended to acquainting them with the reason for his visit to Warwick's lodgings that night. "You seem convinced of Leda's guilt," she said. "Why is that? I must tell you my aunt is not. Or," she added honestly, for the motives behind Dulcie's actions remain wreathed in mystery, "she doesn't seem to be."

"You forget, Miss Montague," Tolly spread apologetic hands, "that I was there. It could have been no one but Miss Langtry, by the valet's own word."

"You said the window stood open," Mignon argued. She had formed the habit of discussing her aunt's investigations with Lord Barrymore, primarily because it effectively distracted him from romance. "Why could not some intruder have entered by that means and exited the same way?"

"You are air-dreaming, Miss Montague," said Tolly in a condescending manner, "for which I must blame your aunt. I fear the window stood open only because Miss Langtry used it to escape." He looked at the chimneypiece, representing Apollo and the Muses as depicted on the sarcophagus of Homer, as if he expected to witness a materialization. "By-the-bye, where *is* your aunt?"

"Dulcie is very busy these days," retorted Mignon, somewhat ungraciously. "I believe this afternoon she is riding with a gentleman friend." She dropped her hands to the piano keys.

"Oh?" Tolly awarded Mignon a curiously intent look. "May one ask whom?"

"One shouldn't," observed the disapproving Culpepper. "It verges on impertinence."

"Sir John," explained Mignon, taking pity. "The Chief Magistrate of Bow Street."

"Bow Street!" ejaculated a figure in the doorway, in all-too-familiar tones that made Mignon strike a hideous discord. "Surely I did not hear you correctly!"

"Maurice." Mignon surveyed the newcomer with overt distaste. "What the devil are *you* doing here?"

"A fine way to greet your brother!" he retorted, stepping into the room. "But then, you were ever a stiff-necked, stubborn, silly girl. I have come, if you must know, because Mama was worried that you might get up to some mischief in the Metropolis. A tiresome business, to be sure, and a *most* painful sacrifice. You have no notion of the inconvenience I have been put to!"

"A pity," said Mignon despondently. "You should have had the sense to stay home."

The Honorable Maurice Montague bore a startling resemblance to his sister, possessing the same flaming hair and freckles and the same green eyes, but in splendor of person he cast Mignon into the shade. Maurice was dressed, as befit a young master of twelve millions sterling with pretentions to dandyism, in a light brown coat, white waistcoat, nankin pantaloons fastened at the ankle with two huge gold buttons, and yellow stockings with large violet clocks. On his feet were black pumps; and above the starched points of his shirt collar showed not one but two cravats, black satin over white linen, designed to give the desired thickness to his neck. "Don't," he begged, observing his sister with an uncordiality that matched her own, "go off into one of your odd humors! I am in no condition to deal with one of your queer turns."

Mignon sighed and introduced Maurice to the other occupants of the room, her spirits only slightly lifted by Culpepper's incredulous expression. "Do you mean to stay here?" Mignon asked, with little hope that he did not. What better way to keep her under his eye? "You might have let us know, Maurice, so that preparations could be made."

"That is not your concern, surely!" retorted her brother, with a pointed look at Culpepper. "You may go now, my good woman, and see that my belongings and my valet are properly housed!"

"My mistress," said Culpepper, the light of battle in her eye, "specifically instructed me to attend to Miss Mignon."

Maurice raised a quizzing-glass to one offended eye. "Do you presume to argue with me, woman? I take all responsibility for my sister upon myself." He waved an irritated hand. "Now do go away!" Culpepper obeyed, leaving Mignon with the happy impression that Maurice had made a formidable enemy.

But a gentleman so grand as Maurice, and so pampered by a

doting mother, could not be expected to concern himself with what servants might or might not think. Quizzing-glass still in hand, he took stock of his surroundings, which included bronze Floras, muses and hermaphrodites, a crystal lustre from which darted aerie creatures in attitudes of flight, and a bright blue carpet ornamented with flowers and insects. His pained gaze then fell upon Mignon, whose fiery curls were piled atop her head in a manner more suited to the unfortunate females who plied their trade in London's narrow streets than to a young lady of gentle birth. "The Baroness," he remarked, letting the quizzing-glass fall, "appears to have rather extravagant tastes. Mama said the rhino runs through Lady Bligh's fingers like water, and I see nothing to prove her wrong! And what were you saying about our aunt and Bow Street? I fear she must be lacking in delicate principles!"

"I take it," said Lord Barrymore smoothly, doubtless recognizing a kindred spirit, "that you have not been previously acquainted with Lady Bligh?" Mignon applied herself to the piano keys, seeking relief for her exacerbated feelings. Maurice, from the aloof superiority of his twenty-six years, made it his purpose in life to spoil her pleasure and cut up her peace.

"No," replied Maurice. After a great fussing with his long coat-tails, he seated himself cautiously in a chair. "According to Mama, both the Baron and Baroness comport themselves in a manner that is strongly to be deprecated. But she could hardly refuse Lady Bligh's well-meant invitation to have Mignon in Town, and for various reasons it was most opportune." Mignon supposed she should be grateful that he did not go on to explain the reason for that invitation's timeliness. Maurice, with his annoying tendency to play off the airs of an exquisite, reminded her of nothing more than a pantin, a pasteboard puppet strung together so that the lightest touch of a finger set it falling into grotesque attitudes. She wondered what Dulcie would make of her brother.

"Do tell me," begged Maurice, "what connection my aunt may have with Bow Street. Surely," he shuddered, "she has not run afoul of the law!"

"No, no," soothed Tolly, looking rather amused. "She has merely undertaken to aid an old friend."

"A friend?" repeated Maurice in an imbecilic manner. "What is this friend's connection with Bow Street?"

"I fear," said Tolly gently, "that the friend is currently lodged in Newgate Prison, where she awaits her trial for the murder of a peer."

This intelligence so unnerved Maurice that, after frantic patting and poking of his many pockets, he had recourse to a vinaigrette. "Murder?" he gasped weakly. "Unthinkable!"

"Not at all," remarked Mignon, delighted to see her brother so overset. "It happens all the time! Just yesterday there was an item in the newspaper concerning a clerk in holy orders who was crossed in love and murdered a bishop's mistress." Maurice moaned. "As for Dulcie's involvement, that must be obvious. Princes often love vulgarity, you know, for its very contrast with the gloomy elevation of their own station. London is very thin of company at this time of year. You will not like it, Maurice."

"Your sister, Mr. Montague, tends to exaggerate!" Lord Barrymore intervened, earning a scowl from Mignon. "There are still the races, the theatre, an occasional supper party to provide excitement." He looked in a kindly manner at Maurice. "If you like, I could gain the *entrée* for you to various of my clubs."

This was rather a set-down for Maurice, who had so long puffed up his own consequence that he fancied his wealth made him welcome everywhere. "You're very kind," he mumbled.

"Good!" said Tolly briskly. "You will also wish to visit the shops—Hoby for your boots of course, and Lock's for your hats. After that," he winked in a conspiratorial manner, "well, we shall see!" Maurice's woebegone countenance brightened considerably.

Mignon, somewhat cheered that her brother would be so well occupied during his sojourn in the Metropolis, wondered if Lord Barrymore suspected, as she did, that Maurice had come to town with the express intention of taking her home with him. She paid little attention to the masculine conversation that was going on around her beyond noting that Tolly and Maurice were on the way to becoming bosom bows. Charity appeared in the doorway, beckoning furtively.

"Excuse me," murmured Mignon and slid from the stool.

"A note for you, miss!" whispered Charity, obviously delighted to participate in something clandestine. "A boy brought it to the door and said particular that I was to put it right in your hand." Poor thing! thought Mignon, looking at the girl's homely features and mousy hair. Her complexion was mottled as if makeup had been inexpertly applied. "Well, look at it!" hissed Charity. "He said no one else was to know."

With a queer foreboding, Mignon took the letter in her hand. She stared at the familiar handwriting, as rigid as if she'd been turned to stone.

Maurice leaned close to Lord Barrymore and smiled, revealing teeth stained by the tobacco he sometimes chewed in place of eating meals that would spoil his fashionable figure. "My sister," he said in a most penetrating whisper, "is wild to a fault! Mama lives in fear that she will never form an eligible connection." He sighed. "Man to man, looking after Mignon has been a most arduous task! You cannot know how relieved I am to learn she has discovered a distinguishing preference for a gentleman as acceptable as yourself." Tolly shot Mignon one of his oddly assessing glances. He smiled.

"Thank you, Charity," murmured Mignon, cheeks flaming. "That will be all." The maid limped away, as if her shoes fit poorly.

Unable to trust herself in her brother's presence lest she denounce him as a misguided marplot or he derive from her manner an understanding of the letter which she held gingerly in her hand, Mignon climbed the ornate marble staircase. Once in the safety of her bedchamber, she dropped the letter on the dressing table and moved to the window, where she stared unseeing at the street below.

The chamber that Lady Bligh had assigned her niece was decorated with various Persian curiosities including a carpet of velvet embroidered with gold and silver. It even possessed a small bath-room, hidden in a niche entirely walled with mirrors. Strewn about the room were large dolls dressed in the Persian manner, with long hair painted red or gold, clad in pretty gauze pantaloons and golden anklets. Dominating all else was a huge bed of ma-hogany inlaid with gold and supported by two bronze swans. On a nightstand sat a golden lamp, beside it a bound history of the exploits of Tamerlaine.

Mignon might have been lodged in a cell at Newgate for all the appreciation she showed for her surroundings. "Oh, *damn!*" she cried, and left the window to stand once again at the dressing table, looking at the letter as if it were an adder poised to strike. The maid, Charity, fancying herself Cupid's assistant, would have been surprised indeed at Miss Montague's reaction to this romantic missive, for Mignon flung herself onto the ornate bed and burst into tears.

Chapter Eleven

Sir John's unostentatious carriage moved slowly along the Ratcliffe Highway to Shadwell, once the scene of horrid and grotesque murders. Only a few years before, an entire family had been slain in a singularly brutal manner. But Sir John had no more thought to spare for the history of the countryside than he did for the beauty of the day. His attention was riveted on his companion, stunning in a pelisse of peacock blue velvet trimmed with chinchilla fur, worn over a gown fashioned entirely of eyelet embroidery. On her silver hair was a lace bonnet with cordings and flowers in diverse shades of blue. Draped about various portions of her superb anatomy was a staggering fortune in sapphires.

"This is a fool's errand you've set us," he said somberly. "What do you expect to find?"

Lady Bligh sighed and twirled her parasol. "I see that you are in one of your disapproving moods, dear John! How very dull of you." Expertly, she fluttered her long eyelashes. "I promise you that we're not chasing a will-o'-the-wisp."

The Chief Magistrate, having through long experience learned the value of her ladyship's promises, reflected wryly that the Baroness was quite capable, if it suited her underhanded purposes, of setting him to chase his own tail. "You are a rogue, Dulcie!" He flicked his whip. "It would save a great deal of time if you would merely tell me what you want of me."

"You misjudge me, John." Dulcie cast him a glance simultaneously provocative and piqued. "As if I only seek you out when I wish favors of you! Have you so little opinion of yourself that you cannot believe I enjoy your company?"

"No" said Sir John, no little bit surprised to feel himself flush. "I was hardly born yesterday, Dulcie! It is not for the pleasure of my company that you have insisted that I escourt you to Shadwell on the *qui vive!* Confess. I know perfectly well that you have some mischief in mind."

"Not mischief." The Baroness was charmingly rueful. "You are determined to think my motives the most base, I see."

"I am," agreed Sir John cordially. "If you think to cajole me into releasing Leda, you waste your time."

Lady Bligh's luscious lower lip protruded slightly. "I think you are also determined to spoil my fun."

It was definitely midsummer moon with Sir John; he thought the Baroness's artful pout the most delicious he'd ever seen. "Minx!" he said appreciatively. "Very well, I will listen to what you have to say. Mind, I promise nothing more!"

"You are truly understanding, dear John." Dulcie abandoned her lounging attitude and sat briskly upright. "Oddly enough, I *don't* wish anything of you, at least not today." The Chief Magistrate was aware of an absurd disappointment. "And I certainly do not wish Leda freed from Newgate! She is in quite enough trouble as it is."

"She is also," added Sir John dryly, "causing more of it than her share. At last report your Leda was simultaneously gathering information on child prostitution and planning prison reform." Further-more, due to the agitation of the Press, particularly the London *Apocalypse*, Sir John was forced to deal with riots almost as wide-spread as those caused by the arrest of Sir Francis Burdett in 1810. "You have not told me why you've made Leda Langtry your concern."

Dulcie wore the expression of one looking backward through time. "Leda was once a friend of mine." She made no further explanation, as if that little was sufficient. Perhaps, thought Sir John, for her it was.

The Baroness was not prone to long periods of abstraction or nostalgia. "I suppose," she said, thoughtfully wriggling a dainty foot shod in a blue fabric slipper with a ribbon bow, "Leda's trial is set for the next session?"

"It is." He was very much aware that Lady Bligh's hand still rested on his arm.

The Baroness leaned even closer, her dark eyes fixed on his face. "I very much fear, John, that if that trial takes place, Leda will hang."

Sir John looked straight ahead of him, resolutely refusing to meet Lady Bligh's imploring gaze. "I thought you wanted nothing of me?" he remarked. "You are correct: it is very likely, consider-ing the evidence against her, that Leda will hang."

"And it matters not to you that she is innocent, for you will have your scapegoat, the public outcry will be stilled, and Prinny and Warwick's rich relatives will be satisfied." Dulcie's tone was mournful. "Would you condemn a woman to death for murder," she said softly, "without any real evidence that she was responsible? I have little knowledge of the law, but it seems to be a proceeding both illegal and injudicious."

Sir John knew that he was becharmed. At that moment, he did not care. He pulled his horses to a halt. "Go on."

Lady Bligh was a practiced weaver of spells, so skilled that her ensorcellments left her victims with no regret. "Dear John!" she whispered, and idly traced the line of his jaw. "Insufficient attention has been paid to the fact that Leda's pistol was stolen from her before Warwick's death. The burglary is no tall tale, you know. It was corroborated by her employees."

"A clever ploy," said Sir John, struggling greatly for coherent thought, "to make it look as if Leda was innocent. She could have staged it herself."

"You must ever doubt me," lamented Dulcie. "You question my word, hold me at arm's length! I think if you will carefully check Leda's activities on that afternoon, you will find she did not have time to return and burgle her own shop."

At arm's length? reflected Sir John muzzily. It was not at a distance that he wanted to hold the Baroness. "Leda could easily have taken the weapon with her when she originally left the shop. Perhaps she arranged with someone else to so disrupt the premises that it looked as if a robbery had occurred. Crump harbors grave doubts regarding one of Leda's employees."

"Willie, no doubt," mused Lady Bligh. "Don't you see, John, that the evidence against Leda is not at all conclusive? Even her motive is insufficient. One does not go about murdering all the people that one dislikes, after all! Warwick, with his fondness for political blackmail, must have had a great many enemies."

"So you knew even that." Sir John gazed rapt upon the bewitching Baroness. "I suppose that is how you persuaded him to sign Leda's release. You truly are a dangerous meddler, Dulcie! How did you find out?"

"Lady Warwick, of course." Lady Bligh was amused. "She has a positive mania for discussing her husband's more unpleasant habits. Poor thing! It is almost the only pleasure left to her."

Sir John reluctantly dragged his eyes away from hers. "You want me," he said severely, "to connive at delaying Leda's trial."

"I would not have phrased it so crudely, but yes." Dulcie's husky voice was laden with regret. "Dear, dear John. If there was world enough and time—but, since there is not, I suggest we proceed to Shadwell."

The Chief Magistrate took up the reins, aware that by his failure to refuse her request he had entered into a tacit conspiracy with the Baroness. He wondered if she was truly convinced of her friend's innocence, and if Dulcie would act differently if she were certain of Leda's guilt . . . .

"Justice," she murmured, and he wasn't surprised that she had so accurately followed his thoughts, "is a very curious thing. Wasn't it Warwick who used to boast that Britain was the only country in Europe without a citywide police force? He attributed it to the people's love of freedom. At the time of the Wapping murders, Warwick went so far as to say he'd rather see a half-dozen throats cut each year than be subjected to the gross indignities of an organized peacekeeping force." He could feel her contemplative gaze. "You yourself had little reason to love Warwick, John."

"No," he replied brusquely. "You can hardly accuse *me* of murdering the man!"

"I accuse you of nothing," the Baroness said indignantly, then wilted on the seat like a tired bluebell, with such good effect that Sir John grew speedily convinced that he'd wounded her feelings.

"Warwick," he said abruptly, damning his indiscretion even as he spoke, "thought he knew who was behind the robberies. He spoke to me about them the very day he died."

"Ah!" Miraculously, Lady Bligh revived. "Did he mention who he thought the guilty party to be?"

"No." With disapproval, Sir John regarded his traveling companion. She was a true pied piper, and he must always dance to her tune. "His excitement didn't prompt him to imprudence. I could not discover precisely what he'd learned."

"Turn left here." Dulcie pointed down a narrow lane, then clutched the seat as the carriage jolted over deep ruts. "It sounds very much as if Warwick suspected someone of an elevated social standing or he would not have been so circumspect." She grinned. "Wouldn't it be marvelous if Prinny was our culprit? The whole world knows how desperately he needs funds."

"Dulcie!" Sir John almost dropped the reins. "Surely you don't think——"

"No." She loosened her grip on the seat to clutch at her bonnet, which had slid to one side. "But wouldn't it be *fun!* You know, of course, that Barrymore called on Warwick the evening of his death and thus was present when the valet found the body. Have you thought to ask what prompted his presence there?"

Sir John had his hands full of mettlesome horseflesh, for his steeds took wild exception to the atrocious condition of the lane, and thus missed Lady Bligh's expression. Had he but seen that extremely guileless look, his suspicions would have been immediately aroused. "Barrymore is a frequent visitor at your house," he said. "What are you trying to tell me?"

"Barrymore," replied the Baroness serenely, "is a most estimable young man. He nourishes a most proper passion for my niece—*too* proper, I suspect, to inspire an answering emotion in Mignon." She pointed. "There is our destination, John."

The Chief Magistrate had only time to stop his carriage in front of the small, thatched, derelict-looking cottage before Dulcie spoke again. "You have been remiss in another matter, John. I won't chide you for it, for I know you have much on your mind, but it is lapses like these which bring down odium upon Bow Street." He waited patiently while she set her disheveled person to rights. "Warwick had a large number of banknotes in his possession when he died."

"We found none." Sir John helped her to the ground. "But it was fairly obvious that there had been a robbery."

"Was it?" Lady Bligh's sideways glance held no praise. "Your men have searched Leda's shop, I'm sure. Did you find any banknotes there?"

Sir John was forced to admit that they had not. "What's the point, Dulcie?" He looked at the mean little cottage. "And what the devil is this place?"

"The point, dear John, is that those banknotes were forgeries." Briskly Dulcie set off across the patch of dirt that served as the cottage yard. Bemused, the Chief Magistrate followed her. The hovel looked rather as if it had been utilized by rustic lovers seeking a trysting place. Lady Bligh rapped energetically on the door.

"Do you think," inquired Sir John humbly, "that I might be told where we are and why we're here? At your convenience, of course! I would not wish to distract you from whatever unmentionable thoughts are running through your scheming little head!"

"Don't take a pet, John!" No response came to her loud summons, and Dulcie turned away from the door. She was frowning. "I have an extremely unpleasant hunch."

"Oh?" The Chief Magistrate had a premonition of his own, that Lady Bligh was going to land him once again in the devil of a fix. He watched as she walked slowly through a neglected garden to the well that stood in one corner. When she stopped dead in her tracks, he moved quickly to her side.

"This is the home of Mary Elphinstone," the Baroness said somberly, staring at the clear footprints that surrounded the well. "The woman whom Leda was visiting when Warwick was murdered. I had hoped she would prove Leda's alibi."

Sir John cared neither for Dulcie's somber tone nor her use of the past tense. Almost reluctantly, he moved forward to peer into the well. What he saw there prompted him to step back hastily.

"Mary?" inquired Lady Bligh, her face pale, and her voice faint.

"Yes." Sir John was overwhelmed by protectiveness. Gently, he grasped Dulcie's shoulders. "I fear she'll assist no one now."

Chapter Twelve

Crump gazed with some complacency around the small, bare Bow Street office, then seated himself with great satisfaction at the Chief Magistrate's desk. It was a severe breach of etiquette, but Sir John was presiding over a hearing in the Bow Street courtroom, and was hardly likely to know.

"I've been thinking," said Crump to his less-than-enthusiastic visitor, "about what you told me concerning the robbery."

"Oh?" inquired Mr. Throckmorton, somewhat testily. Never had he thought that *he* would be summoned to Bow Street. "What about it?"

"Tell me again about that dangerous-looking character you saw lurking about the club."

Mr. Throckmorton grimaced, not at the question but at the pervasive smell of horse dung and soot that came through the open window. "As nasty a villain as you might hope to see," he replied promptly. "Brown-haired, he was, and shabby. And he wore a monocle."

"Ah!" Crump leaned back in Sir John's chair and hooked his thumbs in his quilted piqué waistcoat. "You didn't mention that eyeglass before, guv'nor."

"I daresay in the agitation of the moment it slipped my mind." Mr. Throckmorton glowered at his interrogator in a decidedly hostile manner. "What progress are you making, Crump? I might tell you that Raggett is growing most anxious for the return of his silver plate."

"You tell Raggett that matters are proceeding smoothly." Crump brought forth his pipe. "Very smoothly indeed! In fact, we are in momentary expectation of making an arrest."

"Oh?" Mr. Throckmorton was obviously intrigued. "Can you tell me who?"

"Afraid not, guv'nor." Crump winked in a comradely manner. "But I believe I can show you something in just a few moments that will assure you that Bow Street is on its toes!" Mr. Throckmorton looked skeptical, but said no more.

In truth, Crump reflected as he lit his pipe, this case was not progressing as well as he might wish. It was easy enough to see how Lady Coate's faro bank had been stolen; her servants were shockingly negligent in locking up the house and to open the old-fashioned safe was little more than child's play. And the robbery of Messrs. Rundle and Brydges presented little more of a challenge. It was common enough for a well-dressed thief to enter such a shop, examine small articles such as gold seals and brooches, and then, while looking the shopkeeper in the eye, to conceal several items in the wide sleeves of his coat. The only difference was that these robbers operated on an unusually large scale.

The burglary at White's Club was somewhat more difficult to understand. Further speech with the Negro page, however, had almost compensated Crump for his severe disappointment regarding the chimney sweeps. That enterprising young scamp, as Crump had suspected, had two very sharp eyes in his head. Under duress he had admitted seeing a gentleman near the plate closet the evening before the theft was discovered. The page had thought little enough of it at the time, gentlemen in their cups being prone to wandering here and there, nor could he offer a clear description. All the same, it was a step forward. Crump thought he might speak to the sweeps again. Innocent they might be, though the Runner harbored doubts, but it was possible they might have unwittingly seen something odd.

The door to the office swung open, and a third man was ushered into the room. The arrival of this individual sparked a startling reaction from Mr. Throckmorton: he leaped to his feet with an agility that belied his great girth and sent his old wooden chair crashing to the floor.

"That's him!" cried Throckmorton, pointing a chubby finger, cheeks awobble with the force of his emotion. "That's the man I saw!"

"Egad!" said Willie, starting as if he'd been stung. Propping his feet up on Sir John's desk, Crump puffed dreamily on his pipe.

"Don't bother to deny it!" Throckmorton advanced across the room. "You were skulking about White's Club!"

"*Not* skulking!" protested Willie, offended. "I do not skulk, dear man. I lurk, ears cocked for any interesting tidbits that might be incorporated in tomorrow's news. It has always been the way of the journalist, ever since the very beginning when rich and influential men who had to be away from court employed writers to send them the latest news." He struck a martyred pose. "Just as it has always been the lot of the journalist to suffer persecution, ever since the Star Chamber in the reign of Charles I. It is a hard life, gentlemen!"

Mr. Throckmorton's jaw had dropped open during this volatile speech; now he closed it with an audible snap. "Don't try to deny it!" he repeated. "You were seen sneaking about White's on the very day of the robbery."

"Was I?" asked Willie, unconcerned. "It is quite possible. I pussyfoot all about the city, as innocuous as a lamp post, and you would be surprised at the things I learn." He smiled seraphically. "Did you know that a perfect mermaid, with a comb in one hand and a looking glass in the other, has been blown ashore at Greenwich?"

"No, and I can't say that we care." Crump's neat little feet thudded to the floor. "Throckmorton, you positively identify this man as the one you saw?"

"Use your eyes!" snapped Throckmorton. "Of course I do."

"Then you may step into the hallway and give your evidence to the clerk." Crump gazed benignly upon Willie. "While your deposition is being taken, I'll just have a little chat with this gentleman."

Willie watched with keen interest as Throckmorton, plump cheeks flushed, stomped out of the room, then moved to the window where he perched, long legs dangling from the sill.

Crump remained briefly silent, puffing on his pipe and contemplating the mysterious workings of his own clever mind. He had not believed a word of Throckmorton's tale about the mysterious prowler who displayed such interest in White's august premises; yet here he was, confronted with that very man. No wonder Willie had seemed familiar, though they'd never encountered one another before! And Willie worked for Leda, who Crump was growing more and more convinced was involved in this series of very clever crimes. Perhaps she was the master mind behind them all.

"You positively unnerve me, Mr. Crump!" said Willie, his gloved hands clasped between his knees. "It is delightful to see you again, of course, but I nourish the liveliest apprehension as to why you've called me here. Do you think you might explain?"

Crump chuckled. "It's not *me* as has the explaining to do! You've heard Throckmorton swear he saw you at White's. Mind telling me what you were doing there?"

"Zounds!" Willies eyebrows climbed almost to his hairline. "Am I thought to be a suspicious and dangerous character? You flatter me, Mr. Crump, indeed you do!"

"I'll do more than that if you don't stop your clowning!" said Crump, annoyed. "I'll see you committed to quod for a month as a rogue and a vagabond."

"Name-calling?" Daintily, Willie crossed his legs. "An unworthy pastime, particularly for a thieftaker. People in my profession are merely accused of scandalmongering and lies, whereas people in *yours* are accused of living by catching innocent men and having them hanged." Beatifically, he grinned. "It is to be expected, of course! A thieftaker is hardly paid sufficiently well to keep him honest. I do sympathize, Mr. Crump!"

"There's even less future," retorted Crump, so grimly that Willie blanched, "in being hanged. Answer my questions or it'll be the worse for you."

"Mr. Crump, you misjudge me! I am only too happy to oblige." Willie wore a cautious expression. "What questions were those?"

"What were you doing at White's?" repeated Crump, a great deal more patiently than he felt.

"I was merely waiting to speak with one of the members, not wishing to venture within." He shrugged. "I'm truly sorry to disappoint you, but there it is! The truth is often dull."

Crump greatly doubted that he'd heard the truth, dull or otherwise, but temporarily let the matter lie. "Who," he asked, "is paying Miss Langtry's way at Newgate? Was it you that left a handsome purse for her use?"

"I?" Willie's nose wiggled frantically. "I'm sure I would've liked to, but I haven't a feather to fly with. Nor can I help you regarding dear Leda's comforts, other than telling you she has money of her own."

"Does she, now?" mused Crump. "Odd, isn't it, that she claims she doesn't know who bought her way?" But, then, Leda claimed a number of things that were obviously untrue.

"Actually, it is not," Willie commented gently. "You would not know, Mr. Crump, but the people are firmly behind Leda, as are my fellow Gentlemen of the Press. She is the only female member of the London Press Club, did you know? Absolutely anyone could have left that purse for her, and if he wished to remain anonymous, we would never learn who it was."

Crump said nothing, recalling the gaoler's rather dubious tale of a well-dressed gentleman. "Where does Leda get her money?" he barked. "Don't try to tell me that damned newspaper is a financial success."

Pained, Willie closed his pale eyes. "We journalists do not pursue our craft," he said reprovingly, "for financial gain. To tell the world the truth, *that* is our concern!" He grimaced. "You *do* have hold of the wrong end of the stick, Mr. Crump. Surely you know Leda was visiting with a friend at the time of Warwick's murder?"

Crump's smile was a great deal less pleasant now, and his bright eyes rested thoughtfully on Willie's gloved hands. "Mary Elphinstone?" he said, in tones so menacing that Willie quailed. "I'll tell you something, laddie, since you'll know it soon enough anyway. Mary Elphinstone's body was found yesterday. She was apparently beaten unconscious, then thrown into a well."

For once, Willie had no prompt retort. White as chalk, he teetered on the windowsill. Crump listened to the crash of cart wheels on the cobblestoned streets below, the occasional hearty curses of draymen, as he mulled over the details that he'd withheld. Around Mary Elphinstone's well had been a woman's footprints, prints the same size, or Crump missed his guess, as Leda Langtry's feet; and on Mary Elphinstone's body had been a brooch stolen from the worthy establishment of Rundle and Brydges. It was impossible to determine exactly when the woman had died, but one thing was sure: if Leda hadn't killed Lord Warwick, she had certainly killed Mary Elphinstone. Crump rather suspected Leda was responsible for both murders, and that Mary Elphinstone had died not only because she could disprove Leda's alibi, but because she knew too much about Leda's activities.

"Good God," said Willie weakly. "You are a rum one, Mr. Crump! Poor Leda is in a dreadfully forlorn position now. I suppose you'll next be asking me to unbosom myself to you, to make a full confession of *my* guilt."

"No." The Runner was convinced that he was on the right track, but there were still certain abstruse points to be cleared up. "What I'm asking is that you take off those gloves and show me your hands."

Willie swallowed hard as he slid off the window sill. "It is another of the hazards of the profession," he said gloomily as he stripped off the gloves. "The printer fell ill and I was forced to deal with the press. As you can see, it is not an occupation at which I am adept."

What Crump saw were knuckles as raw and abraded as if they'd beaten the spirit out of an old woman. He contained his excitement, however, and merely rose to lean casually against the back of Sir John's chair. There were moments of sheer joy in this profession of his, when he knew beyond the shadow of a doubt that he was hot on the trail of a murderer.

Yet even Crump had to admit that Willie hardly looked like a bloodthirsty criminal, drooping as he was in the middle of the room, slowly pulling on his soiled gloves. "Who were you looking for at White's?" asked the Runner. He might be convinced that he had solved the puzzle, but Sir John would require proof.

"Mr. Crump, you *do* have an ax to grind!" Willie cocked his head impudently to one side. "And I, alas, have a deadline to meet. Very well, if you must have it, I was waiting for Viscount Jeffries."

Crump had a nasty sinking sensation in the pit of his stomach, for he recalled very clearly that he'd met that gentleman in Lady Bligh's Drawing Room. No matter where Crump turned, he encountered the irrepressibly nosy Baroness! "Why?" he asked sternly.

Willie turned positively coy. "I'm afraid my reasons are personal, and I doubt that you'd approve of them." Crump stared astonished as Willie winked. "Now, Mr. Crump, loath as I am to depart your stimulating company, I must attend to that deadline!"

The Runner made no move to prevent his unconventional

visitor from blithely exiting, for Willie would be closely followed wherever he went. Crump knew evasive action when he saw it: Willie had been patently relieved at the thrust of the questioning. A man with a great deal to hide, concluded Crump happily. Those secrets would be exposed ere long.

The journalist had given him more than a little food for thought. Things were taking on a definite shape, for all there were so many busy fingers set on making a muddle of the pie. So Viscount Jeffries was a member of White's, Crump mused. Now that the chimney sweeps were cleared, it was one of Crump's more tedious tasks to discreetly investigate that select membership. He thought his first efforts might be directed toward nosing out the association between Viscount Jeffries, Willie Fitzwilliam and Leda Langtry.

Chapter Thirteen

Although it was an unreasonably early hour, Lady Bligh was already closeted with her two most loyal retainers in the Breakfast Room. "Well, Culpepper," said the Baroness, elegant in a lacy dressing gown and with an even lacier cap covering her curls, "what have you learned?"

"To heartily dislike oysters!" retorted the abigail, whose ill temper might have been partially excused by the particularly severe bout of indigestion that had kept her awake half the night. "A woman *was* seen leaving Warwick's apartments, by way of the window, very near to the time when the murder took place."

"Ah!" The Baroness popped a well-buttered scone into her mouth.

"She wore black," continued Culpepper. "Though she was heavily veiled, it was noted that she had white hair."

"So do half the dowagers in London," commented Dulcie in slightly garbled tones. She drank deeply of her chocolate. "Surely you can do better than that, Culpepper!" Her shrewd eyes darted to the doorway. "Gibbon, do step into the hallway and ask my niece to enter." The butler threw open the door. Mignon—dressed for the out-of-doors in a forest green spencer over a paler walking dress, and a neck scarf of emerald with lime stripes, beige half boots and kid gloves, and a most elegant green velvet hat trimmed with coque feathers—stood on the threshold, hand upraised to knock.

"How nice you look, my dear!" The Baroness was apparently no whit disturbed that her niece intended to set out on foot into a very dreary morning, an undertaking that would have sent Mignon's mama, had she but known, into convulsions. "Do heed my advice and take one of the footmen along. I shall not ask him to report to me where you've been, I promise, child! Now do have some chocolate."

Mignon, greatly startled, obeyed. How could Dulcie have known she meant to set out alone? She frowned. Could her aunt have also guessed where she meant to go?

Dulcie had turned back to Culpepper. "There *was* something queer about that woman," conceded that worthy, somewhat unhappily. "She displayed the agility of a far younger woman than she appeared to be, dropping to the ground as easily as if she clambered in and out of windows every day."

"That is odd," conceded the Baroness. She eyed her butler. "Gibbon?"

"I have discovered one thing, my lady." He, in turn, surveyed Mignon. "It concerns Lord Barrymore."

"You fear Mignon will betray us to her so worthy suitor?" asked Lady Bligh. Mignon blinked. "We need not regard my niece, Gibbon. What about Lord Barrymore?"

Gibbon obviously did not share his mistress's assurance concerning Miss Montague. He stared stiffly straight ahead. "It is being said, my lady, that Lord Barrymore owed Lord Warwick a considerable amount of money."

"Money," mused Lady Bligh, tapping her long fingers on a table top. "Interesting! However, I daresay Barrymore has a perfectly innocent explanation." She sighed. "Damned if the opposition isn't progressing in leaps and bounds whilst we sit here havering and wavering on the brink."

"Yes, my lady," said Gibbon gloomily.

Mignon, whose nerves were taut as a fiddlestring with combined anticipation and dread, could bear to sit idly no longer. She put down her cup. "You're off then, Mignon?" asked the Baroness brightly. "While you're out, you might match a piece of ribbon for me." She pulled a scrap of lilac cording from the pocket of her robe.

"I would be happy to," Mignon replied, "but I do not plan to be near the shops today."

"Dear Mignon, you will learn that plans are things to be lightly discarded when more pleasant alternatives present themselves. Take the ribbon!" No small bit confused, Mignon obeyed.

In the hallway, she waited briefly for the prescribed footman to ready himself. "Refresh my memory, Gibbon!" demanded the Baroness, clearly audible. "Is not a convict returning from transportation likely to be hanged?" Gibbon's answer was lost; in a burst of prudence that she herself did not understand, Mignon turned and closed the Breakfast Room door.

"Going out, miss?" inquired Charity, who had approached so silently that her voice made Mignon jump. She swung around to find the homely maid surveying her with an oddly approving eye. "I hope you have a pleasant walk! Though it's hardly a day for it."

At last, with her unwanted escort following a few paces behind, Miss Montague stepped outside. She touched the letter that was folded in her reticule. If only she had been sufficiently dishonest to steal unseen out of the house—and if only Lady Bligh had not seen fit to send an escort along! Mignon considered various ways of ridding herself of the footman. Despite Dulcie's promise that no questions would be asked, Mignon thought it would be a great deal more prudent to dispense with his company.

It was indeed a bleak morning. Summer had deserted London, as had most members of the *ton*. If only Maurice had been similarly inclined, thought Mignon. He might have taken himself to New Brighton with its elegant residences facing the ocean, its smart bathing boxes and its graceful terraces. Brighton was a favorite resort of their mother's and Maurice had, some years back, been thrilled to witness Prinny driving his coach-and-four under the tutelage of Sir John Lade. But no! Maurice must present himself in London and fall in so firmly with Lord Barrymore that he had even written to their mama, giving his august opinion that Tolly would be the perfect man to take Mignon in hand. Miss Montague scowled so dreadfully that the footman gulped, afraid he had caused offense.

At least there was some consolation in the fact that Maurice's attention was not firmly on his sister—else, thought Mignon grimly, she would have hardly escaped the house. Maurice was breakfasting with Tolly, and doubtless waxing enthusiastic about a lovely and retiring young widow whom he'd been privileged to glimpse, an acquaintance of Lord Barrymore's and, from Maurice's description, as perfect a female as ever drew mortal breath. Mignon cordially wished her brother success with this new romance, the latest in a series of infatuations. If only Maurice would wed one of the ladies who caught his wandering eye, he might have less time to meddle in his sister's business. Alas, Maurice's marriage was slightly less likely than a second appearance of Christ, for Lady Montague was not only singularly unwilling to share her son's affections with any other female but remarkably skilled in disposing of those ladies who posed a potential threat. Perhaps it would be different, Mignon thought, here in London where Maurice was not so firmly under his mama's thumb.

Though London may have been deserted by the *ton*, the streets were still busy, thronged with vendors selling hot loaves, muffins and crumpets, and countless other wares. Their raised voices blended with the jingle and clatter of horses' hooves striking rough stones. Suddenly visited by a brilliant idea, Mignon stopped so abruptly that the footman almost collided with her. Her clever mind working rapidly, she looked around.

There were cat's-meat men and bellows menders, knife grinders and lavender merchants, playbill vendors and girls selling watercress, milkmaids delivering fresh cow's milk at street doors. Mignon eyed an old woman hawking baked and boiled apples, a white-clad Flying Pieman with steaming hot puddings, then turned to the footman. "I find," she said ruefully, "that I am positively starving! Do you think you might slip into that cookshop and procure for me a pie?"

It was hardly the footman's place to argue with her request, unseemly as it might be for a young lady to walk through the streets eating pastry. He stepped into the store, unaware that Miss Montague was a scheming little minx who had hit upon this subterfuge to make her getaway.

But Mignon was not destined to go far. She paused to watch the Regent's yellow carriage with its maroon blinds, pulled by superb bay horses and escorted by dashing Life Guards, move majestically through the streets. The people around her also turned to stare, in an ominous silence that was broken only by an occasional jeer. It occurred to Mignon that she was deliberately tarrying, and she wondered if she had lost her spirit of adventure, or if it was Leda's predicament that so oppressed her spirits.

"Miss Montague," said a voice at her shoulder, and Mignon found herself looking into Lord Jeffries' undeniably handsome face. Stunned, she noticed first that his eyes were not an ordinary brown, but lightly flecked with green, and second that for some odd reason the Viscount seemed amused. "How fortunate that I have come upon you in this manner," he remarked, "for I particularly wished to speak with you." Speechless, Mignon allowed herself to be helped into his fashionable phaeton with towering wheels and yellow wings, drawn by matched coal-black horses. "It was not kind of you," added Ivor, still in that laughing tone, "to bamboozle your poor footman! The fellow was positively quaking in his boots. I sent him home, with a message to Lady Bligh that you will be perfectly safe with me."

Will I? wondered Mignon, casting another sideways glance at his comely countenance. He wore a well-cut coat of green superfine, an ecru mancella waistcoat, and green kerseymore trousers. Mignon blushed at the thought that she and the Viscount made a nicely matched pair. "You wished to speak to me?" she said quickly. "What about?"

Seemingly in no hurry to answer her question, he turned in the comfortable seat. "I was closeted with Leda's solicitor when I saw you pass by in so very clandestine a manner that I was immediately intrigued. There was nothing for it but to follow you, a presumption that I hope you will forgive."

"It is I who should ask your forgiveness," she murmured, so meekly that she startled herself. "On the occasion of our last meeting, I was insufferably rude."

"So you were," agreed the Viscount cheerfully. "As I recall, so was I. An enlightening experience, I assure you! And one to be forgotten, I think, since the honors were so even."

Mignon had not expected such generosity. "You should not have let me take you from your meeting with Leda's solicitor. I'm sure your business with him was important."

"So it was." Ivor's frown detracted not at all from his charm. "But it was drawing to a close when I glimpsed you. Livingston is a vulgar, dirty, dogmatic old pedant, unutterably boring, one of those learned advocates often heard declaiming at such length in court. Fortunately, he is also bloodthirsty, clever, subtle, full of talent and craft, and very fond of my—of Leda." The frown vanished. "It was not to speak of Leda that I practically kidnaped you."

"Is that what you've done?" asked Mignon feebly, stricken all aheap by the magnetism of the man. "Why?"

Ivor regarded her judiciously. "It's the freckles, I think, that particularly fascinate me." She gazed at him, bewildered, and received a devastating smile. "Tell me, Miss Montague, is this your first visit to Town?"

"It is." Mignon looked with great interest at her gloves. "You do not have to tell me, sir, that those who've never been seen at Almack's are regarded as utterly unfashionable."

The Viscount refused to be provoked. "Almack's?" he said. "I don't care for the place myself, or for the Italian Opera that during the season is so much the rage. People can't appear there except *en toilette*, even in the pit. In front of every box hangs a chandelier, which dazzles one most offensively and throws the actor into shadow."

"It sounds," Mignon said in surprise, "as if you do not much care for Society."

"Between you and me and my very discreet coachman," Ivor grinned, "I don't. If one isn't being crushed half to death at some tedious rout, one is being bored to death by the bluestockings who prattle away in half the drawing rooms of the kingdom about morals and metaphysics and the derivation of languages! You are more fortunate than you realize to be in London at this time of year, Miss Montague."

He was determined not to discuss Leda, it seemed, and Mignon wasn't reluctant to set aside her own worries for a while. "You still haven't told me," she remarked, "why you wished to speak with me."

"Haven't I?" The Viscount quirked a sandy brow. "Perhaps I mean to keep you a long time in a terrible state of suspense. No, I beg of you, don't frown at me, Miss Montague! The truth is I had meant to apologize to you for my hasty words, but you were quicker than I." He smiled. "Though I refuse to retract my remark about your superb eyes."

"You flatter me, Lord Jeffries." Mignon was gruff. "I need only look in a mirror to know I am nothing out of the ordinary."

"Are you not?" Inexplicably, Ivor laughed. "It has long been my contention that the so-called weaker sex is prone to remarkably foolish ideas! But now allow me to atone for my rudeness by showing you some of London's less fashionable sights." Before Mignon could protest, he had leaned forward to issue instructions to his coachman.

Thus Miss Montague was privileged to view the great court of the Royal Exchange, surrounded by covered arcades where the merchants of every nation had their places of assembly; the statues of English sovereigns, most remarkable among them Henry VIII and Elizabeth; and the celebrated Lloyd's Coffee House. She was taken to the vast and beautiful Bank of England, chartered in 1694 to help the government of William III solve its credit problems. There she viewed the Bullion Office where piles of gold and silver ingots appeared to her astonished eyes as more rightly belonging in some Aladdin's treasure cave. And she was taken to the Guildhall where the Lord Mayor in his blue gown and gold chain was in the act of administering the law. When at length she was set down outside the Bligh mansion, Mignon was so dazed that she barely managed to thank her guide.

"Ah!" said Lady Bligh, meeting her niece at the door, "I see you found time to perform my little errand." Mignon stared down at the ribbon which dangled forgotten from one hand. As she recalled what else had temporarily fled her errant mind, her spirits sank as if weighted down by a stone.

Chapter Fourteen

"Preposterous!" sputtered Maurice, not for the first time. He was not feeling quite the thing, having passed the previous evening with Tolly at the Cocoa Tree, where they had clareted and champagned til 5 a.m., finishing off with a Regency punch composed of madeira, brandy and green tea before ambulating somewhat unsteadily homeward. Even had Maurice been in fine fettle, however, he could have felt nothing but dismay at finding himself in this shoddy room at Bow Street. He shook his head. "This is beyond everything."

Sir John was inclined to agree. He studied Maurice, in whom he saw little kinship with Lady Bligh. The Honorable Mr. Montague, having been privileged to meet the brooding Lord Byron, had chosen to model himself after that gentleman. His shirt collar fell over a very narrow cravat of white sarsenet; he wore a black coat and waistcoat and very broad white trousers of Russian duck. Looped up to a button of his waistcoat was a watch chain and dangling seals. Sir John wondered if Maurice's admiration of Byron was sufficient to lead him to strike up an acquaintance with Caro Lamb or begin to scribble poetry.

But the Chief Magistrate had no time to dwell upon Maurice's peculiarities. He turned to his other visitor. "I trust," he said politely, "that you can explain."

Lord Barrymore was very much as ease. "I can," he replied, with equal courtesy. "Shall I begin at the beginning? Very well!" He paused, as if ordering his thoughts. "Being members of White's, Warwick and I were accustomed to laying occasional wagers on various things. The debt that you mentioned was the result of one such occasion when I went down rather heavily."

Sir John was no stranger to London's various gentlemen's clubs, having patronized a good number of them in his own youth, before his taste for drink and play had given way to a passion for justice. It occurred to him that some of those old contacts might have been better cultivated than allowed to languish on the vine. It was not only the poor and luckless who turned to crime. "What," he asked, "did the wager concern?"

"Insufferable!" protested Maurice, from his position near the window. "What can Lord Barrymore's private concerns have to do with Bow Street? This is a shocking invasion of a man's privacy."

"It's all right, Maurice!" Tolly flashed an apologetic smile at Sir John. "I'm sure I wish to do anything I may to aid in bringing to justice Warwick's murderer. Excuse my presumption, but I thought she was already in custody?"

The Chief Magistrate rubbed his lined forehead, behind which throbbed a magnificent headache, half wishing Lady Bligh might suddenly appear to tease away the pain. "There are various minor details," he said vaguely, "still to be cleared up. The wager, Lord Barrymore?"

"Of course." Tolly seemed anxious to cooperate. "It concerned the lovely Miss Browne, and the most likely winner of her hand. Warwick backed Selkirk, while I wagered on Willoughby." He shrugged. "As the world must know, Selkirk won. It was an error of judgment that cost me £3,000. You may verify it in White's betting book."

"The debt was paid, then?" inquired Sir John, ignoring Maurice's fresh burst of outrage.

"Naturally," replied Lord Barrymore, not the least disturbed by the intimation that he might act less than honorably. "We met at the club and I took care of the matter. I would have to check my engagement book but I believe that meeting took place two days before Warwick's death."

Sir John, in those long-ago days before he had abandoned the *ton* to take up his magisterial gavel and dispense justice at Bow Street, had been a formidable opponent at the card table. His impassive features gave nothing away. "How well," he said idly, "did you know Warwick, Lord Barrymore?"

Tolly looked surprised. "Not well at all. We were members of the same clubs, and often met at social functions, but we were far from close friends."

"Oh?" Sir John's bushy brows rose. "Then how did it come about that you called at Warwick's quarters on the night he died?"

Maurice's indignant protests began anew at this unthinkable insinuation, but Lord Barrymore only smiled. "I went there," he replied, "at Warwick's express request. I'm afraid I failed to keep the note he sent, not anticipating its importance, but Warwick's valet should remember. He brought it to me."

Sir John studied this helpful gentleman and wished that he'd dared leave the interrogation to Crump. The Chief Magistrate had little taste for prying into the lives of his fellow men. "Have you any notion of why Warwick wished to speak to you? Perhaps, forged banknotes?"

Lord Barrymore looked very startled indeed. "There was a case some years back," he mused, "in which the Bow Street Justices took part in an inquiry at the Bank of England in connection with such notes. There was quite a to-do made at the time, as I recall.

The Lord Mayor made a sharp protest against what he termed the 'improper intrusion' of Bow Street in an affair outside its jurisdiction. Is it that to which you refer?"

"No." Sir John's head throbbed like a well-played drum. He recalled the instance to which Lord Barrymore referred; it had brought him into an argument with the Home Secretary almost as heated as the one that had taken place more recently when control of the mounted Bow Street Patrol had passed from the Chief Magistrate into his superior's hands. "I refer to the fact that Warwick had in his possession a large number of forged banknotes."

"So you knew that." Lord Barrymore seemed relieved. "I did not wish to betray a confidence, but yes, Warwick had come across notes which he believed to be forged. I do not know that they were. He asked me to look at them, and to give my opinion."

"Oh?" Sir John leaned back in his chair. "What would *you* know about such things?"

Lord Barrymore spread his hands in a curiously foreign gesture. "I have a small knowledge—there was a sad affair, quickly hushed up, when a member of my regiment passed similar items. I became curious, did some reading, looked at all manner of forgeries." His smile was self-deprecating. "Warwick knew of my interest, and wished to know if the notes truly *were* false before he took further steps. Alas, I had no opportunity to give him an opinion of the matter! For all I know, those notes might have been quite legitimate."

Sir John reflected sourly that the Home Secretary would not be happy to hear the the Chief Magistrate of Bow Street had interrogated an ex-officer in the Prince's own regiment, the Tenth Hussars. He further reflected that Dulcie was even less likely to be pleased, since Lord Barrymore was so assiduously courting her niece. "Have you any notion how Warwick came by them?"

"Not the least," said Tolly cheerfully. "I take it, since you're so interested, that the notes are missing? Audacious, these recent robberies!"

This subject Sir John had no wish to discuss. "When Warwick's valet admitted you that night, did you notice anything odd?"

"I'm truly sorry I can't be of any assistance," Lord Barrymore replied regretfully, "but I didn't. The window stood open, of course, but all else appeared to be in order. Poor Simpkin was quite overwrought."

"Very well," said Sir John, and made a neat little speech in which he both thanked them for their assistance and apologized for any inconvenience his summons may have caused. In return, Lord Barrymore professed himself eager to assist Bow Street in any way possible, and the Honorable Maurice declared himself scandalized. They left Sir John gloomily drawing abstract designs on the top of his old, scarred desk.

"Infamous!" declared Maurice once again, as they reached the street below. "Damned if I ever thought to see the day when a gentleman would be required to explain his actions to Bow Street!"

Tolly tossed a coin to the patient urchin who held their horses and swung into the saddle. "Sir John is a gentleman himself," he replied. "In case you've forgotten, he's also a good friend to your aunt."

"My aunt," repeated Maurice gloomily, wondering if his wide trousers were quite the thing in which to go riding. They were more than elegant, but they were also deuced awkward. "A woman has no business to become a public character! Delicacy is lost in proportion to the notoriety she gains."

Lord Barrymore, who had already heard in great detail the reasons for Maurice's annoyance with Lady Bligh, only smiled. The Baroness had no sooner learned of her nephew's high-handed treatment of Culpepper than she assigned to him a chamber containing various relics of Tippoo Sahib, Sultan of Mysore, who before his death had been a friend of the adventurous Baron Bligh. This formidable foe of England had taken the stripes of the tiger as his coat of arms, and claimed he'd rather live one day as a predator than a century as a quietly grazing sheep. Maurice's aversion to his rooms was perhaps understandable: most outstanding among the articles displayed therein was a barrel organ concealed in the belly of a well-preserved tiger under which lay a mauled, scarlet-uniformed Englishman. From this masterpiece issued the mingled sounds of a triumphant snarling tiger and a man in his death agonies.

"I only hope," Maurice said sourly, "that my aunt may not induce my sister to follow in her footsteps. She is hardly the best influence on Mignon."

Though Maurice seriously doubted Mignon's prudence, his was a mind easily distracted from unpleasant things. Lord Barrymore had already proved as good as his word, and had taken his new friend to Hoby, the famed boot maker who also served as a Methodist preacher, from whom Maurice purchased Hessian, Hussar and Wellington boots; and to Lock's the hatters at No. 6 St. James's Street, where Maurice procured a beaver hat, a glossy black top hat and a folding *chapeau bras*. To Maurice's wonderment, he was also taken to a bordello where he gazed with no small amazement upon a naked posture-woman who struck incredible poses on a huge silver tray. He pondered what Lord Barrymore's next surprise might be.

Tolly turned into Hyde Park, where in the season the *ton* convened to see and to be seen. It was almost bare now of the ladies in their fashionable carriages, of well-mounted gentlemen, of dashing courtesans. But Lord Barrymore, with an odd little smile, led his friend down a path. Ahead of them, a carriage had stopped. A woman sat within. Maurice wished suddenly that he had access to a looking glass. He feared that his carroty curls, brushed down over his forehead in the ragged Brutus style, had gotten mussed.

"Good afternoon!" said Tolly, pulling up his horse. "How lucky it is to meet you here." He glanced at Maurice, the amusement more pronounced, but Maurice was staring spellbound at the carriage's occupant. She was a delicately formed lady with a porcelain complexion and jet-black hair. "Maurice, let me make known to you Mrs. Harrington-Smythe."

Stunned by such beauty, Maurice stammered a reply. His awkwardness seemed to gratify the lady. Gently, she smiled.

Chapter Fifteen

Only Lady Bligh and Mignon were in the Morning Room, Maurice having taken himself off to destinations unknown after voicing his usual complaint about his sleeping quarters, this day announcing that his bed was so enormously large that he lay like an icicle in it, the fire being too remote to render any sensible warmth. Mignon was vaguely curious about the ways Maurice filled his time, but they had never been close and she could hardly question him without leaving herself open for a similar interrogation.

The Baroness sighed and dropped her newspaper. She looked fetching indeed in a semitransparent chemise gown belted under her breasts and worn over a sheer slip of thin taffeta. Her heavy peach curls were caught up in an Apollo knot and secured by tortoiseshell combs.

"What is it?" asked Mignon, concerned by her aunt's brooding expression. "Has something in the paper distressed you?"

Dulcie looked not at her niece but into her teacup. "It has been," she murmured vaguely, "a most interesting year. In February a military gentleman appeared at Dover with false tidings of a great victory over the French. The deception was found out, but not before a group of prominent Englishmen had made a fortune on the Stock Exchange. The culprit himself netted a profit of £10,000. Clever! And in July, Percy Bysshe Shelley, despite the fact that he is married and a father, eloped with the daughter of William Godwin. That was slightly less clever, I fear. Due to lack of funds, they have already been forced to return."

Mignon warily eyed the Baroness, who had fallen silent. Lady Bligh was staring into the teacup with a reverence that might have been more aptly awarded the Delphic Oracle. "Mignon!" she said, so abruptly that Miss Montague nearly spilled her tea. "You will recall that you offered your assistance to me."

"I do." Mignon replied cautiously.

Dulcie lifted her dark eyes. "I mean to hold you to that promise." She manipulated her slender fingers so that knuckles cracked. "Starting immediately. I had meant to keep you as far as possible out of this thing, but there were contingencies I did not foresee. Will you trust me, Mignon?"

"Of course." Miss Montague regarded her enigmatic aunt with no small perplexity. "What is it you wish me to do?"

"For a start, to keep rein on your temper." Idly, Dulcie touched the garnets that were wound around her slender throat. "We are shortly to receive an irate visitor."

Mignon had learned the futility of asking questions. She dropped her eyes to the book she held, a volume entitled *Waverley*, published anonymously by Walter Scott, a friend of her aunt's. If only she might confide in Dulcie—but she could not. "It makes no difference," commented the Baroness, in tones that were almost grim. "The die is cast." As Mignon was gathering sufficient courage to question this remark, Viscount Jeffries stepped into the room.

It was a charming chamber with ceiling and carpet of the palest green and walls papered in a floral design, and its occupants were arranged in a most pleasing tableau. Dulcie was posed on an elegant tapestried sofa, her delicate feet propped comfortably on the orange cat's broad back; while Mignon, clad in a becoming long-sleeved blue gown with a small design of scattered flowers, shared with Bluebeard a wing chair. So far was Viscount Jeffries from evidencing appreciation that he looked both bitter and forbidding.

"Forgive my intrusion," he said to Dulcie, in tones that were far from apologetic. "I must speak with your niece." Mignon raised startled eyes.

"You are greatly out of temper," observed the Baroness calmly, "and little wonder! But you will regret it if you ring a peal over Mignon. Despite appearances, she is not to blame."

"Who then?" demanded Ivor, tossing his hat without ceremony onto a Carolian carved cherub. "You? I think not, Lady Bligh, though it doesn't surprise me that you should wish to cover up your niece's deceit and duplicity."

"I beg your pardon!" gasped Mignon, closing her book with so much force that Bluebeard nervously ruffled his feathers. "My *what?*"

"Don't bother to deny it!" Ivor looked down upon her from a great, icy distance. "I suppose this is the way you chose to repay me for seeking to keep my relationship with Leda secret from the world? Fine conduct for a young lady of breeding—but I suppose you were well paid!"

Mignon stared. *This* was the man she had thought a husband to dream of, with his high station in life, his handsome face, and his all-conquering charm? "Paid?" she repeated. "For what?"

With an irritated gesture, Ivor bent to pick up Dulcie's paper from the floor. "You play the innocent overwell," he snarled. "Here, read your handiwork. Not that I imagine you haven't already done so! What evil genius prompted your meddling, Miss Montague? Nothing could be more revolting to propriety."

Mignon gazed at the newspaper and her heart sank to her toes.

Blazoned across it, in unmistakable language, was the information that Leda Langtry, murderess, was the mother of Ivor Jessop, Viscount Jeffries. Even that was not the worst; the item was embellished with intimations and innuendoes that quite took one's breath away. "You blame me for *this?*" she asked faintly.

If any doubt had entered the Viscount's mind, he had not allowed it room to grow. "You do not deny it, I see. What purpose did you think to serve, Miss Montague? Or was it done solely for financial gain?"

"It wasn't done at all!" blazed Mignon, her promise to control her temper already forgotten. "At least, not by me! Even if I wished to sell information to the Press, I wouldn't know how to go about it." She grasped the arms of her chair so tightly that her fingers showed white. "*You* have made a rare mull of it, Lord Jeffries, not I!"

Ivor's teeth flashed in a fierce parody of a smile. "You are an unconscionable little liar, Miss Montague, and I do not intend to leave here until I have the truth from you. By force, if necessary." He stepped toward her with obviously fell intent. Mignon grasped her book, meaning if necessary to hurl it at his head.

"Children, children!" chided the Baroness, and rose to cross the room. Culpepper, even more sour-faced than usual, stood in the hallway. "Excellent!" said Lady Bligh, and again closed the door.

"Dulcie!" gasped Mignon, for Ivor had grasped her shoulders and was shaking her as if he meant to loosen not only her tongue but all the teeth in her head.

"Unhand my niece, young man!" Serenely, the Baroness returned to the couch. "Mignon did not play you false. Nor has she any need for money, possessing a considerable fortune of her own."

The Viscount, though he ceased to manhandle her, retained his grip on Miss Montague. "You must defend her, of course," he said, his brown eyes fixed angrily on Mignon's pale face. "I recall that you warned me she would do precisely what she's done."

"I did no such thing," returned Lady Bligh irritably. "I hinted merely that Mignon has a tendency to trust everyone. I was trying to persuade you not to speak at all, but you refused to listen. It doesn't signify; too many people already knew, including Willie, who can be trusted with no one's secrets but his own." She looked speculatively at Ivor, who clutched Mignon's arm as if he meant to drag her before a magistrate. "Distasteful as it may be to see one's dirty linen washed in public, it was bound to happen eventually. I repeat, you must not blame Mignon. In this matter, she is perfectly innocent."

Mignon, whose head still spun from the combined effects of Ivor's tongue-lashing and his mistreatment of her person, wondered what Lady Bligh might know of other matters in which her niece was less blameless. "If you are through bullying me, sir," she said frigidly, "I should like very much to sit down." With a searching glance, Ivor released her. Mignon sank into her chair.

"If not Miss Montague, then who?" Ivor asked, with no abatement of his rage. "I suppose you know?"

"Not know, suspect." Dulcie toyed with her necklace in a way that made one fear she might strangle herself. "I will not tell you now, for I do not understand the whole, and any steps you take would only make things worse."

The Viscount, it was obvious, did not care for this judicious attitude. "You take a great deal upon yourself, Lady Bligh!" he growled. "I don't see that your previous efforts in Leda's behalf have accomplished any great steps forward. Two people are dead, and Leda remains in Newgate."

"She will continue to do so," retorted Dulcie severely, "until I see this coil unwound. Come, do not take on so! What does it signify, after all, if your relationship to Leda has been published to the world? I had not thought you so poor a creature that you would care about such things! I fear your uncle has taught you to overly value your consequence."

Lord Jeffries might have made a great number of pithy responses, including an elaboration on the fact that Lady Bligh so little valued her own reputation that she was positively notorious. Instead, his look of anger was replaced by surprise.

"I?" he said. "It is not myself, but my uncle who so loathes to hear our name bandied about. I had previously kept all concerning Leda from him, but this I could not. It brought him off his sickbed to confront Leda in Newgate—and God alone knows what will come of that! He loathes my mother so greatly that during all the years of our association he never spoke of her other than to inform me she was dead."

"There is a great deal," interrupted Dulcie severely, "that you do not understand. Jumping to conclusions is a dangerous pastime, young man!" Mignon peered sideways at the Viscount, curious to see how he would take this reprimand. He raised an offended brow.

"So far is your uncle from loathing Leda," continued the Baroness, "that he once offered her his hand in marriage. Leda jilted him to marry your father. But that does not explain your excessive concern for your uncle's peace of mind!"

Ivor, justifiably stunned by this intelligence, gazed upon Mignon's bright hair. So did Bluebeard, who reached forward with his sharp beak to tug at a loose curl. Mignon winced. "My uncle," replied Ivor, absently disengaging the parrot, "has been very good to me. The least I owe him is a consideration of his name. Percy abhors scandal."

"You owe Percy nothing!" snapped Dulcie. "Which is something else you have yet to learn. If not for his stuffy principles, you would have acknowledged Leda straightaway?"

"She did not wish it." Ivor's hauteur had returned. "When I broached the matter, Leda replied that her association with the Jessop family had been far from felicitous, and that she no more wished to claim a relationship with them than Percy wished to recognize her. I fear that whoever leaked this information to the Press has done my mother a great disservice thereby."

A pompous lot, thought Mignon resentfully. Did Viscount Jeffries but know *her* past, he would speedily repudiate their acquaintance instead of lounging so indolently against the back of her chair. "So!" said the Baroness triumphantly. "That's one puzzle explained." She did not share her insight, but stared bemused at the closed door, her fingers buried in Casanova's fur.

Ivor cleared his throat. "I fear I was wrong," he remarked stiffly, "but that does not alter the situation. This is an abominable proceeding and I cannot see what's to be done."

"Of course you can't" Dulcie's dark gaze was unfriendly. "I fear, Jessop, that all too often you don't see beyond the end of your aristocratic nose! If you don't come down off your high ropes, young man, I shall be quite out of charity with you."

Mignon could not see the Viscount, who stood behind her chair, but his anger was a palpable force. Oddly, this did not cheer her, but made her wish even more strongly to cry. At least, if Maurice decided to drag her home, she would be freed of this wretched imbroglio. It was obviously Mignon's destiny to live out her days in the country, playing nursemaid to her invalidish and ill-tempered mother, and never to set eyes again on any member of the opposite sex.

Lady Bligh was immune to the touchy tempers of her fellow men. Her astute eyes flicked from the Viscount's face to rest on her niece's downcast countenance. "There is something you haven't considered," she said somberly. "The worst repercussion of this sad affair is neither Percy's indignation nor Leda's dismay. Can't you see that this disclosure implicates you, by your blood relationship, in Leda's escapades? It has occurred to Bow Street, I assure you! Now the dedicated little Crump will plague you as he does Willie." She frowned. "Perhaps I might be of more assistance to you, Jessop, in the matter of alibis?"

"You need not concern yourself," Ivor replied offended. "I have nothing to hide."

"That is not at all the point!" retorted Lady Bligh, striding briskly toward the door. "But have it as you wish. I must consult with my abigail." She turned, hand on the doorknob, to regard him sternly. "I suggest it would be to your future advantage to apologize to Mignon." The door closed behind her with a decisive thud.

"Pray don't so exert yourself!" said Mignon, staring down at her clenched hands.

Ivor moved to stand in front of her, frowning down at her bent head. "But I wish to," he murmured and extended a hand. Blue-beard squawked and hopped from Mignon's shoulder to the back of the chair.

She could hardly refuse him. Anticipating a formal apology, Mignon placed her hand in his. Instead, she was hauled ungently to her feet.

Nor did he release her immediately. "Did I insult you?" inquired the Viscount, his brown eyes warm with concern. "These past days have been most trying, and I fear I took out my ill temper on you."

"Naturally," said Mignon, staring fixedly at his cravat. "Since you considered me the author of your misfortunes, you could hardly behave otherwise."

"That stung, did it?" Ivor's tone was cordial. "I had meant it to. I could not help but recall that your aunt had warned me against you." His strong fingers moved to her chin and forced her gaze up to meet his.

Mignon glared at him through her tears. "Dulcie explained that," she said gruffly. "I see no reason why we should discuss this again."

"Don't you?" Ivor caressed her cheek in a manner so delightful that Mignon wished to scream. "You aunt explained nothing, as you know perfectly well. What secrets are you hiding, Mignon?"

"None that need concern you." If only she had sufficient force of will to wrench away from him! "Unless you still think that I betrayed you to the Press?"

"I find it intolerable," Ivor replied, cupping her face in his hands, "to think that you would betray me to anyone."

It happened so naturally that, try as she might, Mignon could not later recall precisely how she found herself in Lord Jeffries' arms, being ruthlessly kissed, and responding with a passion that would have made her mother turn crimson with shame. Nor did Mignon break away from that embrace as would have a young lady of proper upbringing and delicate sensibilities; she did not swoon, or burst into tears. Instead, she looked up at the Viscount and requested, somewhat breathlessly, that he repeat the highly improper act again. Ivor, it appeared, was as depraved as she: without the least demur, he complied.

"Well!" said Lady Bligh, choosing that most compromising of moments to reenter the room. "A trifle unconventional, perhaps, but overall an admirable way to reconcile one's differences."

Mignon returned to reality with a painful thud. She cast an agonized glance at the Viscount, who looked as disoriented as if he'd been tumbled out of bed by an earthquake in the dead of night, and without a word fled the room.

Chapter Sixteen

As he made his way toward York Place in Marylebone, Crump chewed thoughtfully on his pipe stem. His investigations might appear to the uninitiated to be making little headway, but the Runner was not the least displeased with the way things were falling out. Nor was he unhappy about the afternoon, spent in close questioning of the latest victims of the criminals who Crump was fast coming to think of as Leda & Company. He smiled. Ah, but they were growing bold! No simple robbery this, but the passing of forged circular letters of credit, documents issued by bankers to enable clients to obtain ready cash in any part of Europe. Normally, such documents contained a list of principal towns and cities at which withdrawals could be made and the names of agents, as well as a space where each withdrawal was noted. In this case, the withdrawal spaces had been virgin white. Clever! thought Crump once again.

There had been, he had ascertained during a long afternoon's labor, three persons involved, a woman and two men, and among them they had played pretty havoc with London's banking institutions. Crump was not dismayed that the descriptions he obtained fit no one he knew. The Runner grew more and more convinced that he was dealing with a very diabolical criminal brain. He would have given a great deal to know how Leda continued to rule her illicit empire so efficiently from a prison cell.

But the gang would undoubtedly grow careless, and then Crump would spring his trap. He had a very good notion of who Leda's accomplices were, and given enough rope, they would hang themselves. Sir John had insisted on distributing handbills with details of the various stolen properties to the City's pawnbrokers, but Crump knew full well that none of the contraband would turn up there. Nor, he thought, would it make its way across the Channel to surface at Frankfort or in France. These thieves had no need of immediate profit. Crump subscribed to Henry Fielding's theory: greed, not want, was the main cause of crime.

He came to the residence that he sought, a small elegant establishment perfectly suited to a gentleman's *petite amie*, and approached the front door. A French maidservant admitted him without so much as a blink of her long and patently false eyelashes and ushered him into the sitting room.

"So!" said Zoe, who wore a shockingly transparent muslin gown which exposed her lovely shoulders. "Bow Street has at last come to call on me. I expected you sooner! Do sit down."

Crump looked around the room, decorated in flesh-colored stucco and gilt, with very large looking glasses and curtains of crimson and white silk adorning the walls, and a crimson carpet on the floor. Since there was no item of furniture large enough to conceal either an eavesdropper or a potential assailant, the Runner obeyed his hostess's command. The fact that he himself might be the murderer's next target had more than once crossed his mind.

Zoe regarded him from the récamier on which she was curled like a plump yellow-haired kitten. Indeed, mused Crump somewhat wistfully, she'd make a comfortable armful for any man.

Opera dancers, no matter how free with their favors, were beyond the resources of the Runner's pocketbook. This one, he reflected, must cost Lord Jeffries handsomely! Not that it wouldn't be money well spent.

He cleared his throat. "I daresay you know why I'm here."

Zoe had long experience of the opposite sex; it was second nature to her to try to charm every specimen of it that came her way. "What is your name?" she asked, wrinkling her pretty little nose. "Your Christian name, I mean. I can hardly call you 'Mr. Bow Street Runner' or 'Crump'! It's so devilish formal." She smiled. "I dislike formality, you see."

Crump blushed all the way up to his shiny bald pate. "Siegfried," he replied weakly and held his breath lest she laugh.

"Siegfried," repeated Zoe, testing the name. Distracted, Crump noticed that she had a delightful little lisp. "How unusual! It suits you perfectly. Now tell me how I may help you, Siegfried. I collect it concerns Lord Jeffries?"

"Yes." Crump reminded himself sternly that this charming female might well be a member of Leda's troupe. "I understand you were questioned by the Chief Magistrate regarding a certain list of times, and that you swore the Viscount spent those hours with you."

"He did." Modestly, Zoe cast down her eyes. "I fear you will think the worst of me, Siegfried, but I cannot deny it. Jeffries has been a particular friend of mine for several years, and we have spent much time together alone. Thank heavens my sainted papa is dead for he would be sorely grieved to see his treasured daughter so hardened to shame."

Crump was far from immune to beauty in distress. "Nonsense!" he said gruffly. "I can't speak for your papa, but I see no reason for you to be ashamed of your, er, position." Zoe raised huge, tear-drenched blue eyes to such good effect that he totally lost his trend of thought. "Shall we," he stammered, "get back to Lord Jeffries, ma'am?"

"Certainly, if that is what you wish." Zoe fished a handkerchief out of the extremely low-cut bodice of her gown. "Although I know little more than I told Sir John!" She smiled sadly. "Ivor was not in the habit of discussing with me the details of his personal life."

"*Was* not, ma'am?"

Zoe pressed her handkerchief to her dainty little nose. "All is at an end, alas! Oh, I had expected it, Siegfried, for the philosophy of the upper classes is quite empty of compassion, you know!" She sniffled. "But I had not thought it would happen like this. What a dreadful scandal! That Ivor should be the son of a murderess! Even now the intelligence makes me perfectly sick."

It was none of Crump's business, and it certainly had no bearing on his investigations, but he had to ask. "Forgive my presumption, Miss Zoe, but did you break off your relationship with Lord Jeffries? Or was it the other way around?"

"Siegfried!" She looked indignant. "How can you think I would associate with a man of such notoriety? A woman in my position can hardly afford such scandal. I could hardly maintain what remains of my reputation were my name dragged further through the mud." Zoe shrugged, ruefully. "To tell truth, Ivor's interest was on the wane."

Crump wondered how any gentleman could grow tired of Zoe, surely the most delightful creature ever to lead a debauched life. "What makes you think that, ma'am?"

She gazed at him, startled. "Good Lord, Siegfried, I hope I may know the signs! Ivor spent less and less time with me, and even when he *was* in my company, it was evident that his mind was elsewhere. It is little wonder, I suppose, since his mother was in Newgate. If only I had known!"

"You weren't aware of the relationship between Lord Jeffries and Leda Langtry?" Crump sternly reminded himself that his purpose was to prove the guilt of a criminal, not to gawk and gape at that criminal's ladybird. It wasn't beyond the bounds of possibility that Zoe was lying mightily in an effort to save her own skin.

"Of course I didn't know!" Zoe responded, rather irritably. "To be blunt, I am a businesswoman, Siegfried, and the market value of the particular commodity that I have to offer decreases in proportion to the unpleasant notoriety that it receives. The mistress of a murderer's son has little more appeal to discreet buyers than the mistress of a cracksman or a highwayman!"

An interesting choice of words, mused Crump: in his opinion, Jeffries might be the most superior cracksman of them all. Why? he wondered. From all accounts, the Viscount was a very wealthy gentleman. "Yet you protect him?"

Zoe glanced pointedly about the elegant room. "Can I do less?" she asked. "It is only the truth, after all. And if I did *not* come forth with the truth, it's apparent Ivor would truly be in the basket."

Crump's genial features revealed nothing of his interesting conclusions. "I'm afraid I don't follow you."

"No?" Zoe's expression was less that of a playful kitten than of a tigress prepared to defend herself. "I am not an unintelligent woman, Siegfried! Ivor's relationship with Leda makes him automatically suspect. You see, I knew Warwick rather well at one time. If *he* knew that Leda was Ivor's mother, it would be to the advantage of both of them to see him dead. Warwick was not beyond publishing such information if it could gain for him some advantage."

Crump looked at her and saw instead the battered features of Mary Elphinstone. The old woman had been greatly disfigured by severe bruises about the head and face, and a cord with a running noose had been tightly tied around her neck. "It occurs to me that you yourself might be in some danger, Miss Zoe."

"From whom, Siegfried?" Zoe leaned her head on a languorous hand, patently amused. "Surely you do not think Ivor would harm me? I assure you we parted on the most amiable of terms."

Crump wondered how long that amiability would last if Zoe refused to support Lord Jeffries' so convenient alibis any longer. There was little doubt in the Runner's mind that Zoe's statements were nothing but lies, and that the Viscount would be very reluctant to let his one-time mistress outlive her usefulness.

"I do not mean to rush you, Siegfried," said Zoe, interrupting Crump's thoughts, "but I am expecting a caller and I do not think he would be greatly pleased to meet a Bow Street Runner. Is there anything else you wished to ask me?"

Crump rose from his chair and looked at her, so lovely and so unattainable to him that she might have been the Queen. "Not right now, ma'am. I thank you for receiving me."

"There's no need for thanks, Siegfried!" Zoe stretched out languorously on the récamier. "I'm glad to be of assistance. Come back any time." The same maidservant showed him to the door.

Crump made his way through the darkening streets, battered pipe in hand. Alluring as Zoe may have been, she did not long occupy his mind. He was not unaware that Ivor frequently visited Leda's shop, thus coming into contact with the perfidious Willie, or that the mysterious financial resources of the *Apocalyse* had yet to be satisfactorily explained. Leda's wealth could well be the proceeds of robberies committed by the three of them. The net was drawing tighter, Crump thought. Now he must figure out a way to ensure that none of his slippery fish escaped.

Then there was the matter of Lady Bligh. He suspected that Dulcie had gained Leda's original release from Newgate by the simple expedient of blackmail and he was very curious as to why the Baroness had so exerted herself. The Runner supposed she was also responsible for the various odd items that had recently begun to appear in the *Apocalypse*. But why should Dulcie concern herself with speculations that transported convicts might be returning to England, hidden in the flood of refugees and travelers from war-stricken Europe? If only Lady Bligh was more inclined to cooperate with Bow Street! It was obvious that he must cultivate her garrulous cook once again.

Crump's idle wandering had brought him to elegant Manchester Square, bastion of the nobility, a spacious street with built-up corners that exuded a snug and sheltered air. He stuffed his pipe in his pocket and recalled smugly his last meeting with White's chimney sweeps. Again his intuition had proven correct, for those two rascals had in their possession an elegantly embroidered gentleman's handkerchief, found on the floor near the plate closet. Though the Runner could not make out the intricate monogram, he had a fair notion to whom that expensive item belonged.

Though Crump might have preferred to witness a cockfight that was even then taking place at Westminster between the gentlemen of Middlesex and Shropshire, he settled himself comfortably enough in the shadowy recesses of a side street. Directly ahead loomed a large brick mansion with a balustrated roof, approached by a forecourt and prominent portico. The Runner touched the scrap of material, souvenir of the robbery at White's, which resided in one of his pockets, and pondered the methods by which he might breach the walls of Lord Jeffries' town house. Unless Crump missed his guess, the evidence he sought lay hidden within.

Chapter Seventeen

"I recall," said Lady Bligh, elegant in a morning dress of white French lawn, "the notorious rake Thomas, Lord Lyttleton. A few weeks after his marriage, he ran off to Paris with a pretty barmaid, about whose virtue he'd just won a bet of £100. Further along in his career, he published a blasphemous parody of his father's verse, spread a rumor of his own death, and seduced in turn three sisters whose ages didn't add up to fifty years. They called him 'the Libertine Macaroni.'" She gazed accusingly upon Lord Barrymore. "You are all too young to remember, of course! The great Charles Fox was a macaroni also—how well I recall him, a rather astonishing figure in his blue hair powder and red-heeled shoes." Willie tittered and she sighed. "Now it is the Regency, and the elegant minuet and snuffbox are being replaced by the waltz and the cigar."

Once again the Baroness held court in her Morning Room.

Present to admire, in varying degrees, her ladyship's surroundings and person were Lord Barrymore, Willie Fitzwilliam and an incredibly handsome young man whom Willie had brought expressly to make the acquaintance of his unpredictable benefactress. Of the three, only Willie seemed at ease.

"So you are Willie's actor!" Abruptly, Dulcie roused from her reverie to stare, rather rudely, at the young man. He looked a veritable Lothario, with curling black hair, worn rather long, luxuriant side whiskers and mustache, sapphire blue eyes and a profile that would have done justice to a Greek statue. "And a heartbreaker, I vow! I take it you do not mean to pattern yourself after Charles Young, Covent Garden's leading attraction, a widower whom no woman's blandishments can tempt to be untrue to his wife's memory. Where do you make your home, Jesse Saint-Cyr?"

"Wherever I may be, Lady Bligh." Jesse smiled, which might have stopped a heart less shrewd than Dulcie's. "I am a nomad by choice."

The Baroness also smiled, a trifle unpleasantly. "I vow that London is excitement enough for me! *Too* much perhaps, with these recent murders and daring robberies."

"Lady Bligh!" Concerned, Lord Barrymore leaned forward in his chair. "Surely *you* have nothing to fear from such cutthroats! Lord Bligh must have left you adequately protected in his absence."

The Baroness clutched her breast. "I am an old woman, Barrymore," she whispered. It may have been a ridiculous statement, but at that moment she looked undeniably frail. "No match for determined villains, I assure you!"

So stirred was Tolly by Dulcie's remarks that he moved to Lady Bligh's couch and took her hand, patting her as he might a favorite dog. "You must not allow yourself to become so overset!" he said bracingly. "It is a great pity that you should be alone at such a time, but I beg that you will call on me for any assistance you may need. I would be only too happy to be of service to you."

Dulcie cast him a grateful look. "You are very good," she

murmured feebly. "It is kind of you to pamper an old woman, Barrymore."

"Nonsense!" replied Tolly, obviously gratified. "I consider myself quite one of the family, you know."

This was all very interesting, but Willie was sufficiently alert to recognize a superb performance. Lady Bligh doubtless would have made a remarkable career on the stage. Though he might wonder to what end she so beguiled Lord Barrymore, Willie was a great deal more concerned with his own pursuits: to wit, one slightly acerbic play. "Baroness," he said, pale eyes gleaming, "I wish to speak to you about the announcement of my play. As I had hoped, it will be put on at Drury Lane." He paused a moment to savor his triumph. "You may not know that newspaper proprietors consider it a privilege to insert theatrical announcements gratis, or that such announcements cannot be inserted without authorization. Have I your permission to go ahead?"

He had meant it as only a courtesy request and never considered that Dulcie might withhold consent. Willie's stomach tied itself into uncomfortable knots as he felt the weight of her thoughtful gaze. "Jesse Saint-Cyr," she murmured, her black eyes moving to rest on that dashing young man. "An unknown provincial actor to follow Edmund Kean, who acted Richard III at Drury Lane earlier this year. And a masterful performance it was! You might be wise, Willie, to consider placing another, better-known, actor in the lead role."

"Unknown but positively brilliant, Baroness!" said Willie hastily. He knew the black look that had settled on Jesse's features and wanted no displays of artistic temperament in Lady Bligh's Morning Room. "It must be Jesse or no one!"

"Oh, very well!" Dulcie looked positively exhausted. "Have it your own way. Go on with your announcements, though I must insist that your Jesse's name does not appear in them. Bill him as a brilliant unknown or whatever you wish, but I want to see no mention in print of the name Jesse Saint-Cyr."

"But, Lady Bligh!" wailed Willie. The young actor looked ready to spit nails.

"Must I recall to you our arrangement?" inquired Dulcie wearily. "One from which *I* have drawn little benefit? Or need I explain what will happen to your play if I withdraw my support?"

"No." Willie's drooping figure was expressive of deep gloom. "Of course it will be as you say."

"It grieves me, Lady Bligh," murmured Tolly, who still retained possession of her hand, "to see you so worn down. Surely Miss Montague could take some of these more trivial details off your shoulders? I am sure your niece must agree with me that you have taken on entirely too much! Her devotion to you is quite delightful to see."

"Ah, Mignon." The Baroness's spirits revived almost miraculously. "She is such a joy to me! My niece has felt the lure of London. She is caught up in a social whirl and has little time to spare for me."

"Oh?" inquired Lord Barrymore thoughtfully. "Naturally Miss Montague will wish to spend a certain amount of time with her brother now that he is in town."

"Maurice?" Dulcie's laughter was so infectious that it distracted even Willie, who was trying to soothe his actor's sensibilities. "It is not her brother's company of which Mignon has grown so fond! A pity she has had to miss this so convivial gathering—but that is the temptation of living so near the center of things, where life is one long love affair."

"Miss Montague is a considerable heiress," reproved Lord Barrymore, "and too young to have learned the ways of the world. I hope she may not perforce suffer a severe disillusionment!" Willie noted with relief that he had succeeded in wheedling Jesse out of his sulks. The actor was following the conversation with interest.

"Set your mind at rest, Barrymore." Serenely Lady Bligh regarded the diamonds that glittered on her wrists and hands. "If I were to accuse anyone of dangling after a rich heiress, it would not be Viscount Jeffries."

* * *

Miss Montague, at that moment, had no more thought to spare for her wily aunt than she had for the man in the moon. She gazed at the small thatched cottage before her. "The reward for convicting a housebreaker is £40," she offered gloomily, "and for compounding a felony it's £40 more."

"You are very well informed," retorted Lord Jeffries, engaged in issuing instructions to his coachman. "Are you also cow-hearted, Miss Montague? If you feel an incipient onset of vapors, I beg you will leave in the coach. Despite your aunt's insistence that you accompany me, I am quite capable of undertaking this enterprise alone."

Mignon glowered at the Viscount, more than elegant in a satin-collared violet redingote, beaver hat, white kerseymore unmentionables and leather boots. He was in a reckless humor, as evidenced by the snappy pace at which they had driven into the country and the high-handed manner in which he had dealt with Mary Elphinstone's man of business. "I'll stay," she said brusquely. Mignon, too, wondered at Dulcie's insistence that her niece accompany Lord Jeffries on this mission. Did Lady Bligh seek to play matchmaker? She might as well have sent Mignon straight into the dragon's den.

The coach rattled away, to return in one hour, and Mignon stiffened as Ivor took her arm. So far was he from amorous intent that he cast her an irritated glance before guiding her roughly across the dirty yard. It served her right, reflected Mignon ruefully, for reading entirely too much into a simple kiss. So far was Lord Jeffries from appreciation of his companion—who was looking her best in a brown velvet spenser, a white muslin gown and a tucked silk bonnet with lace frills—that she might have worn sackcloth and ashes.

The doors were tightly locked, and they skirted the building to stop under a small window. Ivor made short work of it. "Feeling missish, Miss Montague?" he inquired. "I fear you'll have to be the one to enter."

Mignon eyed the narrow opening, well above her head. What-ever Miss Montague may have been, whatever secrets burdened her conscience, she was no coward. "Very well," she replied, with overt hostility. "I trust you are gentleman enough to turn away."

Ivor made no reply, but grasped her waist. With an indelicacy that made her blush, Mignon scrambled through the window. She waited only to catch her breath and to subdue the unbecoming violence of feeling roused by the Viscount's touch, before unbolting the back door and admitting him. The impropriety of the venture struck her as Jeffries once more closed and bolted the door behind him.

"Don't worry, Miss Montague!" he said, as if he had read her thoughts. "These are hardly the surroundings I would choose in which to ravish you, even had I such intent." He spoke absently, looking around the bare room. "I wish merely to find some means to prove my mother's innocence."

Mignon turned hurriedly away, hard pressed to preserve some sense of decorum. It was not often that Miss Montague found herself at point nonplus. "How fares Leda?" she asked, desperate for a change of topic. "I fear that she must find time weighing heavy on her hands."

"Not she." Lord Jeffries moved to rummage through an ancient writing desk. "At last report Leda had offered her services to form an association for the improvement of female prisoners in Newgate. She is now in her glory penning descriptions of the Inner Yard. It abuts on the streets, and every day it is filled with a struggling mass of skinny, half nude females fighting for position near the railing. They hold out sticks with spoons attached and beg pas-sersby for money." He turned and frowned at Mignon. "This seems to be an extremely profitless undertaking! Have you any idea why your aunt sent us here?"

"None." Mignon shook her head. "But Dulcie usually has good reasons, no matter how incomprehensible they may seem." The Viscount returned to his endeavors, looking skeptical.

Mignon wandered idly about the mean little cottage, peering

into an old pot, poking into a cannister of tea, and mulling over what they'd already learned. Mary Elphinstone's man of business, who obviously had borne the old woman no great love, could tell them only that his employer was a gentlewoman fallen on hard times whose only source of income was an allowance that arrived regularly from London. The party responsible for this munificence was, or so he claimed, unknown to him. What a hobble! thought Mignon, and not just in regard to Leda's predicament. She glanced at Ivor, still frowning over the contents of the writing desk, and approached the room's only closet. In it were a few plain gowns and a high shelf that looked bare. Trying hard to forget that the owner of these few poor items had met her death in a singularly brutal manner, Mignon climbed onto a rickety old chair. A dusty sewing box sat at the very back of the dark recess. She stretched out her arm.

"Mignon!" snapped Lord Jeffries, looking up to see her teetering on the chair. "What the devil are you doing? Come down from there!" Startled, Mignon overbalanced. She, the chair, and the dusty box, went flying through the air.

Miss Montague, however, did not tumble ignobly to the floor, for the Viscount caught her in midfall. "Let me down!" she gasped, very much afraid that she would cast decorum to the winds if clasped for long against that strong, hard, and overpoweringly masculine body. Lord Jeffries complied, with such alacrity that Mignon immediately succumbed to a fit of the blue devils.

"You have," he said inconsequentially, "a smudge." He reached out to brush it from her cheek, and Mignon bit her lower lip, hard.

"Look!" she cried, wildly seeking distraction, and pointed at the sewing box, upended with its contents strewn about the floor. It did not serve: Lord Jeffries' thoughtful glance never wavered from her face.

"I think, Miss Montague," he said softly, "that it's time we had a talk. You, I fear, are playing a deep game."

Mignon would have moved away, had she anywhere to go

except backwards into the closet. The Viscount blocked every other avenue of escape. "And you," she said crossly, "are talking fustian! Your coachman will be returning any moment and we haven't finished here."

"My coachman," retorted Ivor, a dangerous gleam in his brown eyes, "will not be back for at least three-quarters of an hour, being engaged in imbibing ale and gossip at the local inn. Are you determined to treat me in a cavalier fashion, Miss Montague? It is a puzzle that you can, er, respond to me so warmly one moment and the next behave as if you are totally indifferent. Or is it your habit, my darling, to go around casting out lures?"

"I didn't!" wailed Mignon, looking everywhere but at the Viscount. Surely he must hear the beating of her heart, for he was standing very close and it was very loud. "Oh, why must you make such a piece of work of it? It is the height of absurdity! We both suffered a, uh, moment of weakness and would come under the gravest censure were it to become known. But it will not, I assure you."

"No?" inquired Lord Jeffries, who sounded oddly amused. "Have you forgotten your aunt's untimely entrance into the room?"

"You need not trouble yourself over Dulcie." To her horror, Mignon's voice was husky, as if she verged on tears. She blinked rapidly. "My aunt does not expect that you will make a rather dowdy looking female the object of your *amours.*"

"Do you suffer such moments of weakness often?" inquired the Viscount smoothly. "What a farrago of nonsense! Mignon, look at me."

"No," retorted the uncooperative Miss Montague.

"I see," murmured Lord Jeffries, "that talking won't pay toll." Without another word he stepped forward and took Mignon into his strong arms. An idle observer, had one been present to witness this scandalous scene, might have noted that Miss Montague, despite her fine words and noble resolutions, offered him not even a token protest.

"Oh, Ivor!" she gasped, when at length she was permitted to

speak again. "Believe me—there are things you do not know—this simply will not do!"

"Moonshine, my darling," replied the Viscount, smiling in a most dizzy-making manner down on her. "My *amours*, indeed!" And then his glance fell upon the shattered sewing box. With an oath, he released her.

"What is it?" cried Mignon, dropping to her knees beside him on the floor. Strewn among the wreckage, scraps of material and spools of thread, was the unmistakable gleam of jewels. "Oh, no!"

"Oh, yes, I fear." Grimly, Ivor extracted a handful of gems. "From the robbery of Rundle and Brydges, I'll wager."

Stunned, Mignon sank back on her heels. "Bow Street surely searched here? How did they come to be overlooked?"

"Bow Street," mused Lord Jeffries, searching through the wreckage. "I am rapidly coming to rue the day when Henry Fielding was forced to turn from the penning of political satire to the practice of law." He flicked a piece of broken wood. "Here's our answer, I fancy. A false bottom. Apparently whoever planted these items here gave Bow Street credit for more initiative than they displayed."

Mignon's head was whirling. "You think the jewels were placed here in hope they *would* be found?"

"What other explanation is there?" asked Ivor, his face grim. "Other than that Leda is somehow mixed up in the robberies? Think how it must look! Mary Elphinstone was financed by someone, and in her cottage are discovered the proceeds of robbery. What would seem more obvious than that she was paid to keep silent?" He picked up a piece of paper from amid the rubble and scanned it, his lips compressed into a thin line. "Paid by Leda," he added somberly.

"What is it?" Mignon asked feebly.

"The deed to this cottage." Ivor's glance was searching, as if he meant to seek out her loyalties. "We were sent here to help Leda, and it seems we have opened Pandora's box instead. Things would be bleak indeed if these things fell into the wrong hands! You see, this property is in my mother's name."

Chapter Eighteen

It was midnight. The woman crept along Piccadilly until she came to an elegant complex of buildings set one hundred feet back from the street and protected by a high wall topped by ornamental lamps. This magnificent structure—once Melbourne House, later York House—was the Albany, a most luxurious and convenient hotel which was sacred to bachelors and widowers. Among its illustrious residents were Lord Byron, complete with his macaw and his silver funerary urns from Greece. Also in residence there was Monk Lewis, a gentleman who possessed a taste for the super-natural and macabre, as witnessed by his phenomenally successful book, *The Monk*, and his play, *The Captive*, so convincing a por-trayal of madness that it threw Covent Garden into hysterical confusion during its sole performance. The woman thought she'd as lief not encounter either of those gentlemen.

It meant ruin, of course, for any lady to be seen entering these male premises. She slipped through the gate, beneath its tall classical pedimented arch, then ducked into the shadows as a porter passed by. He was an impressive figure in his coat with scarlet cuffs and collar, scarlet waistcoat and leather-lined velveteen breeches. Indeed, she reflected sourly, the porter was a great deal finer than she.

Even though it was late, and the night windy and tempestuous, traffic roared past the entrance, filling the air with the loud clacking of wheels on stone. The woman shivered, not entirely from the cold, and made her way to a certain ground-floor apartment near the entrance. Effecting an entry was no problem; she had her own key. She knew at once that he was there. Cigar smoke hung heavy in the air.

This was not his home, though it was certainly splendid enough, possessing not only kitchens and cellar in the basement, a living room which connected by fine double doors with a bedroom, a dressing room with water closet and hip bath, but a garret on the top floor. He was doubtless in the bedroom which looked onto the Rope Walk. As she moved quickly through the living room, sparing a glance for the silks stretched on the walls, the woman pulled off the wig that concealed her lovely hair.

"You're late," he said. The bedroom was almost in darkness, lit only by a single candle in a massive silver stick. He had a mania for such things, taking no chances that his true identity might become known, for he had long ago taken these apartments under an assumed identity. The woman looked at him as she stripped off the drab clothing that was so repugnant to her. The cigar burned in a saucer on a table by his chair.

"I could escape no sooner." She reached into the wardrobe for a frilled, beribboned dressing gown. "From my watchdogs! Faith, but I'll be glad when this thing is done."

"Did you come alone?" He tapped off the cigar's long burning ash. "Or were you followed by a strong force of Bow Street Runners, with a company of Guards in reserve? I trust I needn't tell you what discovery could mean. We could all be committed for trial on the capital charge."

The woman tied her dressing gown, so loosely that it threatened, at the least provocation, to slip off her shoulders and probably to the floor. A far cry from her usual appearance, she thought smugly, as she gazed into a gilt-edged mirror and effected certain changes to her face. "Don't you want to know what I've learned?" she asked. "You know as well as I that Bow Street is ineffectual. At any major disturbance, the military is called."

"By the statute of the 3rd and 4th of William and Mary," he murmured, as he crossed the room to stand behind her, "all and every person and persons that comfort, aid, abet, assist, counsel, hire or command any person to rob another shall be hanged, and without the benefit of clergy. It seems of little consequence who brings us in."

"Clergy!" she mocked, meeting his eyes in the mirror. "Since when have you concerned yourself with the clergy?" It was a bitter pill to swallow, for she knew perfectly well that a gentleman of his birth and position was not likely to marry her, for all the pleasure he derived from spitting in the faces of his venerable ancestors. "While I sneak about with my ear to keyholes, you have other fish to fry. I congratulate you that you have found so agreeable a way of passing the time!"

"Ah." His hands rested on her shoulders. "Jealous, my pretty? You must know by now that I far prefer sluts without morals to insipid Society chits. Tell me what you've learned."

"Everything went off perfectly well." She completed the repairs to her face, then turned and threw her arms around his neck. "There! Do something for me?" Her voice was husky. "Open the safe?"

He looked down at her, wryly amused, then turned to swing aside one of the many paintings that hung on the walls. These were of an inflammatory classical nature: Lucretia struggling in the arms of Tarquin; Andromeda lashed naked to a rock. His visitor found far more titillation in the sparkling gems that glittered in the safe's dark recess. Her eyes glowed.

"My avaricious little beauty!" He draped her about with jewels. "I fear I have taught you extravagant tastes."

The woman had moved back to the looking glass, there to stare greedily at the diamonds and pearls, rubies and sapphires that hung around her neck. "Please," she whispered, "let me keep just one thing."

"The devil!" he retorted. "Did I but leave matters to you, we'd quickly be brought to a standstill. You'll have jewels aplenty in time, but you must wait."

"That's what you always say!" She sulked. "I'm tired of waiting. Don't I deserve some reward for all the help I've given you?"

With a pair of silver scissors, he operated on a fresh cigar. "What you deserve," he retorted, "is a whipping. May I remind you of the small matter of Warwick's banknotes?"

"That wasn't *my* fault!" she cried, stung. "Take the blame for someone else's carelessness is a thing I will not do!"

"Am I my brother's keeper?" he murmured, and lit the cigar. "It is entirely your fault that the notes are not again in our possession— though I believe that failure may yet work to our advantage." He looked at her. "I do not mean to argue with you, my pretty, but there is very little that you will not do. For instance, you will leave here tonight and return from whence you came, much as you dislike the notion, and you will continue to play to the man in the pit and to make the best of a bad audience."

Perhaps it was due to the priceless jewels she wore that the woman grew so bold. "What if I refuse?"

"Refuse?" he repeated, his voice cold. "You have no choice, being much too deep in this thing to turn craven now. To be perfectly blunt, I will wring your neck myself before I give you a chance to turn King's evidence."

She stared at him, chilled, for she knew he spoke only the truth. No matter that she loved him, to this man she was merely a convenience, and easily expendable. "I spoke in jest," she whispered through cold lips. "Good God, you must know I wouldn't inform on you."

"Come here," he said, and smiled. "Don't you want to know what I next plan?" Slowly she walked across the room. He pulled her down into his lap. "What would you say," he murmured, "if I told you I meant to join the hordes of hopeful aspirants to extinct titles and dormant funds that keep the courts so busy?"

"I'd say it was a hubble-bubble notion," the woman retorted, a trifle waspishly. She was feeling sadly unappreciated and the cigar smoke made her head ache. "You already have one title, isn't that enough?"

"There is no such thing as 'enough,'" he reproved, as he toyed with the tie of her robe. "Although the laws *do* enjoin scrupulous fulfillment of dispositions of the deceased. Did you know there is a counting house here in England where a fully dressed corpse has been standing at a window overlooking its former property for twenty-five years?"

Despite herself, the woman's flesh crawled. She liked this talk of corpses no more than she cared to look on them. She was firmly caught, as he had said; if she rebelled, he would see her, too, dead.

"I should not tease you," he murmured, as he pushed open the robe, "but it is so great a temptation! Very well, my pretty, think instead of the Bank of England, that marvelous institution governed by men of enormous power that has mobilized capital, helped make currency reliable, given strength to the whole structure of banking."

"What of it?" she asked absently. Perhaps there was some way to make off with a single strand of pearls, so fitting to her youth and apparent inexperience in the world of crime.

"I have a plan. And I have a key, borrowed long enough from a certain unsuspecting porter for wax impressions to be made. All that remains is to await the proper time."

It was, the woman thought, the proper time for her endeavors to be repaid, if not in jewels then in coin of another sort. She sat up, allowing the robe to fall to her waist, then placed her hands behind her head and arched her back provocatively.

"The Society for the Suppression of Vice still thrives," he said, his voice suddenly deeper. "I wonder what Wilberforce would say to you! But you distract me. I have not yet told you of my plan."

She stretched her arms into the air, sighed, and let them fall. This one was a devil, with his scheming and his ruthlessness. He lifted the cigar and she shrank back. It would not do to rouse his temper, lest that glowing tip come into contact with her skin. "Go on," she whispered, all passion fled.

"A plan to rob the Bank of England," he murmured, "and every bullion merchant in the City of London." The woman goggled, then gasped as he forced her to her knees in front of him. "A plan which, with your cooperation, my pretty, must inevitably succeed."

Chapter Nineteen

Lady Bligh swept like a spring breeze into the stuffy Bow Street Public Office. "Dear John!" she said, and bent to hug him. "Do not trouble to rise or say that you are pleased to see me! I would have come sooner, had I not been positively overwhelmed with trivial matters. You will overlook my tardiness, I know!"

The Chief Magistrate looked regretfully at the papers spread across his battered desk, then raised his tired eyes to study the Baroness. She wore a pelisse of deep red satin, a Vandyke double pereline, its flat collar spreading to her shoulders, and a chinchilla border and muff. On her golden curls was a black velvet hat, and on her feet light walking shoes.

"It grows cold, dear John!" Like a delicate bird, she flitted about the small room. "This season is of them all my least favorite, with its accursed fogs so thick that one must see one's way to breakfast with a taper and light candles in the middle of the day. But soon, in consequence of the opening of Parliament, Society will begin to be more lively again. I believe that I must plan a small party."

Sir John might have resented this interruption, and this irrelevance, had he not possessed a fair understanding of the working of Dulcie's mind. As he watched, she alit at last on the old wooden chair. "Do you recall the great frost this February last that turned the Thames to solid ice between London Bridge and Blackfriars? Freezeland Street, they called it, and on either side were booths of every variety—butchers and barbers and purveyors of gin and beer, brandy balls and gingerbread. There were bookstalls and printing presses, skittle alleys and toyshops, and even gambling establishments."

Whatever the Baroness had on her mind, she was approaching it in a singularly roundabout manner. The Chief Magistrate put down his pen. "What's the point, Dulcie?"

She pressed the muff against her cheek. "Merely that we are no longer young," she said wistfully. "I remember the balls when you would dance with me, and then while the other young ladies were very correctly strolling on their partners' arms, you and I would slip away. Just think how long ago it was, dear John! So long that we never even shared a waltz, for it was unheard of."

Sir John thought of that dance, with its vulgar intimacy which had made an Oriental ambassador almost faint, and rubbed his forehead. "You have a husband now, madam!" he said repressively. "I am sure that if you wish to waltz, Maximilian will be happy to oblige."

"I might, and have, called Bat many things," retorted Lady Bligh, "but 'obliging' is not one of them. You have missed the point, John! Times are changing, rather drastically. I daresay the day will come when the horse is replaced by Trewithick's wretched steam engine that runs on tracks." She sighed. "Even Brummell's star is on the wane. What a career the Beau has had! From Eton and a coronetcy in Prinny's own regiment to an exalted position as the absolute *arbiter elegantiarum* of fashionable Society."

"Dulcie." The Chief Magistrate was growing annoyed. "I didn't ask you here to discuss Brummell!"

"Of course you didn't." Lady Bligh stroked her chinchilla muff, obviously preoccupied. "The Beau, I fear, will not reign much longer. He is on the outs with Prinny, largely due to his championship of Maria Fitzherbert—though no one can deny our Regent has treated his morganatic wife abominably!—and he is running deeply into debt. He claims his bad luck stems from the loss of a lucky coin."

Sir John rose irritably. The Baroness ignored him. "I wonder," she mused, "to what I might attribute *my* ill luck."

"What's this?" growled the Chief Magistrate, unwillingly concerned. "*What* ill luck?"

"Dear John." Dulcie was mournful. "There can be little point in telling you, since you will refuse altogether to share in my suspicions. So I will allow only that I am exceedingly worried about my niece."

It grew apparent to Sir John that, in the midst of a spate of the most brilliant robberies of all time, requiring him to conduct frequent acrimonious conferences with the Home Secretary, he was to be called upon to intervene in Lady Bligh's domestic affairs. He stood at the window, looking down at the ancient tavern across the street. "Why?" he asked reluctantly.

The Baroness frowned. "Poor Mignon has got herself in quite a tangle," she said, "and though I hope she may make a recovery, I wouldn't wager on it." She glowered at the Chief Magistrate so intently that he turned to face her. "I vow I must be growing old, dear John, for I am inordinately concerned for the girl."

Ah, but she was a Circe, and he was far from deaf to her siren song. Sir John crossed the room and tilted up her face. She looked little older than when they'd shared those long-ago dances and those forbidden interludes. Only the tiny laughter lines around her fine eyes betrayed the fact that she was no longer in her youth. "If you are so worried," he said, bemused, "why don't you simply take a hand?"

"I cannot." Her dark eyes filled with tears. "There is nothing I can do that would not make matters even worse. Poor Mignon must muddle along as best she can, and I only pray that she will not be left wearing the willow or, even worse, be coerced into some action that will prove disastrous."

Feeling inordinately helpless, Sir John proffered his handkerchief. Things must be in a very bad case to reduce the indomitable Baroness to tears. "What can I do?" he asked, resigned.

"You can immediately inform me," she replied promptly, with a look that melted his bones, "if my niece is hauled before you, probably by Crump." Briskly she blew her nose. "I give you my word that her involvement is purely circumstantial. Mignon hasn't a cruel or avaricious bone in her body, which is a great deal more than I can say for various of her associates."

"Involvement?" Sir John turned away. "Are you telling me your niece is mixed up in murder and robbery?" Lady Bligh said nothing and he strode irritably to his desk. "You mentioned Crump. Perhaps you would like to know why I asked you here." He glanced over his shoulder to find the Baroness hard on his heels. Before he could step away she had snatched the piece of paper he held in his hand. As she read it, her arched brows sank into a frown. Well might Dulcie scowl! thought Sir John. That note put an end to her theory of Leda's innocence.

"What an extraordinary thing!" announced the Baroness at length, her dark eyes glittering but not with tears. "This is a positive masterpiece of vague and incriminating remarks that give much credence to the notion that Leda is a criminal mastermind. Brilliant, in fact! We are dealing with no ordinary felons, John. May I ask how you came by this?"

The Chief Magistrate sat down heavily in his chair, hoping an official manner might inspire Lady Bligh to behave. He was tired to death of this case and of her ladyship's shenanigans. "Crump intercepted it," he said.

Dulcie was not one to be cowed by a pompous attitude. With a mischievous grin and a rustle of satin, she perched on the edge of his desk. Her heavy perfume filled Sir John's nostrils, making him think of deep and mysterious forests, amber and jasmine and musk, the stately chime of crystal and silver bells.

It was with some relief that the Chief Magistrate greeted the advent of two more people in the small room. "Speak of the devil!" murmured Lady Bligh. "It is our astute and courageous little Crump." The Runner's unhappy companion received a gimlet stare. "And, if I am not mistaken, Lord Warwick's valet."

Crump was a more-than-discreet individual, well-suited to his duties at Tattersall's Subscription Rooms on summer Mondays when debts were settled, at the Bank of England on days when dividends were paid, at Drury Lane and Covent Garden where he stood in the saloons and watched for pickpockets; and thus he displayed no surprise at seeing Lady Bligh perched so insouciantly on the Chief Magistrate's desk. He did note, however, that Sir John looked unusually flustered, and that the Baroness seemed pleased with herself.

Simpkin was less broad-minded and furthermore labored under considerable distress. He goggled open mouthed. "So," said Lady Bligh thoughtfully. "I perceive you have solved one of our little mysteries. How clever of you, Crump!"

The Runner was inclined to agree. With an ungentle hand, he propelled Simpkin farther into the room. The valet, as if his knees had grown too weak to support him, sank down on the wooden chair. "I fancy," said Crump cheerfully, "that this rascal can make a number of things clear." He hooked his thumbs into his waistcoat, canary yellow embroidered with blue.

"I didn't know they were forged!" cried Simpkin, wiping his feverish brow. "To that I'll swear."

"As you'll swear that the murderer of your master was Leda Langtry?" Lady Bligh arranged herself more comfortably on the hard desk top and leaned back on one hand, thus presenting Sir John with an excellent view of her enchanting profile. "I think we'd benefit greatly from hearing how you arrived at that notion, Simpkin."

The valet was more than eager to comply, not looking forward to a discussion of forged banknotes. "So," mused the Baroness, when he had done, "you only *assume* that Leda remained hidden on the premises because you did not conduct her to the door. Why not, I wonder?" Simpkin swallowed hard. "And when you later saw the woman in your master's room, you saw only a *figure* clad in black—not, in fact, her face."

"That's true," Simpkin conceded, while the Chief Magistrate fiddled with his pocket watch, relic of the great Henry Fielding, and Crump fumed.

"Then," continued Lady Bligh serenely, "you cannot in point of fact swear that the woman who interrupted Warwick was Leda Langtry."

Simpkin would have agreed to anything at that point. "No," he said, hopefully.

"Excellent!" The Baroness beamed. "An interesting point, is it not? I suspected as much. Now you may have your turn, Crump!"

And high time, thought the Runner, though he could hardly chastise Lady Bligh for interference in the due processes of the law when the Chief Magistrate sat so pointedly silent. It was plain as day that, in regard to Lady Bligh, Sir John was soft in the head. "It's a very curious thing," he said, "about this scamp. One day he's all to pieces, and the next he's so plump in the pocket that he's spreading the rhino all about town."

"Rhino?" inquired Lady Bligh.

"Rolls of soft," explained Crump, irked at the interruption. "Money!"

"Ah," murmured Dulcie. "To be precise, forged banknotes. Fascinating!"

"It would be even more fascinating," interrupted Sir John wryly, "if you would let Crump proceed."

"I didn't know they were forged!" wailed Simpkin, ashen. "I swear I didn't!"

Crump found relief for his feelings in a very loud snort. "Tell us another one!" he growled rudely. "Have you any notion of the penalty for passing forged banknotes?"

"I believe it is extremely severe," mused the Baroness, while Simpkin looked ready to swoon. "Every bit as severe, in fact, as the penalty for outright theft. I suggest it might be in your best interests, Simpkin, to tell us all."

Simpkin had no intention of being so cooperative, not fancying his head in the hangman's noose, but he found he could not remain silent. Like metal to a magnet, Lady Bligh's stern eyes pulled the truth from him. "I stole them," he said faintly, "from Warwick's desk." And then it all came out, from the pilfering of the first few notes to the subsequent removal, practically under Lord Barrymore's nose, of the remainder of the stack.

"I wonder," mused Dulcie, "how Warwick came into possession of those notes, and why he left them sitting out in plain sight."

"I can answer that," said Sir John, awakening as if from a trance. Crump glowered, not best pleased at this turn of events. "He had meant to show them to Lord Barrymore, who is something of an expert on forgeries."

"Ah!" Lady Bligh wriggled with pleasure. "I was correct in assuming that there was more to Tolly than meets the eye. It is frequently true of young men who appear in no way remarkable."

Crump wasn't interested in this sidelight on human character. "Those notes *are* forgeries," he said. "There can't be two opinions of the matter. We've managed to round up most of them." He shot the Baroness an unfriendly glance. "It's my opinion that they were printed on Leda Langtry's press, and furthermore that such forgeries were the source of her income." This brilliant deduction earned for him no praise. Sir John raised a shaggy skeptical brow, while Lady Bligh remained remarkably silent.

Simpkin could no longer stand the suspense. "What," he whispered in broken tones, "is going to happen to me?"

"I daresay it won't be pleasant," observed the Baroness absently, "but it will be a great deal *less* unpleasant than what would be your fate if you went free." She turned her head to regard the Chief Magistrate. "Has it occurred to you, dear John, that in this case there actually was no robbery? It does not follow the pattern of the other crimes. I conjecture that there were two purposes to be achieved in the matter of Warwick: the retrieval of those notes, which Simpkin unwittingly foiled, and Warwick's death. I think we may safely conclude that his suspicions were too close to the truth."

"Nor did Mary Elphinstone's murder follow that pattern." With a jerk of his head, Sir John indicated that Crump was to escort Simpkin from the room. "It would appear that she, also, knew too much, which brings us back to Leda Langtry."

"I think you will find," said Dulcie, hopping down from the desk, "that Mary Elphinstone died because she didn't know enough." She peered at him intently. "Have you considered, John, that high rank is no indication of a moral character? Look at John MacMahon, Prinny's Keeper of the Privy Purse and Secretary Extraordinary. *He* is the natural son of a butler and a chambermaid, who started life as an actor, gained an ensigncy for his efforts as a pimp, and the rank of lieutenant colonel by loaning his wife to a royal duke. Now he serves Prinny in a similar capacity and has demanded an Irish peerage and the Order of the Bath as the price for his silence."

Sir John gazed upon her, thinking not of corruption in high places but of his first sight, countless years past, of that beguiling countenance and those golden curls.

"Dear, dear John," murmured the Baroness. "How you would like to keep me well wrapped in lamb's wool! What were we discussing before Crump appeared?" She pondered, lovely head tilted to one side. "Ah, yes, my victory fête. I cannot say precisely when it will be, but I have already written to inform Bat that his presence will be required. One trusts he will choose to absent himself sufficiently long from Mme. de Staël's salon! She is a woman who is masculine in build as well as mind, though in conversation she has no equal and in her home has entertained kings. I hope very much, dear John, that you too will be able to attend!"

"A victory fête?" inquired the Chief Magistrate. Sir John reflected that he would rather not encounter the unpredictable fifth Baron, who was as likely to salute him in the French manner on both cheeks as he was to call him out for impinging on the Baroness's virtue.

"Humph!" said Lady Bligh, and leaned across the desk to tweak his nose. "I trust there will be a victory to celebrate, but if matters continue as they have begun, it is more likely to be a wake."

"Dulcie." Sir John's smile faded as he registered her extreme anxiety. "You can't seriously believe your niece is in actual danger?"

"Can't I?" retorted the Baroness dryly. "It's easy to see, John, that you do not know Mignon."

Chapter Twenty

"So Warwick's valet stole the banknotes," mused Lord Jeffries. "I wish it might work to our advantage, but I do not see how it may."

Our advantage? thought Mignon, but refrained from comment. "Have you seen the *Apocalypse* today?" she asked. "It is full of the most startling speculations—such as that Simpkin himself may have murdered his master and made up the tale of seeing a woman in Warwick's rooms simply to save his own skin."

"Which would let Leda off the hook," reflected Ivor. "At least in that case. I suppose this is your aunt's doing? If nothing else, it may buy us some time."

Again that plural pronoun. Mignon reflected that with every passing moment she was caught more firmly in the spider's web. "Time in which to do what?" she murmured. "Every new discovery we make only implicates your mother further."

"I fancy," retorted the Viscount, with a speculative glance, "that

Leda's implication is precisely what's intended. Nor is she herself
offering us any great assistance, being quite damnably close-
mouthed. She refuses to explain her association with Mary
Elphinstone, you know. I trust the evidence I left with you is safely
tucked away?"

"Yes." Mignon did not elaborate. It seemed to her that Lord
Jeffries' position was more than a little precarious, and she had
prevailed on him to let her take the jewels and the deed to Mary
Elphinstone's cottage to Bligh House. She had meant to entrust
them to her aunt, but the Baroness had been in one of her
unapproachable moods, sitting in the Hymeneal and staring fero-
ciously at the portrait of her rakish spouse, so Mignon had secreted
the items in her own room.

"I wish you might trust me!" said Lord Jeffries, rather testily. "I
cannot rid myself of the conviction that you are playing a lone
hand, and for disastrously high stakes."

If it was a game she played, Mignon thought wearily, it was
with a deck stacked against her.

"Or can it be," Ivor added grimly, "that you do not believe in
Leda's innocence? Perhaps you think along with Crump—who has
most recently invaded my home to look at, of all things, my
pocket handkerchiefs!—that I am her accomplice?"

"You are talking nonsense." Mignon wished she might honestly
assure him that she questioned neither Leda's innocence nor his
own honesty. "What I may think has little to do with the matter."

Ivor looked down at her, his sandy brows drawn into a frown.
"I could not blame you," he said, to her surprise, "if you did
entertain doubts. Even I have wondered if Leda might be involved
in all this, for it is obvious that she has something to hide. But I
cannot shake the conviction that my mother, despite her mania for
newsmongering and stepping on people's toes, is not capable of
murder." He sighed. "What a wretched imbroglio this is! I expect
to be apprehended myself at any moment."

"Mr. Crump can hardly do that," Mignon replied, with more

confidence than she felt, "without a particle of evidence against you."

"Evidence!" Lord Jeffries' tone was vicious. "I've come to detest that word. Even now Crump is doubtless following us, hoping at least to witness another robbery." Suddenly, he smiled. "What do you say, Miss Montague? Shall we treat our tenacious little shadow to a slight diversion?"

"I rather suspect," replied Mignon, torn between vexation and relief by the formality of his address, "that my aunt had something of that nature in mind."

They were in The Strand, the thoroughfare that linked the mercantile City with the fashionable West End. With a grin that betokened devilment, Lord Jeffries guided his companion—more than elegant in white muslin and a golden-brown cloth redingote with satin collar—toward Exeter 'Change, by Burleigh Street, the main thoroughfare for foot traffic.

"How is your uncle?" asked Mignon. "I believe you said he was going to visit Leda in Newgate."

"He did," Ivor replied promptly, with a repetition of his smile. "I do not know what passed between them, though I'll wager a contretemps ensued. Percy returned home and took straight to his bed after vowing, most volubly, that Leda was the most fractious and vile-tempered female he had ever seen."

Mignon gazed bemused upon a fat lady of at least fifty-five who was dressed in black velvet with white trimmings and a turban with floating ostrich feathers, and who had two homely daughters in tow. "I hope he is not seriously ill."

"No." In the crush of people, Ivor took her arm. "His physicians pronounced his malady to be nothing more than a colossal case of the sulks. Now we are going to temporarily forget my uncle and my mother and this abominable fix! You and I, Miss Montague, and consequently Mr. Crump, are going to view a huge old lion called Nero. We shall also pay a visit to an elephant so well behaved that Byron has claimed he'd like to have it as a butler."

Miss Montague was a lively, good-tempered girl who viewed the world about her with amiable pleasure when not caught up in gloom, and so she gazed with interest upon the various marvels to be seen in Exeter 'Change. The lower part was very spacious and had the appearance of a large bazaar. Among the various shops laid out on either side of a large gallery were a substantial dealer in ladies' workboxes and other fancy articles, milliners and seamstresses, hosiers and bookstores. Over this was a large menagerie, at the entrance to which stood a huge powerful-looking man dressed in the costume of Henry VIII's Yeomen of the Guard.

"Look here!" he cried, handing descriptive bills to the passersby. "The most extraordinary animals in the world to be seen alive for the price of one shilling! The wonderful elephant Chunee, and Nero, the largest lion ever seen in the world! The boa constrictor and the laughing hyena, the orangutan, birds of paradise and ostriches." Mignon watched through lowered lashes as Lord Jeffries paid the admittance fee. Heavens, but he was a fine figure of a man! Why, then, this unwavering conviction that she was rushing on headlong to her doom?

It was too precious an afternoon to waste in morbid imaginings. Mignon wrinkled her nose at the smell of the animals and, imagining the Runner's chagrin at discovering their destination, gave voice to a delightful giggle. The Viscount, once more at her side, glanced down at her.

"What is it?" asked Mignon, for he was studying her face with an intensity that was attracting no small attention to them. "Why are you staring at me?"

Ivor's brown eyes held an expression that made her flush. "I am counting your freckles," he replied, and his tone was dangerously close to a caress.

"Oh?" inquired Mignon coolly. How like him to remind her of those freckles and that she was a far cry from the Society beauties who doubtless doted upon him wherever he went. "It is a singularly odd way in which to pass one's time."

"It is," agreed the Viscount, taking her arm in a grip so firm that Mignon felt the warmth of his hand even through the cloth of her redingote. "And a fascinating one! Strange that I should never before have remarked the allure of red hair and freckles and big green eyes."

"You are teasing me," Mignon said gruffly, wondering what Crump might make of this conversation. "You are also making us very conspicuous."

"I had not thought you possessed of such a strong sense of propriety," murmured Lord Jeffries, but he guided her expertly through the crowd. Mignon bit her lower lip and cursed the heat that rose so easily in her cheeks. "It was not my intention to make you uncomfortable."

Miss Montague gazed gloomily upon a rather moth-eaten lion. It yawned. "Freckles," she announced perversely, "are nothing to jest about, Lord Jeffries. Ask anyone unfortunate enough to possess them. Try as I may, the wretched things will not go away." He was looking at her with obvious amusement and she hastened to turn the subject. "It seems singularly callous to be idling away our time in amusements while your mother languishes in Newgate."

"I doubt," said the Viscount dryly, "that it is in Leda's nature to languish anywhere. There is one odd thing that came up in Percy's confrontation with her, of which you may wish to inform your aunt: Leda has no notion of who is paying her way. She assumed I had made financial arrangments with her gaoler, but I had not." He smiled at Mignon's puzzled expression. "In truth, I never thought of it, having had little prior experience with prison protocol."

Mignon erred greatly when she allowed her eyes to meet his. Her breath was taken quite away.

"You misunderstood me," said the Viscount softly, and she blushed again at the warmth of his tone. "I was not teasing you about your freckles." He touched her cheek. "Indeed, I *do* mean to count them, every one. I anticipate it will take an entire lifetime."

But then the animals burst into a dreadful roaring, and Lord Jeffries looked away. Mignon, considering the location of various of her freckles, could only be glad the moment had passed. It was the elephant who had started the uproar, battering his strong trunk and wicked tusks against the iron-banded bars of his cage. Panic swept quickly through the crowd, and the fear that Chunee's great strength would become uncontrollable and that he would let loose the whole menagerie to terrorize the neighborhood. With grim efficiency, the Viscount hustled Mignon outside.

"Good heavens!" she gasped, for the elephant's angry bellows were perfectly audible even in the street. "Byron wants *that* creature for a butler? What happened to enrage it?"

"You remain mightily calm in a crisis, Miss Montague!" Lord Jeffries' countenance could only be called mischievous. "I am glad to see it. As to Chunee, he is generally very docile except in the rutting season, when he becomes increasingly irritable each year." His lips twitched. "It is not a condition reserved to elephants."

Seeking rather desperately for any means by which she might avoid the Viscount's gaze, Mignon reached for her reticule. "Ivor!" she gasped, for it no longer hung from her wrist. "I've lost my reticule."

"Was there anything of value in it?" Lord Jeffries appeared not to notice that, in the excitement of the moment, she had used his first name.

"A few shillings, nothing more." Mignon winced at the noise of the milling crowd. "It is no great loss, I suppose. All this excitement has given me a bit of a headache. Would you mind taking me home?"

The Viscount hesitated, and she thought he might refuse. "Not at all," Ivor replied politely, "though I had thought you were made of stronger stuff, Miss Montague." He glanced at the building from which issued such a loud and confused mêlée. "It is some consolation, I suppose, that we have doubtless lost our shadow. Crump will not soon forgive me that! No doubt he will think I deliberately provoked Chunee so that he might be trapped inside."

Mignon had not lied; her head ached so abominably that there was a roaring in her ears. Thus when the Viscount spoke again, words of incredible sweetness, she glanced at him with bewilderment, sure that she had not heard him right. "It doesn't signify," murmured Ivor, for her distress was apparent. "I hope the day may come, darling Mignon, when you listen by choice to all the various things that I have to say to you."

Lord Jeffries had severely underestimated both Crump's dedication and his agility. The Runner had indeed trailed his quarry to Exeter 'Change, but he had not followed them into the menagerie. He secretly harbored violent antipathy for the prize elephant there—a ferocious looking beast that had been brought from Bombay in 1809. He leaned against the side of a building and chewed contemplatively on his pipe stem while the Viscount and Miss Montague disported themselves within.

Crump had a great deal to mull over, and it was no easy task to make order of the various seemingly unconnected details that danced through his mind. There was Warwick, who had possessed not only forged banknotes and an uncharitable character but a passion for his Regent's wife, Princess Caroline. Lady Bligh had blackmailed him into signing Leda Langtry's release from Newgate. Had Warwick been murdered by his valet, as was so baldly suggested in the *Apocalypse*? If so, where did that leave Leda? Those footprints surrounding the well where Mary Elphinstone's body was found had been made by Leda's shoes. Crump had found them hidden in Leda's home, just recently, with the mud intact. The Runner frowned. The pieces were falling into place, and with a precision that seemed to him a trifle too pat. Crump had a strong aversion to being made a dupe.

As Crump pondered the progress of his investigation, he followed the progress of Lord Jeffries and Miss Montague along The Strand. They were far too engrossed in one another, he thought, to take any heed of him. Odd, though, that the handkerchief he had found appeared to be no part of the Viscount's wardrobe. Nor could he link it to Willie Fitzwilliam, who was far too scruffy to own so elegant a scrap.

2

Unhappily, Crump considered the Baroness. If Jeffries was guilty of complicity in robbery, as it very much appeared, there was little hope that Miss Montague was not similarly involved. One need only see the girl's face when she looked at the Viscount to see that her emotions were seriously engaged. Crump did not like to think of Dulcie's reaction were her niece to be taken for trial.

Nor was Mignon the only member of Dulcie's retinue whose behavior had caught the Runner's gimlet eye. Just that morning, on the theory that anyone exiting the home of the devious Lady Bligh was worth watching, he had followed Miss Montague's brother to a rendezvous in Hyde Park. There he had overheard the Honorable Maurice make a passionate declaration to a stunning lady with dark hair and an enviable figure. The lady had, quite properly, been overcome. Crump might have thought little of his encounter, had not something in her appearance struck a chord of memory.

He stepped behind the thick trunk of an old and barren oak tree as his quarry approached a stately mansion in St. James's Square, and watched as Miss Montague sped with unladylike haste up the steps, almost colliding in the doorway with an impeccably dressed gentleman. Why such haste? mused the Runner. His blue eyes narrowed as Lord Jeffries and Lady Bligh's caller, deep in idle conversation, passed him by. It was not the least curious that Brummell should call upon the Baroness, but it was startling indeed to see so disturbed an expression on the Beau's supercilious face.

Chapter Twenty-One

The Royal Patent Theatre at Drury Lane had seen no small excitement in recent years, from the fire in 1809 that raged with such fury that it illuminated Lincoln's Inn Fields with the brightness of midday to the debut only last summer of a morose and ugly little actor named Edmund Kean whose dramatic abilities took London by storm.

This evening, too, the theatre was crowded, even without the inducement of the bewitching Eliza Vestries displaying her elegant legs in the role of Macheath. The subscription boxes were filled with royalty, including Prinny himself, members of the quality who had elected to spend autumn in town, and the demimonde. Prostitutes turned the Green Room into a veritable hunting ground; likewise the lobby, where loitered procuresses shepherding herds of innocent-looking girls. In "Fop's Alley," young gentlemen gossiped and strolled; in the saloon, Crump idly lounged, his bright eye alert for pretty pickpockets, his services procured for a guinea a night.

Crump was not the only representative of Bow Street thus to grace Drury Lane: Sir John was a prominent, if reluctant, member of the party in Lady Bligh's box. "I'd give a great deal," he said, "to know why you enticed me here."

"Enticed you, John?" The Baroness wore a revealing gown with traces of the Greek influence in its Ionic sleeves and the palmette border at its hemline. Her golden curls were caught up in a Grecian knot, and disposed about her lissome person was a fortune in rubies. "Nonsense! Have you no curiosity about Willie's play? He is a brilliant dramatist, whatever else he may be." She smiled. "Too, dear John, I thought it would benefit you to experience a taste of family life."

Sir John withheld reply. The antics of the family Bligh bore closer resemblance to the caperings of a dozen chattering monkeys than to any model of domestic tranquility. He glanced at Mignon, demure and withdrawn in her gown of white satin and jaconet muslin, and wondered what Dulcie found in that quiet little creature to cause her unease. His weary gaze then moved to an opposite box where Maurice, staggering in a violet satin frockcoat, white satin waistcoat and breeches, the whole enlivened with jeweled buttons and gold and green embroidery, was deep in animated conversation with a dark-haired lady. As he watched, Lord Barrymore entered the box and bowed to the woman before speaking to his friend.

"Maurice," said Dulcie, as she pinched the Chief Magistrate's arm, "has more hair than sense." She peered sideways at her silent niece. "I fear it is a common failing in the Montagues! But we shall speak no more of that just now. Tell me, John, do you recall the Chevalier d'Eon, whose sex was so long a matter of debate? The Chevalier was not only a distinguished member of the French diplomatic corps, but he excelled at dueling; he also posed most successfully as a woman during negotiations with Empress Elizabeth of Russia."

"Of course." Sir John was a trifle huffy. Did Lady Bligh think advancing age had weakened his mind? "The Chevalier toured English towns and watering places as a woman fencer until wounded during a duel in, I believe, 1796. To what purpose is this conversation, Dulcie?"

"Dear John," lamented the Baroness, "I vow I worry about you! Must a conversation have a purpose? Cannot one talk for the sheer pleasure of it?" She leaned against his arm."I meant only to point out to you the efficacy of clever disguise."

Whose disguise? wondered Sir John, but Dulcie's soft body was warm against his arm and her heady perfume was in his nostrils; his effort at coherent speech resulted only in a groan.

Beside Miss Montague sat Viscount Jeffries, stunningly handsome in his coat of blue superfine and white marcella waistcoat. "You are very quiet," he murmured. "Have I offended you?"

Mignon smoothed her white kid gloves, well aware of the distinguishing preference signaled by Ivor's presence at her side and of what the world must think. "Not at all," she replied, and hoped her face did not betray the effort necessary to maintain that cool tone. She looked across the auditorium at her brother. "Tell me, Lord Jeffries, if you know anything of a Mrs. Harrington-Smythe?"

"Is that what she calls herself?" Ivor quirked a brow. "I'm afraid I do not, Miss Montague—and to be blunt, neither should you!"

Mignon frowned. From something Maurice had said, she had thought Mrs. Harrington-Smythe to be no stranger to polite Society. "Are you saying," she demanded, "that she is a ——"

"Ladybird, pretty horsebreaker, high-flyer, take your pick." His amusement was more pronounced. "You see what a broadening of your horizons, darling Mignon, may result from association with me?"

To the relief of both Mignon and Sir John, Willie bounced into the box. "Oh, my shattered nerves!" he twittered, and sank down beside the Baroness. "The play is about to begin." Sir John gazed upon the young man, pale and tremulous with excitement, and wondered for what incomprehensible purpose Lady Bligh encouraged so unprepossessing a specimen. It was due to Dulcie's influence that the theatre was filled to overflowing with not only commoners but every member of the *ton* who remained in town, from Brummell to the wicked Duke of Queensbury.

"Don't fret, Willie," soothed the Baroness, and patted his hand. "Your play shall have as tremendous a success as *Timour the Tartar,* the play in which real horses trod the stage of Covent Garden for the first time." She lowered her voice. "You might bear in mind, Willie, that for my efforts payment is still due."

"I've done all you wished," he muttered, with a feverish look in his pale eyes, "even to the announcements. Jesse has been kept incognito, though I have been plagued on all sides to reveal the name of my principal."

"You *would* have him," retorted Lady Bligh, "despite my advice." Her thoughtful gaze moved about the theatre, casting opprobrium upon the decorations in salmon pink, the burnished gold ornaments and crimson upholstery, and coming to rest, with little more approval, on Mignon. "Ah well, I've done the best I can."

Miss Montague had so much to occupy her thoughts that she scarcely noted when the play began. Chief among those perplexing matters was the theft of her reticule. The purse had been returned to her later the same day by Charity with the mumbled explanation that it had been left by a child. No child, thought Mignon unhappily, had penned the note she'd found inside. One could not make one's problems disappear by simply ignoring them, it seemed.

"Pay attention, Mignon!" hissed Lady Bligh, then turned to the Chief Magistrate. "Things could be in a worse case, dear John, and I suspect that shortly they will."

The curtain rose to display a masterpiece of scenic art. Clouds painted in semitransparent colors on framed, stretched linen rose diagonally by way of a winding machine. Behind the clouds stood mountains, and in the foreground lay a sand pit covered with moss and lichen. Thunder rattled, lightning flashed, and a pale moon rose. Willie's moment had come.

The audience sat rapt through the melodrama, which combined

such disparate elements as Satan portrayed by a *chef de cuisine*, and a teapot, milk jug and cup which executed a *pas de trois* while spoons and forks danced around them as *figurantes*. The hero played expertly on musical glasses and suffered an unfortunate addiction to apricot tarts; the heroine served as a scullery maid; and a large Newfoundland dog was in the habit of biting Satan in the seat of his pants. Even the Chief Magistrate laughed himself into stitches, while Lady Bligh expressed a vast appreciation for a half ruined Moorish castle and a wish to use a certain temple of glowworms at her next rout.

Throughout it all Miss Montague sat silent, her green eyes riveted to the stage. Only when the curtain descended did she make a sound, and that was merely a soft little expulsion of breath. With a flourishing bow, Jesse Saint-Cyr retired through one of the doors, with brass knockers on them, which stood always open upon the stage.

"He is no William Charles Macready," observed the Baroness, "but I suppose that, temporarily, he will do." Willie did not argue the point, being overwhelmed by enthusiastic applause. With fluttering hands, he screwed his monocle into one eyesocket, where it did not long stay, being quickly dislodged by the restless hopping of his brows.

Lady Bligh's box was soon crowded with appreciative spectators, among them Brummell, whose approval was all the more valuable for being restrained, Lord Barrymore, and Maurice. It was not difficult, under cover of the confusion, for Mignon to slip away.

Maurice may have appeared a ridiculous figure, his eyes faintly bulging and his breath constricted by the tightness of his cravat; but, despite his dizzying infatuation with the elusive Mrs. Harrington-Smythe, the Honorable Mr. Montague was not entirely a fool. Additionally, he had the benefit of a lifelong acquaintance with his enterprising, if addlepated, sister. It was no more than two shakes of a lamb's tail before Maurice realized Mignon was gone.

"Where is she?" he demanded, looking wildly around the crowded box. "I swear I'll wring her neck for this!"

"Your shirt points are sadly wilted," commented the Baroness with marked distaste. "In fact, nephew, you look a regular quiz. Do you not mean to congratulate Willie on the success of his play?"

"I mean," Maurice retorted, flushed with rage, "to take my sister back to Yorkshire and lock her away!" He looked at his aunt's stern face. "Well, think of the scandal! I would never have allowed her to come to you, Aunt, had I thought you would encourage her madness."

"If there is scandal," Lady Bligh said calmly, "it will be of your making, Maurice. I suggest you be seated and drink some of my lemonade." With a forceful hand she pushed him down in the chair. Rendered impotent by Dulcie's eagle eye, Maurice drank. He bitterly regretted the impulse that had brought Mignon to London. The family had thought her restored to her senses—but clearly she had none.

Mignon had as little thought for her brother's inevitable displeasure as she had enthusiasm for the task she must perform. She made her way through the backstage confusion, her nostrils filled with that extraordinary compound of odd scents peculiar to the theatre. Aware of the curious glances that followed her, and that this undertaking was at the least unwise, Mignon's cheeks flamed. There was little alternative, as the note had made clear. She had no difficulty in locating the dressing room.

"Well, puss!" He took her hand and drew her inside. "It has taken you an unconscionable long time to seek me out. I had nearly begun to despair."

Mignon looked at this well-built young man with his thick and curling dark hair, his devilish smile. How magical it had seemed that so glorious a creature should care for her! Mignon was a trifle too honest to see herself as Cinderella, transformed by love from a rather dowdy female into a stunning belle, but she could not deny that Jesse was well qualified to play the fairy-tale prince. And so he had, she thought bitterly. His passionate avowals had been no more than another role. "I had no choice," she replied, and tried unsuccessfully to remove her arm from his grasp. "It is the last time I will meet you, Jesse."

"So reason has prevailed." His smile was crooked, his eyes as cold as ice. "I thought it might in time. What shall I do, Mignon, now that you've shattered my hopes? Would it gratify you if I put a period to my life?"

"You're talking nonsense." Mignon gritted her teeth against the pain of his grip. "I can't imagine that your feelings for me are sufficiently deep that you could even briefly consider such a thing."

"Once you thought differently." Jesse's fingers were so brutal that Mignon cried aloud. "Once you would risk all for a moment in my arms. What has happened, Mignon, to change your mind? Have you met another man who can offer more than I?" His voice was vicious. "What would his reaction be, I wonder, if he learned of our relationship?"

"You wouldn't!" gasped Mignon, with little conviction. "There is nothing to tell, save a few indiscreet meetings. It would be your word against mine. Who do you think would believe you, Jesse? You're nothing but a strolling actor and a mountebank." Her eyes filled with tears at the pain he inflicted, not with his hands but his words, but Miss Montague would not go down without a fight. "And, I suspect, a fortune hunter in the bargain!"

"Very discerning of you, puss." Jesse flung her away from him, and Mignon came up smartly against a wall. "You have been very foolish, behaving in a shockingly forward and unmaidenly way, making a dead-set at me and taking my fancy to an alarming degree. Now you think you may simply cry off." He seemed a total stranger, his face set in grim lines.

"What do you want?" whispered Mignon, rubbing her bruised arms. "Money? You must know I cannot touch my capital without the consent of my trustees."

"Your capital," mocked Jesse, and ran his fingers through his dark hair. "Ah, God, I've made a mull of it! I cannot blame you for thinking the worst of me. It is my accursed temper—but you accused me of wanting only your money, and it is a taunt I cannot stomach." He moved toward her and took her face in his hands. "I cannot bear to think that I should lose you, Mignon."

Miss Montague wondered what had happened to her, for his ardor no longer roused in her an answering spark. "You threatened me," she said stiffly. "I would hardly call it a loverlike act to promise to publish my letters to the world."

"As if I would," Jesse murmured, his eyes now warm. "It was the only way to bring you to me, and for it I apologize. You must know, puss, that I wouldn't harm a hair of your head. Come, tell me you forgive me and that our misunderstanding is at an end. There is nothing I wish more in the world than to make you my bride."

"What of *my* wishes?" hissed Mignon, seeking refuge from her bewilderment in a display of rage. "Do you think to so easily bend me to your will?" Jesse stepped back, pale. "What a happy relationship we would have, you and I and my obliging trustees! It will not serve, Jesse. I will not marry you."

"Won't you?" His handsome features twisted as he grasped her shoulder. "There is more than one way to bring a reluctant damsel to the altar, Mignon."

Miss Montague was no bread-and-butter miss to swoon away at the threat of ravishment. Green eyes shooting fire, she drew back her hand and applied it with satisfying force to Jesse's mocking face.

"An enlightening scene, indeed," murmured Lord Jeffries from the doorway. "If you are through enacting a Cheltenham tragedy, Miss Montague, I will return you to your aunt."

Chapter Twenty-Two

Culpepper was irate. First Charity had disappeared for several hours, returning at last with a weak tale of her sick mother, and then Gibbon had vanished. No doubt the butler was about some business for the Baroness, thought Culpepper sourly, but his timing was in the largest degree inconsiderate. Since there was no butler in evidence, his duties fell upon the abigail, second highest in the domestic hierarchy. What next? Culpepper wondered. As if it were not enough to be courted by a drunken watchman, now she must collect coats and hats and see that Lady Bligh's impromptu party ran smoothly. With a martyred expression, Culpepper made her way to the Ballroom.

She need not have worried: Lady Bligh's entertainments were as famed for their perfection as for their eccentricity. Even on short notice, the Baroness had procured an excellent orchestra; Indian jugglers who performed in an anteroom; and a craniologist who carefully examined and remarked upon the skulls of his fellow guests. In yet another chamber was a big buffet table laden with the most delicate and choice refreshments of every kind. Behind it stood a sulky Charity, assisted by two other maidservants dressed in white uniforms and black aprons. Still later a supper would be served by male attendants in a room connected with the kitchens. Culpepper supposed the guests would drive home by sunlight. Hopefully Gibbon would have made a reappearance by then.

The fifty-foot-long Ballroom was an exquisite chamber with marble floors and green wall panels on a white ground; the surroundings were pale buff. The richly molded ceiling had been painted by Florentine Cipriani, who was also responsible for the allegorical pictures on the panels of the State Coach first used by George III in 1782. At one end of the ballroom, a large bay window looked onto the gardens; at the other end stood a colonnade of Ionic arches. Statuary marbles were placed at various intervals around the room.

"Sometimes I wonder," remarked Lady Bligh to Sir John, "what my father would have thought of Bligh House. He was a vulgar soul, I fear! I well recall him swallowing his peas off a knife, eating oysters by sucking them off his wrist, enlivening a dull dinner party by removing his false teeth in front of us all." She smiled. "He fancied himself an artist, and it was his habit to moisten his clay by spitting on it in the presence of his models."

The Chief Magistrate gazed at her. "Your hair is coming unpinned," he said inconsequentially, imagining it cascading down her back as she tumbled into his arms. "You seek to distract me, Dulcie. I cannot delay much longer in the performance of my duties. Indeed, I may have already tarried too long."

His stern tone had little appreciable effect on his hostess, who turned her enigmatic eyes to the tremulous Willie, deep in conversation with his fellow guest of honor, Jesse Saint-Cyr. "When pallor became the fashion," she observed, "French ladies applied leeches to draw off their blood so that they could faint away becomingly in company. Do you mean to have Willie do the same in the midst of his victory feast?" She placed her bejewelled hand

on Sir John's arm. "Come, let us mingle with the crowd! It will do
no harm to allow our playwright his moment of triumph before
you frighten the wits out of him."

Leaving Sir John engaged with his amiable and long-winded
Prince Regent, Dulcie slipped away and drew Maurice aside.

"I must protest!" said her nephew, tugging at his tight cravat
and glaring in the general direction of his sister. "How *can* you
allow Mignon to disappear unescorted, for a good half hour, and
demand from her not a word of explanation?"

"Pooh, Maurice!" Lady Bligh guided him firmly across the
crowded Ballroom. "Mignon came to no great harm. You are only
out of sorts because your lovely friend pleaded a headache and
would not accompany you here."

Maurice looked stunned. "How did you know that? Mrs. Harrington-Smythe is both shy and retiring. No doubt she felt she
would be out of place in such a magnificent assemblage."

"Doubtless," replied Dulcie serenely, "she would have been. You
would do much better, Maurice, to devote your efforts to your
ladylove and leave your sister to me." Maurice opened his mouth
to protest. "Monsieur Trouffant!" cried the Baroness gaily. "My
nephew has agreed to be your first subject!"

Aristotle Trouffant was a stout little man with cherubic features
and a pince-nez. He surveyed Maurice, a staggering spectacle in
what could only be described as a court habit, complete with lace
wrist frills, white silk stockings, and black pumps with gold buck-
les. Aristotle allowed no hint of derision to appear on his features.
He was a professional.

"Ah, so you entrust yourself to me!" Trouffant flexed plump and
well-tended fingers. "You are most discerning! For I, along with
Spurzheim, studied under the great Francis Joseph Gall. The skull
being molded on the brain, you know, its surface reproduces the
shape thereof."

Maurice, rendered acutely uncomfortable by the gleam in Monsieur Trouffant's eye, sank down in a chair. "Dulcie!" he protested
weakly.

"You will find, Monsieur Trouffant," said the Baroness, "that my nephew is a coward, among other things. Continue, please!"

"As the brain is the seat of our faculties," explained the craniologist enthusiastically, "it has been noted that persons having a particular talent, vice or virtue, seem to have the same part of the skull particularly developed." He smiled, revealing a gold tooth. "Craniology, monsieur, is the study of the individual based on the peculiarities of his skull."

If not for his aunt's restraining hand, Maurice would have leaped from his chair and taken to his heels. With a vague notion that Trouffant meant to somehow dissect his brain, perhaps in the manner of the surgeons who dismembered felons hanged at Newgate, he gulped as the Frenchman laid inquisitive hands on his head.

"Ah!" said Monsieur Trouffant. "Never have I seen a better developed area of self-esteem. You see? It is situated at the intersection of the circumference of the skull and an imaginary straight line starting at the extreme tip of the chin and passing through the greater part of the exterior ear." As he spoke, he traced that line. Maurice shuddered.

"Fascinating," murmured Lady Bligh. "And that means?"

"If normal, excellent moral restraint." Monsieur Trouffant's voice was disapproving. "But this is excessive, indicating pride and disregard of others."

"Truly remarkable!" The Baroness's dark eyes were speculative. "I suspect you may prove invaluable, Monsieur Trouffant!"

Maurice was not the only one to derive little enjoyment from Lady Bligh's rout. Mignon cast a harried look at the glittering company. Thus far she had managed to avoid conversation with either her brother or Jesse, but she had little faith that her luck would hold.

"You are looking positively blue-deviled," murmured Lord Barrymore. "If I may offer a word of advice? Do not judge your brother too harshly. He is a well-meaning soul, and he has only your best interests at heart."

Startled, Mignon glanced at her companion. Tolly looked very fine in his formal attire, a chocolate brown cloth frock coat with self buttons, beige drill breeches buttoned and tied, a white waistcoat. "You seem to know a great deal of our affairs," she said, in stifled tones. "Maurice has confided in you, I suppose?"

"Do not think ill of him," Lord Barrymore repeated. "He was beside himself when he learned that you had left your aunt's box, and disclosed to me the reason for his concern. I beg you will trust me, as your brother does! Your secrets are safe. As I told Maurice, I have little fear that you will make the same mistake again. If I may be presumptuous, dear Miss Montague, it is not the first time that a young girl has been led astray by an unprincipled blackguard!" He frowned. "I cannot think what your aunt is about, providing you so little chaperonage."

"I am surprised at your forbearance, Lord Barrymore!" said Mignon spiritedly. "You have been apprised of my past indiscretions, which nearly ended in a clandestine elopement, yet seem not in the least affected by the event."

"My dear!" Tolly's gaze was warm. "Surely you cannot think I would harshly judge you for what could only have been the mildest of flirtations? Rather it is to your credit that you possess so trusting a nature and so innocent a heart." He shook his head. "No, I must blame your mentors for not better protecting you."

"A classic case," remarked Viscount Jeffries, pausing behind Mignon, "of the wolf and the lamb? I believe, Miss Montague, that you have promised me this dance."

Mignon had done no such thing, but she accepted his arm. Ivor doubtless meant to rip her character to shreds. Let him then, and be done with it! It was no more than she deserved for having acted with foolish scorn of all possible consequences.

"Your brother," observed Lord Jeffries, as he led her into a waltz, "is looking sulky as a bear. He is also making frequent assaults on the punch bowl! I daresay you will forgive me, darling Mignon, if I say that, drunk or sober, Maurice has not the least semblance of being a clever man?"

"He is feeling thwarted," Miss Montague replied absently. "Only his fear of scandal has prevented Maurice from reading me a thundering scold and asking me questions without end." The impact of his words belatedly struck her. "*What* did you call me?"

Ivor smiled down at her stunned face. "It's as crowded as the very devil in here," he remarked, and whisked her skillfully into an anteroom where were displayed ancient coats of mail, Indian shields made of rhinoceros hide, and an occasional skull. The chamber ended in a rounded bay twenty feet across, and its walls were covered in a paper with details reminiscent of King Arthur's castle. "This," said Mignon unnecessarily, "is the Armory. My uncle is a wide traveler and has a taste for the macabre. The chimney piece was inspired by various tombs."

"Your uncle," retorted the Viscount, "is of scant interest to me, and this room of even less." Mignon gazed at him apprehensively. "My poor darling, you have truly landed yourself in a damnable fix."

"The cursedest dilemma possible." Mignon turned to pace the length of the room. "You don't know the half of it. But you surprise me, Lord Jeffries! I had thought a high stickler like yourself would have only contempt for my foolishness."

"I can see," said Ivor, so close behind her that Mignon jumped, "that you have not altered your initial opinion of my character. I cannot blame you, I suppose! Nor can I condemn your behavior when I have been at least as foolish myself." Startled, she stared at him. "It is a lowering reflection," he added. "I was accustomed to thinking of myself as, er, a nonpareil, and now find myself condemned as the offspring of a murderess and suspected of various unspecified vile misdeeds by Bow Street. It is extremely deflating to one's pride."

"It is," Mignon retorted heatedly, "utter nonsense!" The Viscount smiled, and she flushed at her display of hot partisanship. "I must thank you," she added gruffly, "for coming to my rescue. I shudder to think what might have happened if you had not."

"It was not one of my happier moments," Ivor admitted. She dropped her eyes and Ivor gently tipped up her chin. "I am, it seems, a jealous man! But it would be hardly reasonable of me to hold against you an indiscretion that happened even before we met."

Mignon had an unwelcome and unpleasant suspicion that was speedily borne out. "Much as I would prefer to stay," murmured the Viscount, drawing her closer, "I must take my leave of you. Do not think yourself in a cleft stick, darling Mignon! I will see you clear of it. The task will prove a great deal easier now that I know the truth." And then he enfolded her in a crushing, passionate embrace that was suitable only for one of those infamous creatures known commonly as lightskirts. "When we are freed of this coil," he added, smiling down at Mignon with an unmistakable warmth, "I mean to set before you an arrangement for your future that I think will prove of mutual, er, convenience to both of us."

Miss Montague was finding in herself a remarkable capacity for violence. For the second time that evening she slapped a gentleman's face, then fled the room in tears.

Chapter Twenty-Three

While Monsieur Trouffant happily analyzed various illustrious brains, Willie Fitzwilliam underwent an examination of another sort, one which filled him with the deepest misgiving. "I swear I don't know," he said nervously, "what you're talking about."

"Don't you?" Sir John paced about the Armory, so recently the setting for a very different scene. "I beg to differ! It will go much easier for you if you confess."

"Confess!" Willie swallowed hard, averting his gaze from a grinning skull. "Egad, Sir John, you fill me with the liveliest apprehension!"

Sir John folded his arms, his weary face revealing none of his thoughts. It had been neither a particularly enlightening nor entertaining evening for the Chief Magistrate, placed by the crafty Baroness in the position of seeming to condone the activities of a criminal—although, as she had gaily pointed out, one might expect to encounter all sorts of people at the theatre. And, as Dulcie had further pointed out, though opinion was overwhelming as to the Viscount's guilt, no one was certain of the exact nature of his crime. But it was not Ivor's sins that currently occupied Sir John. "If not for Lady Bligh's intervention," he said severely, "I would have had you at Bow Street before now. Come, tell me about those forged banknotes!"

Willie, who looked almost unexceptionable in the formal garb that the Baroness had provided him, carefully adjusted his monocle.

"I might add," remarked Sir John, "that I already know you made the plates. There's little use in denials! I urge you to cooperate."

The casual remark affected Willie most extremely: his pale eyes took on a glassy sheen, and sweat beaded his face. "How fleeting is triumph!" he lamented. "One moment success, the next instant ruin. Even while I wear the crown of laurels, a gallows rope is being slipped round my neck." He gazed at Sir John gloomily. "Very well, if you must have it! Though it goes sorely against the grain to easily give myself over to the law. It was all for the sake of the play, of course. 'Twas a prodigious undertaking, Sir John, and I saw no other way to bring it about."

"So you made and passed false banknotes," summed up the Chief Magistrate, rather surprised that Willie was proving so cooperative. "How did they come into Warwick's possession? You were acquainted with him?"

"Certainly not!" said Willie, with a look of extreme hauteur. "You've got the wrong horse by the tail—several of them, in fact."

Sir John hefted a broadsword with an expertise that made Willie blanch. "Were the forged notes insufficient for your needs?" the Chief Magistrate inquired. "Is that why you and your confederates embarked upon this series of robberies? I'll have the truth, Fitzwilliam!"

Willie, eyes fixed on that broad blade, shrieked and collapsed onto a settee. "I'll confess to anything!" he cried. "Only I beg you, do not decapitate me!"

"John!" reproved the Baroness, materializing like a somewhat disheveled genie in the room. With a gesture, she brought the Indian jugglers to toss up and catch their burning torches just outside the door. "There is always a way to insure one's privacy, if one is sufficiently ingenious!" She frowned, draping herself provocatively across a chair. "Now," the Baroness announced, "you will explain to me why you are browbeating poor Willie. It is not like you, John, to make a scene."

"Poor Willie," retorted the Chief Magistrate, somewhat discomposed at discovering that he still gripped the broadsword, "has just admitted his responsibility for the forged banknotes." He glared at that unhappy individual, who looked as though he would have very much liked to sink through the floor. "He was just on the verge of confessing to his complicity in murder and robbery."

"Oh?" Willie squirmed under the Baroness's thoughtful eye. "I had thought I might have to repent of my choice, but not quite so grievously. Well, Willie, what have you to say for yourself?"

"He might as well say it at Bow Street," interjected Sir John. "I'm sorry this has not fallen out as you wished, Dulcie, but I confess I'm glad to have it so tidily tied up." Carefully, he replaced the sword in its place on the wall. "Crump was right all along, it seems."

"No," retorted Lady Bligh crossly, while Willie moaned. "I had thought you possessed a superior understanding, John, but you have shown me little evidence of it! No more than Leda is Willie involved in your murders and your robberies."

"Have you no regard for the evidence, Dulcie?" snapped the Chief Magistrate, victim of a fleeting impulse to impale the annoying Baroness on a primitive spear. "How do you mean to explain it away?"

"I don't care a button for your evidence," replied Lady Bligh, and tucked her feet under her. "It would be to your benefit to listen—without comment!—to Willie's tale."

Sir John thought he'd heard enough of Willie's taradiddles for one evening, but he was not proof against Dulcie's pleading glance. "Very well," he replied coolly. "I will listen, and then I will take him in."

"Dear John!" Lady Bligh smiled. "I am persuaded, once you've heard the truth, that you will not behave so. Proceed, Willie! The stage is yours."

"I thought the notes were to be a prop," Willie said reluctantly, his slender, gloved fingers clenched and entwined. "A device to add verisimilitude." Even in his extremely compromising position, he could not resist a malicious glance at Sir John. "I'd no notion the things would fool anyone when closely seen!" The Chief Magistrate made an annoyed gesture, and the playwright continued hastily. "I suppose I should have smelled a rat, but the fact is I did not! It seemed a straightforward request, and I needed the money that I was promised when the things were done."

"You were fortunate," murmured the Baroness, "not to be paid in your own coin. What a hobble! I don't suppose you'd care to tell John who commissioned that pretty piece of forgery?"

Willie winced. "I must protest, *not* forgery! Merely an imitation of the real thing, only accurate enough to seem real when viewed from a distance, as on the stage." He spread his hands. "What can I say? My only defense is that I abhor shoddy work. It seems I am a truer artist than I knew."

Sir John, keeping his temper on a tight rein, reminded himself that Willie had already proven himself the possessor of an extremely fertile artistic imagination. "I'm waiting," he said, though with little evidence of patience, "to hear who commissioned those notes. Perhaps, Leda Langtry?"

"Dear John," sighed Dulcie, "that won't fadge! Leda has no need of money, having more than enough to support her peculiar mode of life, and she obtained it through perfectly legal means, though I will not acquaint you with their precise nature, since it is none of your business!"

"Dulcie," growled the Chief Magistrate, sorely tried, "do hush! I would hear the prisoner's explanation from his own lips."

"Prisoner!" gasped Willie, greatly distressed. "Egad. But the Baroness is correct, Sir John. Leda had nothing to do with those notes—in truth, I doubt she even knew of their existence. They were requested of me by someone in the theatre whose name I have, alas, forgot, though perhaps it may come back to me. I have no idea what happened to them after that, or how they came into Warwick's hands."

Sir John did not demean himself by responding to this palpable nonsense, but stalked toward the door. Perhaps Willie would prove more informative after a few days' solitude in a gaol cell. "John!" said the Baroness. "Oddly enough, Willie has told you the truth, or what he knows of it. Leda is not involved in the forgery."

The Chief Magistrate might have made any number of scathing comments, had not Monsieur Trouffant just then pussyfooted around the Indian jugglers and into the anteroom. The Frenchman paused on the threshold to survey its occupants, perhaps with an eye to brains yet unplundered. They were an interesting assortment: Sir John was obviously ready to commit bloody mayhem with any one of the ancient weapons that hung upon the walls; Lady Bligh was engaged in a silent tête-à-tête with a grinning death's head; while Willie, like a deflated balloon, had collapsed in his chair. Mousieur Trouffant tactfully cleared his throat and approached Dulcie.

"All is as you requested, madam," he said, though with no small private curiosity. "I thought you would wish to know immediately what I have learned."

Dulcie's dark eyes moved from the skull to him. "And?"

Indeed, she was the strangest of ladies, this Baroness with the soul of a cocotte and the sensibilities of a black widow spider! "The organ of destructiveness," Monsieur Trouffant replied obediently, for after all he had been well paid, "makes a ridge somewhat behind the ear. The ridge indicates a tendency dangerous to social life, a perversity prevalent in carnivorous animals. In humans, it may mean one who beats animals, who ill treats children and women." Monsieur Trouffant looked unhappy, for he believed most firmly in the disclosures of his art. "In short, madam, I have never before encountered a ridge so highly developed. There is no question that the subject is inclined toward evil."

"What can be more evil than murder?" mused the Baroness. In one fluid motion, she rose and stood before the Chief Magistrate. "It will not serve as proof, of course, but you would oblige me vastly, dearest John, if you would let Willie go."

Maurice's beloved Mrs. Harrington-Smythe was not the only absentee from Lady Bligh's impromptu fête, and it was perhaps fortunate that Crump was prevented from viewing yet another proof of Dulcie's striking influence over his Chief Magistrate. Nor was Crump, as he proceeded toward York Place in Marylebone, doomed to a solitary journey, for he had a very unhappy Gibbon in tow. "You're very wishful to go to Newgate, laddie!" the Runner remarked. "I *might*, for the sake of old times, be willing to make an exception in your case, if you'll tell me what you were doing at that apartment in Crown Court."

Gibbon knew a hawk from a handsaw, and furthermore he'd been caught in a criminal act. He made an extremely rude remark concerning what Crump might do with his exceptions.

"Very suspicious!" said the Runner, unruffled. "I thought you had reformed, my lad! Sir John will be very disappointed, to say nothing of the Baroness. Aye, I can hardly disbelieve the evidence of my own eyes! There you were, perched like a climbing monkey on a window ledge." In a comradely manner, he applied his elbow to Gibbon's ribs. "What was it, laddie, robbery?"

Gibbon, a staunch believer in the virtue of silence, made no reply. Crump led him to a small elegant establishment and raised his hand to knock at the door. It swung open. "Mighty queer," mused the Runner, and cast his unwilling companion a sly wink. "It looks like Miss Zoe may be entertaining company."

Lady Bligh's butler may have had his minor failings, but he also possessed a strong moralistic bent. "Have you brought me out here," he demanded, gaunt features horrified, "to visit a *Cyprian?*"

Crump proceeded down the hallway, leaving Gibbon no choice but to accompany him. "Don't sermonize over *me*, laddie! You're already under a cloud." The Runner was in good spirits. "This isn't just any bit of muslin but Lord Jeffries' ladybird, and I'll wager you've never cast your winkers on a prettier wench." He smiled genially. "Or a bigger liar! We're here at her invitation, her having sent me a note regarding new developments. You'll be witness, my laddie, when Miss Zoe confesses that she lied about Jeffries."

"You're out there!" muttered Gibbon gloomily. He'd a fair notion how his mistress would react to this development. Not only was he to serve as witness for the prosecution, he'd been caught red-handed whilst committing a capital offense.

Like Siamese twins, a relationship prompted by the pistol in Crump's capable hand, they moved into the sitting room. The Runner thought with complacency that he'd come a long way since the days when his duties consisted of serving summonses and executing assault and peace warrants. With the solving of this case, his fame would almost equal that of Townsend. He looked around the sitting room, approving again of the flesh-colored stucco and gilt.

Gibbon, whose wits were not dulled by dreams of grandeur, and who in addition was accustomed to dwelling in far more luxurious surroundings than these, was conscious of a growing unease. The house was far too quiet. If its occupant was entertaining a caller, presumably male, she was doing so with a demureness unlooked for in a lady of her profession.

"Miss Zoe!" called Crump cheerfully. "Where are you?"

Gibbon had hardly dreamed to see a time when he was grateful for Crump's companionship, but that day had come. "Look." He nudged the Runner. "Behind the settee."

Crump looked instead at Gibbon, whose countenance had taken on the pallor of wax. With reluctance he followed the butler's gaze. From behind the récamier protruded a bare and obviously feminine foot. With an oath, Crump crossed the room.

"I never thought to say this," remarked Lord Jeffries, entering the room through another doorway, "but I'm glad to see you, Crump." Observing Lady Bligh's dignified butler in handcuffs, the Viscount raised a brow. Then he continued, "You will find the body of Marie—the maid—in the kitchens."

Crump's wits temporarily deserted him; he didn't know what to think. The Runner looked at Lord Jeffries, as self-possessed as ever, albeit a trifle pale, and thought inconsequentially of such bruisers as Savage Shelton and the terrible Randall and prizefights held at the Castle Tavern in Holborn. Crump would have wagered that Ivor was as handy with his fists as the renowned Cribb, who'd so easily defeated Belcher at Epsom Downs. He pointed his efficient-looking pistol at the Viscount. "You have some explaining to do, guv'nor," he said.

Gibbon, remarkably cool in the face of these developments, glanced about the room in search of telltale signs. His gaze fell upon a small end table on which sat a remarkably familiar-looking snuffbox.

"I believe you labor under a misapprehension, Mr. Crump," Ivor was saying smoothly as Gibbon inched forward. "I arrived only moments before yourself, as my coachman will confirm. If you carefully inspect both bodies. you will find that they have lain thus for some time. The flesh is quite cold."

Crump had little wish to perform so intimate an examination. Too clearly he remembered the enchanting creature who had called him Siegfried. With an impatient gesture, Ivor stepped forward.

"Don't press your luck!" the Runner said grimly, raising his pistol. "I'd as soon empty this barking-iron into you as look at you, and that's God's truth."

Lord Jeffries ignored the warning, moving not toward the doorway to freedom but to the récamier, his silk-lined opera cloak in his hands. He looked down upon the sprawling, naked body, the yellow hair matted with congealed blood, the face battered beyond all recognition, its nose crushed, one eye dangling from its socket. Gently he spread the cloak over all that remained of a lively little opera dancer, who had once been addressed with proposals of a libertine nature—by a royal duke, a lofty marquis, and a cit of considerable fortune—conveyed through milliners and mantua makers and their ilk. Never again would hopeful suitors send their agents to Zoe.

Aghast, Crump stared at the blood stains on his lordship's clothing and at the mark upon his cheek as if he'd been struck. "Gibbon!" snapped Crump, anticipating a need for assistance. There was no reply, and he glanced cautiously over his shoulder. Lady Bligh's butler, handcuffs and all, had fled.

Chapter Twenty-Four

"I know," said Lord Barrymore ruefully, "that I'm not a regular out-and-outer, but neither am I a dashed loose-screw! I suppose I'm a rather dull fellow, with too strong a sense of propriety, but I can't help but see that you're fretting yourself to flinders. Is there nothing I may do, Miss Montague?"

Mignon regarded Tolly, dressed for an expedition to the races, with an unprecedented warmth. His face had positively lit up with delight when they met by chance in the hallway, where he awaited Maurice, and so appreciative a reaction was balm to her wounded sensibilities. "I thank you," she replied, "but no."

"It is curst irregular in me," and Tolly took her hand, "but I can remain silent no longer. Dear Miss Montague, I have a great regard for you—indeed, I have gone so far as to befriend your brother, not for his sake but your own, since it is apparent that his presence grates on your nerves." He smiled. "Too, I did not wish that Maurice should remove you from Town."

"It is very good of you," replied Mignon, no little bit surprised. What next? she wondered. She was not to be kept long in suspense.

"No, it was not good of me," retorted Lord Barrymore wryly. "It was entirely self-interested. Let me finish, Mignon, before Maurice makes an appearance and another opportunity is lost. I am not one for romantic effusions but I'm sure we would deal well together. If you would consent to be my wife, I believe it would make me the happiest man alive."

Mignon stared, as stunned as if a piece of furniture had suddenly spoken to her. "I am truly sensible of the honor you do me," she murmured.

"And you are very much obliged!" Tolly recited angrily. "Fustian, my dear. I will not press you for an answer. This is neither the time nor the place."

True, thought Mignon. Few damsels could claim to have received a proposal of marriage in the entry hall while waiting for their brother to descend. "Nevertheless," she said, "you have paid me a great compliment, and I must count myself honored by it. I regret that I cannot give you an answer now, but I do not know my own mind."

"Don't trouble yourself." Lord Barrymore cast a distracted glance at the staircase. Various irascible noises indicated that Maurice was about to descend. "For now, it is enough to know you do not hold me in disdain."

Mignon had no wish to meet her brother and undergo yet another scold. With the slightest of curtseys she turned away and proceeded at a good pace down the hallway. Lord Barrymore's proposal had affected her more strongly than she would have thought possible, for during it he had revealed himself as another, more appealing man. Had she always been prone to such errors of judgment? Odd that she had never before noticed that Tolly possessed qualities admirable in a husband: gentleness and strength, concern and tolerance. What did it matter if Lord Barrymore didn't send her senses reeling or her pulse fluttering? *He* at least would never idly gamble his wife's fortune away.

Dulcie, clad in a rose silk gown with embroidered bands and a lacy frill around the neck, was seated beneath the stained glass window in her Grand Saloon. Sunlight streaming through the colored glass caused a rainbow to nestle among her pink curls. "My husband," she remarked to her captive audience, pausing only briefly as Mignon stepped into the room, "is currently on Elba, where he is being treated firsthand to an explanation of Napoleon's code of etiquette, a manual of manners eight hundred pages long. Bat confirms Castlereagh's misgivings that the island is too small to contain Napoleon's restless energy, and too close to the mainland to prevent his hearing all the latest news." She stretched out a ruby-laden arm to the circular table beside her chair. On this sat the orange cat and a skull brought for some inexplicable reason from the Armory. "Did you know that in Dresden the living are thrown with the dead into the river? Death is all around us. But at last I know who *our* murderer is. Shortly these misdeeds will be solved, and their perpetrators brought to light. And to trial!"

Alarmed by the sound of rattling china, Mignon took the tea tray from Charity, who had followed her into the room. "Silly twit!" reproved the Baroness. The maidservant fled.

Mignon set down the tea tray on the table by her aunt, where it made a bizarre arrangement in juxtaposition with the skull and the tomcat. Neatly avoiding so much as a glace at Viscount Jeffries, she retired to a far corner of the room and seated herself near one of the tall velvet-draped windows. Tolly, she thought, would never have treated a lady so shamefully. Bluebeard, hanging upside down from the draperies, crooned tunelessly into her ear.

Dulcie appeared to be in fine fettle judging from her energetic manner. This happy state did not extend, however, to the rest of her household. Gibbon, who had been freed from his handcuffs by his knowledgeable mistress, labored in a state of severe perturbation, terrified lest Crump appear to take him under arrest. Culpepper, having overindulged in champagne the night before, had so grievous an indisposition that she winced and blanched at the slightest noise. Nor were Dulcie's guests possessed of merrier spirits.

Viscount Jeffries looked as grim as the dread reaper, while Willie was sunk in deepest gloom.

"Culpepper!" The Baroness jerked her lovely pink head toward the door. Her abigail exited. "Now," said Dulcie, beaming upon her guests, all of whom had been presented with tea, "we will get down to business. Jessop, 'twould be vastly diverting to hear how you came by that bruise."

Absently, the Viscount touched his cheek, and Mignon stared fixedly into space. "An inconsequential encounter," he replied brusquely. "Nothing to signify except that Crump thought it resulted from a struggle with Zoe." He set aside the teacup that had been pressed into his reluctant hand. "You say you know the murderer. Will you name him, Lady Bligh?"

"No," retorted the Baroness baldly, and reached for the skull which she deposited in her lap. Piqued, Casanova thudded to the floor and draped himself across Ivor's gleaming boots. "Tell me more about your interview at Bow Street."

Lord Jeffries looked as though he wished to refuse. "Crump was sure I had murdered Zoe and her maid and made a good case around the blood stains on my clothing. He was not particularly inclined to believe I'd obtained them when I knelt by Zoe's body to ascertain if she was dead." A muscle twitched in his lean jaw. "Fortunately, Sir John was a trifle less credulous. As he pointed out, I could have escaped without Crump ever seeing me, had I so wished."

"You could also," mused the Baroness, absently inserting a slender finger into the skull's eyesocket, "have acted precisely as you did in an effort to appear sublimely innocent."

"That," remarked Ivor, with a lowering glance, "is precisely what Crump said."

Dulcie's enigmatic eyes rested on him, then moved to her niece. "Mignon! Jessop is in need of some stimulant, I believe. You will find brandy in the sideboard." She smiled at the Viscount. "My husband is not a patient man, and uninclined to wait for servants to fulfill his various whims." She looked rather nostalgic. "Hence there are bottles of brandy and other delicacies readily available in practically every room of Bligh House."

Miss Montague complied grudgingly. With hands that were not quite steady, she opened the rosewood cupboards, lined with brass inlaid in a honeysuckle motif, and extracted both a decanter of brandy and a crystal glass, which she placed on a table at Lord Jeffries' elbow.

"Mignon," observed her aunt, "you are looking fagged to death. You take things a great deal too seriously, child!"

"It's nothing." Miss Montague was very conscious that Ivor's eyes rested on her face, pale and shadowed from a sleepless night. She was briefly tempted to announce that, in the space of twenty hours, she had received a threat of ravishment from a handsome actor, an offer of marriage from an earl, and a proposal of a less honorable sort from a man who might well be a murderer. "I suppose I am not accustomed to keeping such late hours."

"One must expect to encounter various small inconveniences in the pursuit of justice," reproved the Baroness. "Do sit down, my dear, before you fall asleep on your feet. Now, Jessop! Continue with your tale. How did you persuade John to let you go free?"

Lord Jeffries' gaze followed Mignon across the room as he replied. "By showing him the note that I received from Zoe, in which she said she'd been bribed to disprove my alibis. Crump could hardly deny that she had written it, since he had one himself, and in the same handwriting."

"They underestimated her loyalty." Lady Bligh clasped her hands on the skull's gleaming dome. "What else did the note say?"

Ivor's smile was so lackluster that it resembled that of the death's head. "That, much as she could use the money, Zoe would not play me false. She asked my protection, fearing her refusal would bring unpleasant consequences."

"You did not believe her," Dulcie stated in stern tones. "I fear, Jessop, that a lack of faith in the fair sex is among your chief shortcomings!"

Scowling, the Viscount ran a hand through his red-gold hair. "I had the note too late," he responded, "to do other than I did. It was directed to my home. My valet, a most discerning individual, suspected it might contain something of import, and delivered it to me here." His gaze was unfriendly. "You may confirm that if you wish! Bow Street has already done so."

"Oh, do come out of the sullens!" snapped Lady Bligh. "Were the various members of your family not so quick to take offense, we would not be in this fix." She eyed her butler, who was so terrified of reprisals from Bow Street that he leaned in a most unbutlerlike manner against the marble fireplace. "Gibbon?"

He started, then struggled mightily for self-control. With shaking hands, he reached into his pocket. Without comment, Lord Jeffries retrieved his snuffbox from Gibbon's extended hand. "This," mused the Baroness, "is a trifle too much. In the matter of planting incriminating evidence, our villains are greatly overplaying their hand."

Miss Montague was a discerning girl, except in matters of the heart, and thus concluded that Lord Jeffries' snuffbox had been left in Zoe's home. Had it been placed there on purpose or left behind in careless oversight? Were Ivor and his mother being made to look the villains—or were they guilty indeed? It seemed to Mignon that Dulcie might have spoken more truly than she knew when she said that the evidence was overwhelmingly against Leda Langtry and the Viscount, so much so that it seemed false. Was it a case of maligned innocence? Or was it only meant to seem so?

"How progressed your endeavors?" inquired Lady Bligh of her butler. "Before you were interrupted by Crump? I vow the man may be clever, but he is on the way to becoming a curst nuisance." She frowned. "Well? Do not bother to explain to me how it was that you were caught."

Gibbon was a picture of chagrin. "I found nothing, my lady," he said, and drew from another pocket a packet of letters. "Save these."

"Those are hardly of interest," said the Baroness, with marked disapproval, "though excessively foolish. Give them to Mignon, if

you will. The King bought back various of Prinny's letters for
£5,000, though the bond was later canceled." Miss Montague,
recognizing her own handwriting, felt as if for the first time in her
life she might swoon. "Disappointing," mourned Dulcie, "but no
more than I expected. Reward yourself, Gibbon, with a flag's
worth of lightning." She smiled at her dumbfounded niece. "That,
my dear, is four pence worth of gin."

Mignon felt it incumbent upon her, considering the various
speculative glances that were being cast in her direction, to speedily
change the subject. "If Lord Jeffries is innocent," she said deliberately, "then who did kill Zoe?"

"As I have said," replied the Baroness, "they have overplayed
their hand. Zoe had to die, of course, once they had been so foolish
as to approach her, and once she had so nobly refused, but they
acted with too much haste and made a sad botch of the thing."
The Baroness continued: "There is another possibility, one that I'm
sure Bow Street has considered: you yourself could have killed Zoe,
Jessop, after forcing her to write those notes."

"When could he have done it?" queried Mignon, despite her
extreme reluctance to do anything to help the man. He was
remarkably cool, she thought, about the brutal murder of a woman
who had been his mistress for several years. "Lord Jeffries was with
us at the theatre, and then later here."

"Brilliant!" cried Lady Bligh, throwing her arms into the air
with such uninhibited enthusiasm that the skull tumbled from her
lap and rolled gruesomely across the floor with Casanova in animated pursuit. "I applaud your acumen, Mignon! Of course that is
how the thing was done. There was more than ample time between our departure from the theatre and our reconvening here.
Not that we can prove it, for there is no way of telling precisely
how long Zoe had been dead before her body was discovered."

Mignon stared, the letters crushed in her cold fingers. Was
Dulcie saying that Ivor *was* a murderer?

Willie gazed upon the skull that had come to rest at his feet,
and sighed. "One thing I can tell you," he offered un-

enthusiastically. "Zoe truly was offered bribery, and some days before her death." He glanced unhappily at the Viscount. "It seems she at first agreed to it, then later changed her mind." When he encountered the Baroness's steely gaze, he shook like a blancmange. "I know no more! Gossip travels fast in theatrical circles, Lady Bligh, and much of it must be discounted."

"You know," Dulcie retorted, "a great deal more than is good for you, Willie! Had I a less magnanimous nature, I would leave you to Bow Street." The skull being out of reach, she leaned over and drew the orange cat into her lap. Casanova rolled over on his back, purring loudly in an excess of ecstasy. "We have limitless suspects, it seems. By pausing in transit between the theatre and Bligh House, any of our guests could have killed Zoe. Even my nephew is not beyond suspicion, for he arrived here belatedly."

The letters dropped from Mignon's hands to the floor. "Maurice?" she gasped. "He was late because he escorted Mrs. Harrington-Smythe to her home!"

"No, he did not," said Willie, unhappily recalling the words of the craniologist and wondering who among Lady Bligh's guests of the previous evening had such a highly-developed murderer's ridge. "I cannot say with whom the lady left, but she was not in your brother's company."

"Oh, no, Dulcie!" cried Mignon. "What reason could Maurice have? You cannot think him a murderer!"

"Can I not?" mused the Baroness, up to her wrists in orange cat fur. "Perhaps you are correct. But your brother, dear Mignon, may have more motive than you think." Abruptly she stood, and Casanova tumbled protesting to the floor. "That will be all! I thank you all for coming, but have no more need of you today." In the general exodus, Mignon too made an escape to the privacy of her room.

"Culpepper," said the Baroness, when she and her abigail were alone. "How did it go?"

Culpepper, who had spent the past hour in a stern vigil in the hallway outside the Grand Saloon, reached into the bodice of her drab gown and drew forth a string of pearls. She held them as if they were hot coals. Lady Bligh quirked an inquiring brow and the abigail nodded. "Where you said, my lady," she murmured. "That's not all. The house of that opera dancer was robbed, but in such haste that half the valuables were left behind."

"An afterthought." Dulcie picked up the skull. "Very interesting. Culpepper! You may go."

Silence descended rapidly upon Bligh House as its occupants, with some exceptions, resumed their various pursuits. Chief among these exceptions was Gibbon, who had locked himself in the butler's pantry in anticipation of a siege by Bow Street. Culpepper was stretched out like a corpse on her narrow bed, a damp cloth on her aching brow; and Miss Montague, having torn up the letters that had caused her so much trouble, had cried herself to sleep clutching one of her aunt's priceless Persian dolls.

The Baroness, however, was not so easily prostrated by adversity. She sat at a dainty writing desk, the surface of which was cluttered with sheets of pristine foolscap. Bluebeard slumbered atop the grinning skull, and Casanova made desultory swipes at the inkwell. Scowling, Lady Bligh tugged at an unpinned pink curl. Literary or deductive brilliance did not come easily that day. "Hell and the devil confound it!" cried Dulcie, and threw down her pen.

Chapter Twenty-Five

Crump had passed an exhausting forty-eight hours, beginning
with a journey to the races in the wake of Maurice Montague and
Lord Barrymore. There he viewed a wide heath covered with
herds of racehorses showing their paces in a morning promenade.
He had followed his instincts back to London, where he lately saw
Lady Bligh blithely enter a certain apartment in the Albany, to
which she apparently had a key. The purpose of this visit remained
unclarified, for the Baroness was inside only brief moments before
she exited again, nearly catching Crump with his eye to the keyhole. The place looked unexceptional enough, he thought, save for
the shocking paintings on the walls. The Runner could not be
expected to recognize Mars and Venus sporting on a couch, or
Cleopatra with Antony's head on her naked bosom, but he knew
what he liked, and scenes of such perversion were not among them.
Nor obtained he any enlightenment from the manager of the hotel:

the name of the gentleman who leased those apartments meant nothing to Crump.

After that came a visit to Leda Langtry in Newgate, which could not be said to have improved the Runner's frame of mind. Leda obviously nurtured scant reverence for the law and had laughed in his face when he pointed out the seriousness of her situation. But she had at last revealed the source of her income. Part of it was her divorce settlement, part of it payment rendered in return for Leda's resumption of her maiden name and renunciation of all further claim on the Jessop family. It seemed an odd concession for so spirited a female to have made; Crump would have thought it far more characteristic had Leda made an all-out effort to trample the noble Jessops in the mud. Yet the Runner was convinced she was telling the truth. For once, he thought sourly.

Even then Crump was not allowed to rest, for he was forced to sally forth on information received that there was to be a duel between two gentlemen at Wormwood Scrubs. The Runner had arrived in good time, interrupting the contestants in an astonishingly forceful manner and whisking them off to Bow Street. Sir John read them the usual severe reprimand and then released them. He tried to convince himself that the mere fact of having been taken before the Chief Magistrate would dissuade the duelists from trying again.

Only then had Crump been free to retire, and little enough sleep he'd found, with unanswered questions and visions of battered corpses whirling through his brain. With Zoe's death, this case had taken on a more personal aspect for him. The Runner did not lament the death of a man like Warwick, from all accounts a damned cold fish, or the reclusive Mary Elphinstone, but he regretted Zoe's. She had been a lively lass, and might have looked forward to several prosperous years before she met the fate of others of her kind, from starvation, the pox, or the hands of a drunken lout whom she'd picked up on the streets. Crump was not alone in his displeasure. Lord Jeffries had offered a staggering reward for the capture of Zoe's murderer.

This generous gesture could have been the cleverest of ploys, equal to the other strokes of genius that characterized this case, but Crump had begun to entertain doubts. If he took Jeffries and Leda at their words, it was evident that someone had seen in them excellent scapegoats, and in him a supreme dupe. But why Leda? mused the Runner. Had she been merely convenient due to her antagonism to Warwick, or was there some more sinister reason for her involvement?

Yet if there were any truth in his reflections, then all previous conclusions were false. If not Leda, who was behind these robberies? It was clear to Crump that the crimes had been planned by a person of no little brilliance and executed by underlings. That very day the Runner, pausing to catch his breath in a filthy and rat-infested grog shop, had heard rumors of a daring plan to rob the Bank of England. If only the Chief Magistrate were less skeptical, but Sir John didn't believe a word of it. To Crump, the rumors had the ring of truth.

If Leda was innocent, he thought, then what of Willie, who obviously was not? Crump would have frightened the truth from that sly fellow, had not the Baroness persuaded Sir John to let him go free. Crump was well aware that Willie possessed information that could prove illuminating to Bow Street; he would have spared no efforts to loosen Willie's tongue, with red-hot pincers if need be. He frowned. And what of that accursed handkerchief he'd found at White's, with its intricate monogram that even experts could not decipher? One thing was certain: The monogram did not match the initials of anyone suspected in this case. Crump sighed. Perhaps his best course would be to cast aside all his conclusions and to start over again. Methodically going through the calendar of crimes—the robberies of White's, Rundle and Brydges, Lady Coates; the murders of Lord Warwick, Mary Elphinstone and Zoe—he walked down St. James's Street to Bligh House.

Had the Runner been less well-acquainted with the eccentric workings of that establishment, he would have been shocked to be admitted not by one of Lady Bligh's countless servants, but by Miss

Montague, clad in a spotted cambric dressing gown, her red hair making a wild, unruly halo around her head.

"Mr. Crump," she said, with an odd lack of animation. "Thank heavens you've come. My aunt is in her Sitting Room."

Crump, teeth clamped around his unlit pipe, followed Mignon down the hallway. She was a deuced good-looking young woman, he thought with some surprise, for all that her eyes were deeply shadowed and her features drawn as if from some great anxiety.

Crump stepped into the Hymeneal, and into a circus scene. Culpepper, hair hidden beneath a huge mob cap, held a sleepy-looking Charity by the ear; Maurice, clad in a garish silk dressing gown, brandished an ancient blunderbuss and spoke with great enthusiasm to the room at large. Miss Montague, as if her legs would no longer support her, had leaned against a massive marble topped sidetable and was staring fixedly at a tasteful arrangement of yellow canary feathers and crepe under glass, all that remained of Bluebeard's predecessor. By a window stood Gibbon, impeccable in his butler's livery but frantically wild-eyed. In his arms was the huge orange cat, which was eyeing with malevolent intent the blue macaw that perched on the back of the chair where Lady Bligh sat enthroned. The Baroness gazed impassively at the portrait of her spouse which dominated the room.

Maurice turned to stare owlishly at the Runner. "Hallo, Mr. Crump!" he said in slurred tones. "I damned near caught a robber, don't you know?"

"Correction, Maurice," the Baroness interrupted severely. Crump cautiously eyed the burnished barrel of Maurice's blunderbuss. "*I* damned near caught a robber, and would certainly have done so had you not intervened."

"Ungrateful," muttered Maurice, then beamed. "One must protect one's womanfolks! No need to thank me, it was only my duty."

Crump, to whom it had rapidly become apparent that the Honorable Maurice was drunk as a lord, cautiously drew forth his Occurrence Book. "There was an attempt at robbery?"

"Robbery?" Maurice blinked rapidly, as if he encountered diffi-

culty focusing on his surroundings. "Nothing of the sort! It was all
aboveboard. The betting post stood about one hundred paces from
the goal, and there the betters assembled after they'd seen the horses
saddled and had thoroughly examined all circumstances of the race.
What a noise and clamor! Peers and livery servants, sharpers and
black legs! Each called aloud his bet, and when it was taken,
entered it in his pocketbook. All straightforward and unexceptionable, I assure you!"

"Maurice!" Mignon wrested the musket from her brother's
hands. "You are making an ass of yourself! Kindly hold your
tongue."

"As you may have noticed, Crump," remarked the Baroness,
"my nephew is a trifle foxed. It is most vexatious and ill-timed of
him." Culpepper, features grim with disapproval, glanced at the
maidservant beside her. Charity looked to be asleep on her feet,
and Culpepper yanked her ear.

"If we may get down to business?" said Crump, not best pleased
to see that weapon in Mignon's hands. "I assume it was Mr.
Montague who discovered the burglary?"

"It was." Maurice preened. "I'd stepped outside to blow a
cloud—for it is the perfect ending to a good evening, you know,
and we dined at an excellent inn run by a French *émigré* on an
excellent light supper of cold meats and fruit." He frowned, having
lost his train of thought. "Tolly allowed me to see his racehorses in
the stable, did I say? A signal honor indeed."

"You have told us that, several times," interrupted Mignon.
"Try and concentrate, Maurice! You had stepped outside to smoke
a cigar."

"I did?" In a supreme effort at concentration, Maurice scowled
dreadfully, "Ah, yes! I saw the intruder slip through the gardens
and into the Ballroom. Naturally, I sped thither as quick as my
legs would carry me, grasping a weapon from the Armory, and
sounded the alarm!" He looked fuzzily in the general direction of
his aunt. "I cannot conceive how the scoundrel entered, unless the
servants failed to lock up. Shocking negligence!"

"Not at all!" snapped the Baroness. "Those doors were left open on my instructions. How else would a thief gain admittance? The keys to this house are not only kept under close guard, they were fashioned by the incomparable Joseph Bramah, whose ingenuity has defied three generations of lock pickers! Unless I wish it so, no intruder may enter Bligh House."

Crump gazed unhappily at Dulcie, enfolded in a shawl of English cashmere that must have measured at least six yards long. He supposed he should not have been surprised at anything the Baroness did, and in truth he found it no matter of astonishment that she had dyed her hair pink, or that beneath the shawl she wore naught but the sheerest of nightgowns; but unless the Runner was to doubt the fidelity of his own ears, Lady Bligh had *wished* to be robbed, which exceeded even his credulity. He shifted his weight uncomfortably.

"Poor Crump," sympathized Dulcie. "You are quite worn out with fuss, fatigue and rage! We must delay you no longer with our little disagreements, having already been so inconsiderate as to drag you from your bed. Pray continue with your questions! We will do our utmost to help you nose out our would-be robber."

The Runner saw no reason to believe any assurances offered by a lady who was in the practice of daily dissimulation, but he persevered. "Perhaps we should determine," he said, "if anything was taken, though it looks as if your robber was frightened off too soon. It might be a good idea if everyone searched his room."

"An excellent notion!" applauded Lady Bligh. "It has already been done."

Crump was speedily becoming aware that he was out of his element. What underhanded machinations was the Baroness involved in now? "And?" he asked patiently.

One by one they assured him that their belongings had not been disturbed. Crump looked last at the silent maidservant, whose eyelids had once more closed. Culpepper shook the girl vigorously. "Charity!" Her efforts had little effect until Lady Bligh took a hand. Briskly Dulcie removed fresh-cut flowers from a vase and emptied the water over Charity's head.

The maid's eyes flew open, and in them was a look of utter astonishment. "Charity," demanded the Baroness, "Bow Street is here to make inquiries. Is anything missing from your room?" But the maidservant was of little help. succumbing promptly to hysterics, drumming her heels on the floor and shrieking like a banshee. All but Lady Bligh stared, appalled.

"Good God!" said Maurice, roused from his trancelike abstraction by the din. "What a caterwauling! Has someone died?"

"Someone may!" announced Culpepper, and slapped the screaming girl, hard. "Now, miss, come down out of the boughs and answer the question. Have you noticed anything missing from your room?"

Charity looked positively ashen, and Crump felt sorry for the homely lass. "I doubt this is necessary," he protested. "Few in her position have anything worth stealing."

"Necessary?" repeated Dulcie absently. "Of course it's necessary. Answer the question, Charity!"

"No, ma'am, nothing," said the maidservant meekly. She looked a sodden mess, with water streaming down her face and dripping from hair so ugly that it might have been a wig. A wig? Crump frowned.

He was given no chance to pursue that errant thought: the Baroness motioned Culpepper and Charity out of the room. "Laudanum," she explained vaguely. "We were determined that the poor girl should enjoy at least one night's good sleep. She is remarkably restless at the best of times." Trailing her shawl and exuding a sweet perfume, she touched the Runner's arm. "You will wish to inspect the means of the villain's entry. Gibbon will escort you."

"Ah, yes, Gibbon!" Crump rocked back on his heels. "Thank you for reminding me, Baroness, that I'm wishful of having a word with that lad, about a certain case of breaking and entering."

"Now, now, Crump!" his hostess interjected hastily. "You must not be worrying poor Gibbon to death! He was only acting on my orders. *I* will provide whatever explanations are necessary to John."

"Why," asked Crump, with little hope of an honest reply, "did you order your butler to engage in housebreaking?" He had even less confidence that Lady Bligh would make a clean breast of things to Sir John.

"Why, I have a voracious craving for knowledge!" replied the Baroness, with an enchanting smile. "I suppose you might consider that Gibbon satisfies my hunger." The butler blushed a furious red. "Go now, the two of you, and inspect the door. Though it was unlocked you may still find some sort of evidence."

"Lady Bligh!" Along with his energies, Crump's patience was exhausted. "One more question, if you will! Have you any idea what your robber might have wished to steal?"

"Bligh House is full of treasures, dear Crump, more than you might think. He might have been after any number of things." Dulcie drew the shawl more tightly around her, as if to combat a sudden chill. "I confess this night's proceedings have been a sad disappointment to me! We can only hope that he will try again."

Chapter Twenty-Six

Miss Montague was in the Gallery, a handsome chamber enlivened by columns of white-and-purple-veined Derbyshire alabaster, walls covered with crimson Norwich damask, and a ceiling modeled after that in Henry VII's chapel in Westminster Abbey. The Gallery housed collections of paintings, marbles, and bronzes that the various Barons Bligh had acquired on their Grand Tours. The mementos that the present Lord Bligh had brought back from *his* Grand Tour could not be displayed so publicly. Maximilian's only addition to this room had been a vivacious portrait of Dulcie at the age of eighteen.

Mignon herself was as artfully arranged as her surroundings. She wore a very becoming tobacco brown velvet tunic, trimmed with pearl beads and yellow disks, over a white muslin gown. Her red hair was caught back in a fashion that accentuated her high cheekbones and drew attention to her huge green eyes. The effect was slightly spoiled, however, by her scowl.

"My aunt is not here," she said rudely, "having gone to confer with Sir John. And Maurice is keeping an appointment with Prinny's dentist, having presented himself a fortnight ago and finally having been granted an audience. You have wasted your time in coming here. I suggest you depart immediately."

Lord Jeffries, as Miss Montague speedily learned, was very difficult to snub. "Excellent!" he replied smoothly. "Since it was you I wished to speak with, and privately."

Mignon risked a glance at him, then wished she had not. The Viscount looked remarkably fine in his great coat with its deep capes and long wide sleeves, his beaver hat and black leather boots. He also looked to be in a dangerous temper. She lowered her eyes to the handsome Moorfield carpet. "I cannot see, sir, that there remains anything to discuss."

"Then I must open your eyes." The great coat and hat were deposited abruptly on a plump festooned settee. "You see, Miss Montague, Willie has been induced to confess to me who commissioned those forged banknotes."

"Oh?" Mignon was icily polite. "You terrorized the poor man, I suppose." She looked now at the painted glass window which bore the Bligh coat of arms, an eagle and a calgreyhound—a rare monster with the head of a wildcat—on a field of sanguine, with the motto *Cave*, "beware." "What has that to do with me?"

"How well you play the innocent!" Lord Jeffries was so contemptuous that Mignon could only stare at him. "We will go on much better if you refrain from telling me any more Canterbury tales!"

Miss Montague devoutly longed for the musket that she had returned to the Armory. "I haven't the faintest notion," she protested, "what you're talking about."

"You seem to have equally little notion," retorted Ivor, "of what happens to females who follow the path you tread. Do you fancy turning Haymarket-ware, a straw damsel to be sold to the highest bidder? Perhaps I should take you on a tour of St. Giles, one of

London's foulest rookeries, a city of vice within the Metropolis. Or introduce you to Mother Windsor, a notable procuress in King's Place."

Had Mignon been less stubborn, she might have informed Lord Jeffries that he was laboring under a severe misapprehension. Miss Montague might have in the past acted with less than prudence, but she was far from a Paphian girl. However, Mignon had a temper as fiery as her hair. "You forget my fortune!" she reminded him. "I am not yet at my last prayers."

"The question is academic," snapped Ivor, propping one muscular leg on a delicate footstool. "You will be hanged before you can turn into a fubsy-faced old maid. It might behoove you, Miss Montague, to listen to the proposition I mean to make you."

"Hanged!" echoed Mignon, turning pale. She searched his face for some sign that he engaged in a monstrous jest, but found only cold resolution there.

"I have told you I know who paid Willie to forge those banknotes," Lord Jeffries said impatiently. "Consequently, I know who was responsible for the robberies." His steely eyes stabbed her. "For the murders as well, of course, though I do not suspect you of *those*. If I did, I would hardly propose to save your neck!"

"Wait." Mignon's hand flew to her throat. "You make serious accusations, sir. On what grounds?"

Ivor's booted foot thudded heavily to the floor. "Your self-possession is vastly edifying. But someone unjustly accused would hardly be so cool."

Mignon said nothing, having prudently taken refuge behind the plump settee. The Viscount stood firmly between her and the doorway, barring any avenue of escape. Miss Montague longed desperately for rescue. Was she to meet violence—or worse!—at the hands of this devilish unpleasant lunatic?

He looked as though he wished to strangle her. "I would not have suspected this of you, Miss Montague, did I not have proof."

No, reflected Mignon bitterly, he would only think her a baggage who'd thrown her hat over the windmill and consequently had turned bachelor's fare. "Proof of what, my lord?" she asked, assuming a calmness she did not feel.

"Proof that you have been involved in all these crimes, by keeping your cohorts informed of your aunt's progress in tracking them down." His expression was as severe as ever Sir John's could have been. "Proof that you let Leda go to prison, knowing she was innocent."

Mignon's head whirled. "My aunt," she said, grasping at the only sane words she'd thus far heard. "Think you my aunt wouldn't know of it, if what you said was true? Or do you suspect her also of complicity?"

"Of course not." Ivor made an annoyed gesture. "Lady Bligh may very well know of your guilt, and seek to somehow extricate you. She did warn me against you, after all! Or she may be, as I very nearly was, taken in by your clever act. If so, she will suffer greatly for her misjudgment! I wonder you can reconcile it with your conscience, Miss Montague!"

"I think I must not have one," retorted Mignon, fingernails digging into the upholstery of the settee. "How could I, and be involved in robbery and murder? At least you do not think me capable of shooting Warwick, or bludgeoning women to death. I suppose I should thank you for having such supreme confidence in me." She glowered at him. "You have not thought, Jeffries! What is to prevent me, now that you have found me out, from having my 'cohorts' dispose of you? Since I collect you have come to me with your suspicions instead of proceeding to Bow Street?"

"So you threaten me!" The Viscount wore a stern mask. "It is you who have not considered, Miss Montague! I am a wealthy man—wealthy enough to buy you freedom, of a sort."

"Freedom!" Mignon's temper strained violently at its tight leash. "You offer to buy me freedom when I have conspired to send your mother to Newgate. What sort of a man *are* you, Lord Jeffries?"

"Freedom of a *sort*," corrected the Viscount. "You will pay, and dearly, for any harm you have done Leda." Mignon's lips parted and he motioned her to silence. "Are you thinking you may buy yourself off? You cannot. A fortune you may have, but not sufficient influence to hush up the thing so completely that it never reaches the ears of the Quality. You might contrive to escape the hangman's noose, Miss Montague, but your reputation would be gone."

"Ah, my fortune." To hide the trembling of her hands, Mignon folded her arms. "Just what *is* your proposition, Lord Jeffries? I might tell you that I care little for the opinion of the *ton*. Persons of the first consideration are so often very dull."

"I am offering you," said Ivor stiffly, "the protection of my name."

"Oh? How prodigiously kind of you." Mignon's smile resembled a snarl. "In return you gain control of my fortune and an excessively obedient wife, for if I ever threaten to run counter to your wishes, you will menace me with exposure. A sad comedown for a girl who wished for herself a love match."

"You can hardly expect from me declarations of devotion and adoration!" There was a distinctly feral gleam in Lord Jeffries' brown eyes. "The truth is that I want you, and at any price."

"I see." Mignon was thoroughly shaken. Fool, to have fallen in love with a man who, if he wasn't a murderer, was undeniably mad! She inched around the settee. "Since you are so desirous of settling in matrimony, Lord Jeffries, I suggest you might find a more fitting mate among the ladies of St. Giles, or the Haymarket, or King's Place! You see, I would rather go to Newgate than marry you." On this Parthian shot, she scrambled out from behind the settee and bolted for freedom.

But Miss Montague, having burned her bridges behind her in a gloriously foolhardy style, was to be allowed no respite. No sooner had she gained the hallway than she ran smack into Charity. "I must speak with you," hissed the maidservant, who'd obviously been eavesdropping outside the door.

"Very well," replied Mignon, with a sinking heart. "In my room." Mignon grabbed Charity's arm, fearing that Viscount Jeffries would at any moment burst through the Gallery door.

"Whatever you say, miss." Charity's voice was servile, but her plain features wore a decided smirk. Once inside Mignon's bedchamber, the maidservant closed the door.

"Frittering away your chances, aren't you, miss?" she asked maliciously. "First Jesse, then Barrymore, and now Jeffries."

Mignon sank down on the bed. "You go beyond the line of being pleasing, Charity. Do you wish me to report your behavior to my aunt?"

Uncowed, the maid tossed her head. "Hoity-toity!" she mocked. "You won't tell the Baroness, being afraid I'll tell her what I heard. I wouldn't care if I was turned off anyway, me being used to better things."

Miss Montague took little objection to this insolence, her thoughts being otherwise engaged. "You mentioned Jesse," she said faintly. "I suppose you read the notes I had from him."

"I didn't need to." Charity picked up one of the Persian dolls. "Knowing already what they said. You were a fool to try and play a May game with Jesse, thinking he'd let you be shabbing off and making a cake of him."

"Dear heaven!" gasped Mignon, rather idiotically. "You know Jesse?"

"Haven't I just said so?" Charity's expression was unpleasant. "Jesse's a gentleman, he is, and he'll keep mum about what's passed between you. Providing you give him a chance to apologize! You're to meet him at his lodgings tonight."

The return of her letters had accomplished precious little, thought Mignon gloomily. Her lost love was proving himself damned tenacious. "And if I refuse?"

"Then I fear you'll regret it." Unconcerned, Charity turned the doll head over heels and inspected its underpinnings. "It makes a good story, the heiress and the actor, doesn't it? I doubt the

Baroness would like the scandal if the tale was published." Again, that knowing smile. "With suitable embellishments."

"I can hardly visit Jesse's lodgings," protested Mignon frantically, though she didn't believe for an instant that he would deliberately do her harm, "without making a byword of myself!" And how on earth had Jesse become acquainted with Charity?

"You're mighty concerned for your name." Mignon winced as the maidservant carelessly tossed the doll aside. "All I can say is if you *don't* go, it's dead certain Jesse will lose his temper again, and you know what that means."

Mignon watched in glum silence as Charity sauntered from the room. It was speedily being borne in on Miss Montague that she had behaved in a skitter-witted fashion indeed.

Chapter Twenty-Seven

"The poor King," remarked Lady Bligh, "is blind and mad and nearly helpless. I saw him myself recently, flitting across the terraces at Windsor in a velvet cap and dressing gown. Do you recall his Jubilee, John?" The Chief Magistrate was given no opportunity to reply. "Debtors were released, Army and Navy deserters pardoned, and an ox was roasted whole at Windsor with one and a half bushels of potatoes in its belly." She brushed dust from the sleeve of her high-collared spencer, made of rich wine-colored velvet fringed with fur and heavy with embroidery. "I suppose we should not be surprised that the King wrote to Young's *Annals of Agriculture* under the name of Ralph Robinson, or kept a model farm at Windsor, or ate brown bread and boiled mutton and turnips for dinner, considering that he was suckled by a gardener's wife! Although that does not explain why he liked nothing better than to make buttons in the days when he was sane."

Sir John was a busy man, his days filled with all the minutiae of law and crime, as well as with the daily sittings which were held from 11 A.M. to 3 P.M. and again from 7 to 8; and he considered it unjust that what few free moments he possessed should be taken up by people who wished to cajole or bully him. He hardly needed to be reminded of Lady Bligh's high connections, of her influence at Court. Nor was Dulcie the first to visit him that day in regard to the Langtry case.

"So Percy finally has been moved to try and save Leda from an ignoble end!" mused the Baroness, toying with the wide brim of her elegant bonnet, which was turned up at the side with a lavish trimming of ribbon and lace. "I thought he might. Came you to any agreement, John?"

"No." The Chief Magistrate recalled that encounter, during which Lord Calvert had exhibited equal parts of blustery indignation and effrontery. "You are mistaken; he came not in behalf of Leda, but of Jeffries. It seems to me that a great many people are very anxious to protect that young man."

"So they are." Dulcie surveyed her one-time beau with an amused, slightly pensive look that caused his mouth to water. "Dear John! I think it is time I was frank with you."

"So do I!" he agreed sincerely, and leaned forward on his desk. "It is hardly the thing for a delicately nurtured English lady to go about hoodwinking representatives of the law. Crump does not appreciate being made to look the fool."

"It would not have been necessary," retorted Lady Bligh, "had not Crump threatened to bungle the thing so completely. To act the dupe has been an edifying experience for him, I'm sure! Don't you wish to hear what I have to tell you?"

Sir John gazed upon the wily Baroness, her captivating features caressed by the dusty rose curls that escaped from beneath the absurd bonnet, her elegant figure displayed to good advantage as she leaned against the back of the old wooden chair. "Of course," he said. "Dulcie, it is unthinkable that you should be involved in these ghastly matters. Confounding as you are, I would not wish anything to happen to you, and your meddling is dangerous. Why do you not content yourself with teas and routs and pleasure trips, and leave the pursuit of criminals to Bow Street?"

"Dear, dear John," murmured the Baroness. "How good of you to concern yourself with my welfare! But back to Jessop. You wished to know why both Leda and Percy are so anxious to protect the Viscount."

As usual, reflected the Chief Magistrate, he had risen, nibbled and swallowed her bait. "I do."

"It is a well-kept secret, and one that would cause considerable scandal were it to be known," Dulcie said gaily, "but Jessop is a legitimate bastard. In short, dear John, he may be Leda's offspring, but he is *not* her husband's son."

The implications of this disclosure were staggering. The Chief Magistrate would have liked to ask a great many questions concerning Ivor's paternity and the means by which Dulcie had resurrected this skeleton from the Jessop closet. However, Willie burst like a tornado into the room.

"I demand protection!" cried that individual, whose homely features were ashen and whose clothing was filthy and torn. "Lud, but things have reached an alarming state when innocent citizens are set upon in the street!"

"Innocent?" repeated Lady Bligh, absently. Her gaze was unfocused. "They really do flatter themselves against all evidence into a belief that they may yet go free."

"They?" inquired Sir John. Willie collapsed sideways onto the chair and craned his neck to stare at the Baroness. "You don't seem very surprised," he said resentfully. "I tell you, I barely escaped with my life! Were I not exceptionally nimble on my feet, I would have already received my death blow." Rather dramatically, he pushed back lank hair to reveal a purplish swelling on his forehead. "Look!"

"An iniquitous act," soothed Lady Bligh, "and one that I confess pleases me beyond measure. In regard to their own impunity, our villains are a great deal too credulous. They are rushing their fences, and most carelessly."

"*Pleases* you!" gasped Willie, goggling with outrage.

"Suppose," interrupted Sir John, not at all anxious to witness high melodrama, "you tell us exactly what happened."

Willie was only too anxious to oblige. He had been taking an idle stroll, he said, his mind busy with plans for his next play, his ears alert for any scurrilous tittle-tattle on the lips of his fellow pedestrians, when he was set upon by footpads and dragged into an alleyway. "Fortunately," said Willie smugly, and drew open his tattered coat to reveal a pistol tucked into his waistband, "I was prepared! I told the thugs that if they advanced one step farther, I would have their lives."

"After which show of bravado," observed Dulcie unappreciatively, "you let them get away. Remarkably impractical of you, Willie!"

Sir John, more than a little intrigued by this tale, or rather by its omissions, leaned forward. "A pistol is hardly a common accoutrement for a journalist and playwright," he observed. "Just why did you feel it necessary to carry a weapon?"

Willie wore the expression of one who realized belatedly that he has leaped from the frying pan into the fire. "These dreadful crimes," he muttered weakly. "A man must protect himself."

"Hogwash!" said the Baroness. "You must know, John, that Willie has been on pins and needles for some time now, barricading himself in his room at night and generally going in fear of his life—and not without reason!" She walked around the chair and stood looking down at the unhappy playwright. "It is time, Willie, that you ceased behaving in this hugger-mugger fashion and admitted the truth."

"Baroness!" wailed Willie, not a little bit alarmed. "What can you mean?"

At that most inopportune of moments, Crump stalked into the room, dragging with him Gibbon, shackled. Upon espying his mistress, the butler moaned. "I warned you," said Lady Bligh sternly, "about that stickpin."

Sir John had a most unmagisterial impulse to flee the scene. When Dulcie was about, the pursuit of justice turned into a raree-show. "What's this about?" he inquired wearily of Crump.

"Passing stolen goods," replied the Runner jovially, the frustrations of the past week largely alleviated by the fact that he had Gibbon in tow. "Namely, one diamond stickpin." He glanced at the Baroness. How had she known? "It seems that Gibbon here is involved somehow in the robberies, since that stickpin is part of the stolen merchandise."

Dulcie returned his gaze, and in a manner that caused Crump considerable unease. "Fiddlesticks!" she said bluntly. "You know perfectly well that my butler is as innocent as a newborn babe."

Gibbon, trying to look the part, succeeded only in presenting a face of perfect guilt. His anxious eyes met those of Sir John and his mouth turned dry as he recalled the unfortunate history of the Chief Magistrate's pocket watch.

"Now, now, Baroness!" said Crump, though with an absence of his earlier geniality. "There's no use trying to put a good face on it! Your butler was caught with stolen goods." His eyes rested on Gibbon's corpse-white face. "Added to his earlier offense of house-breaking, that leads to some very serious conclusions! I'm afraid it's Newgate for you, my lad, if not the gallows. A sad end for a onetime member of Bow Street, but the law must be served."

"Housebreaking?" inquired Sir John.

The Baroness sighed. "I fear that must be laid at *my* door." As seductive as any nautch girl, she undulated across the room. "I will explain all to you, John. I will even recount to you the fascinating history of that stickpin, if only you will release poor Gibbon." To the Chief Magistrate's horror, she sank to her knees by his chair. "All, I assure you, is not as it seems."

Sir John glanced unhappily at the witnesses to this moving scene. Willie gaped open-mouthed; Gibbon's pallid lips moved silently, as if in prayer; and Crump ground his teeth in frustration. Then he looked at Dulcie, whose pleading eyes were suspiciously damp. Once again passion triumphed over reason. "Very well," said the Chief Magistrate wearily. "Crump, release him."

"Now!" Briskly the Baroness rose and brushed dust from her skirts. "Where were we? Ah yes, Willie!" He flinched. "You were going to reveal to us all that you have so carefully concealed."

"You malign me!" mourned Willie, as Crump walked to the window and stared in a disgruntled manner down into the street. "I have held back nothing, I swear. Indeed, I have helped you in every way I can." He glanced rather frantically at Gibbon. "I thought that you were going to explain to Sir John a small matter of stolen goods and housebreaking."

"A small matter, indeed," retorted Dulcie, "in comparison with what *you* have to say. Out with it, Willie! Or do you wish to fall victim to a murderer's blow? I assure you they will try again, for this knowledge of yours is very dangerous." Nervously, he fingered his shattered monocle. The Baroness sighed. "In return for your cooperation, Willie, I offer you the safety of my house."

Under other circumstances, Willie might have been rapturous at the opportunity to be Lady Bligh's cossetted houseguest, but now he only looked more dejected. "But my play!" he remarked inconsequentially.

It was obvious to Crump that these proceedings were leading nowhere. He turned from the window to gaze sourly upon the Chief Magistrate.

"I have come to certain conclusions," the Runner announced abruptly. "They might have some bearing here."

"So they might," remarked the Baroness cheerfully, "and for the most part you are correct. You have been very astute, dear Crump, save in the matter of that monogrammed handkerchief. But we are concerned with other matters at the moment. Willie!"

"Oh, very well." Willie was glum. "I'll tell you who paid me to make those wretched notes. I might as well! Ivor already knows."

"You told *Jessop?*" So extreme was Dulcie's reaction that only Sir John's quick assistance kept her from tumbling off her perch on the arm of his chair. "I hadn't bargained for that. What possessed you, Willie? Now I must contrive a miracle!"

"I thought you were convinced of Jeffries' innocence," interrupted the Chief Magistrate, thoroughly distracted by the contradictory stories.

"Innocence has little to do with it," replied the Baroness, obviously deep in thought. "On consideration, it is not an entirely unfelicitous turn of events." She regarded the Runner, who wore an expression of the deepest disapproval. "On one point you are far off, Crump! The jury will certainly return a flat verdict of 'Not proved' if Leda stands trial."

It occurred to Sir John that he had received no answers to a great many questions that had been raised. Rather diffidently, he mentioned the fact. "Poor John!" murmured Lady Bligh, leaning against his shoulder in a fashion that sent Crump back to the window in outrage. "You must trust me, else your master criminal will go free, and you will be left with only his underlings. You do not wish that, surely?"

"No." What Sir John *did* wish was to clear his office of all but himself and the Baroness, and not for purposes of adminstering the law. "You know, Dulcie, that there is going to be a day of reckoning."

"Yes." Smiling impudently, she pinched his cheek. "Won't it be *fun?* But it must wait." She looked at Willie, now a great deal closer to the door. "When I was a child," she remarked pointedly, "I was privileged to witness a hanging at Tyburn Fields. My nurse and I stood on a stony hill which commanded an excellent view of the gallows and the carts which carried the condemned men, some already in their shrouds, and the Ordinary of Newgate and the black-clad prison chaplains who exhorted confessions from the prisoners so they might publish and sell them. By the gallows gathered soldiers, the sheriff and the executioner. It was quite a thrilling moment when the faces of the condemned men were covered with black cloths—almost as thrilling as when the horses were driven off and they were left dancing in the air." She paused.

"I will not help you, Willie, if you do not cooperate! In fact, I promise that if you are not murdered, you too will hang. Do you mean to pay so great a price to protect your play? If not, give us a name."

Willie's hands fluttered in one last protest. "Have it as you wish!" he murmured gloomily. "Amazing, the convoluted workings of Fate. If not for those accursed banknotes, I doubt I would have made the acquaintance of Jesse Saint-Cyr."

Chapter Twenty-Eight

Mignon sat at the mahogany table and gazed blankly at the bowl of soup in front of her, a cold puréed mixture of asparagus and celery. The Dining Room was a majestic oblong chamber balanced by fluted columns at each end. Niches with dark grounds nicely displayed antique statues of Roman emperors, the Apollo Belvedere and a large bronze of the Dying Gladiator. In arched recesses stood sideboards and ornate cabinets. Miss Montague had little appreciation to spare for this beauty. The deed to Mary Elphinstone's cottage, as well as the jewels that Mignon and Ivor had found there, had been stolen from her room.

"This chamber," remarked the Baroness, as her servants moved around the table with dishes containing a fresh salmon soufflé, a huge and rosy ham, and big round brown potato pies served cold with sweet-sour tomato pickles, "dates back to Bat's Classic period. You will note the Hope moldings of Roman forms."

Maurice and Willie obediently remarked upon the antiquities on display. Mignon glanced up from her untouched plate only to lock eyes with Charity. The maid wore a black stuff gown, with frilled apron and cap, and the look she gave Miss Montague was unquestionably triumphant. Hastily, Mignon addressed herself once more to her food. The meal, though delicious and served in exquisite Wedgwood ware, seemed interminable. Could it have been Charity who had ransacked her room? If so, why?

Mignon was not the only one to feel constrained. Maurice, applying himself in a desultory manner to cheese and salad and raw celery, had no greater appetite. Had not his aunt brought home another houseguest, Maurice would have made his excuses and skipped the meal. It would not do to appear overly eager, of course; gentlemen of the world kept assignations with an indolent sangfroid. He looked at Willie, sitting by the Baroness, eating with appalling gusto and chattering inordinately, and wondered why Dulcie had given this person free run of her home. Maurice wondered, too, why his sister looked so lachrymose.

"Mignon," he whispered, as the servants whisked off the tablecloth and set out an assortment of deep juicy fruit tarts and brandied blackberries. "You are looking quite knocked-up. Are you sure you do not wish to return home?"

Miss Montague started, and little wonder, for this was the first civil word spoken to her by her brother for several days. "No," she replied tersely, out of charity with him. "Don't concern yourself with me, Maurice. I'm sure you have more important considerations with which to occupy your mind."

Maurice was feeling unusually magnanimous. His sister might be a tiresome chit who tended to imprudence, but he was fond of her. "We only wished the best for you," he said awkwardly, "Mama and I. There are any number of fellows on the hang-out for rich heiresses, you know."

Mignon did know, a fact that did not inspire her with any great admiration for her brother's powers of insight. "Don't worry," she replied gloomily, "I don't intend to be talked into any more elopements." Across the room, Charity was busy at a supper Canterbury, a tray that stood on four legs and was partitioned to hold knives and forks, with a round end for plates. "You served me a good turn, Maurice, though it would have been better if you'd called him out and killed him in a duel."

Maurice looked rather surprised at this *volte-face* on the part of his sister. "How could I?" he demanded, "when you refused to tell me who the rotter was?"

"It was then," remarked the Baroness to Willie, who was grimacing at a gaily painted Chelsea tureen in the form of a rabbit, "that the Prince began first to notice me, and to stop his horse and talk with me when he met me in the streets." Mignon glanced at the deep windows with richly paneled shutters that stood about the room. It was not only in the streets outside that villains lurked. She shuddered.

"I hope this means," ventured Maurice cautiously, "that you mean to exercise more prudence in the future."

"How can I behave any way other than properly?" retorted Miss Montague. Constitutionally unable to tell a falsehood, she had learned early to dissemble. "With you forever at my shoulder to see that I do not?"

Equal to any situation, even sibling battles in her dining room, Lady Bligh rose and fetched three decanters—claret, port and madeira—to the table, then sent the servants from the room.

"My play!" lamented Willie. "So brief a burst of glory, so quickly dimmed."

"What do you mean?" asked Mignon, toying with her apricot tart.

"I mean," replied Willie glumly, "that my principal actor is like to find himself in Newgate." Miss Montague's fork clattered to the tabletop.

"Mignon!" The Baroness took command. "There is nothing so vulgar as to make a noise with your eating utensils. Come, child, we will leave the gentlemen to their libations and retire to the drawing room."

Had Miss Montague been less stunned, she might have retorted that it was equally vulgar for a hostess to festoon herself so liberally with jewels that she resembled a sultan's concubine. Instead, she followed her aunt meekly from the table. Willie leaped to open the door. "Never mind," remarked Lady Bligh. "Your play will not expire so prematurely, Willie. Perhaps, like the phoenix, a new triumph may rise from the ashes of the old." Silently the ladies proceeded into the drawing room.

"Now," said Dulcie brightly, sinking into a chair, "we may be private. I think I must visit Paris, my dear. Bat has told me of a celebrated fortune-teller, Mademoiselle Le Normand, who predicted Marie Antoinette's ride to the guillotine, and the French retreat from Moscow simply by consulting the cards."

"You knew all along," Mignon broke in ruthlessly, twisting her hands. "About Jesse, I mean. Who told you? Why didn't you tell me?"

"What a hobble!" sighed the Baroness. Fire flashed from the rubies on her hands. "You must know by now, dear Mignon, that I have an instinct for such things." Her niece received a frown. "It is not such a terrible thing, you know! Fortunately, you rallied your wits in time to prevent a mistake that would have ruined your life."

"And a pretty to-do there was over that!" Mignon sank down onto a footstool near the fire. "It seemed forever that I was locked in my room, with Maurice and our mama constantly badgering me to learn the scoundrel's name. They were unaware of Jesse's existence, for I met him first by chance."

"And after that, in secret." Dulcie's eyes were half closed. "Calf love, my dear! You are the sort of female who must always prefer a rough diamond over a pattern of respectability." She edged about sideways in the chair. "Speaking of rough diamonds, how progress you with the Viscount?" ·

Mignon hugged her knees. "Lord Jeffries' behavior," she said gruffly, "is that of a man who has neither sense, good nature nor honesty. It is not Ivor I wish to discuss, Dulcie! Why did Willie say that Jesse may be imprisoned?"

"Why does Willie say anything?" countered Lady Bligh, looking

remarkably frail. "He is overfond of the sound of his own voice."
Mignon's lips parted and the Baroness raised a protesting hand.
"You are going to be confidential to a degree that almost frightens
me, and I beg you will not! Continue with your observations on
the Viscount's character, if you please."

"I will never have confidence in him," announced Miss Montague, who was suffering an understandable affliction of the nerves.
Any number of people could have gained access to her bedchamber
during Dulcie's party, and any number could have slipped in at
any time during the day. The thief could have been Willie, or
Maurice, or Dulcie herself. But Lady Bligh was obviously unin-
terested in her niece's conclusions, or her difficulties. "Or in any
person who forces him on me! In short, Jeffries is not only depraved, but I strongly suspect he is a voluptuary!"

"Ah!" mused Dulcie. "Sits the wind in that quarter? Were I to
hazard a guess, I would say young Ivor has offered you a slip on
the shoulder. A trifle ill judged of him, but no small compliment,
my dear! Jessop's taste in ladybirds is accounted peerless."

Mignon was saved a reply by Willie's appearance. Looking a
trifle disheveled, he grasped the decanter of port in one hand.
"Maurice wouldn't drink with me," he announced, in tones that
were both regretful and slurred. "Claimed a previous engagement,
but I know he didn't want my company." He weaved across the
room, narrowly avoiding entanglement with a delicately worked
table and a tapestried footstool. "What'd you mean, Baroness,
about my play?"

"There is always old Brahman," suggested Lady Bligh, watching
with overt amusement as Willie tumbled into a chair. "He has
long been first singer at Drury Lane and invariably receives applause."

"Is that the best you can do?" Willie regarded the decanter
gloomily. "Brahman may have great power of voice and rapidity
of execution and a thorough knowledge of music, but he is hardly
a dramatic actor." He hiccuped. "Besides, a more abominable style
is difficult to conceive."

Dulcie laughed. "I was roasting you, Willie," she apologized.

"Since Brahman will not serve, what say you to Edmund Kean?"

Willie had a great deal to say, and the two of them passed a pleasant hour with much mocking and irreverence. Mignon made little contribution to the gaiety, being preoccupied with the perplexing matter of Jesse Saint-Cyr. What among his sins could be so severe that it condemned him to Newgate? It was obvious that Lady Bligh did not mean to enlighten her niece.

Miss Montague stared blindly at her hands, the fingers so tightly interwoven that the knuckles ached. Jesse had been kind to her and an enjoyable companion while his star was on the rise. It was no more than he deserved that she should warn him that he was suspected of some crime. *Crime?* Mignon jumped as if bee-stung. Why had she not thought sooner of Dulcie's fascination with the recent murders and robberies and of her determination to prove Leda innocent? Surely Lady Bligh did not mean that *Jesse* should take her friend's place on the gallows? Miss Montague might sympathize greatly with the unfortunate Leda, though she was by no means convinced that the old woman was innocent. She also might have suffered a great confusion of feelings for Jesse Saint-Cyr; but she would by no means stand idly by while an innocent man hanged, even when the man was so accomplished a deceiver. But *was* Jesse innocent? He had been in Bligh House and could easily have learned the location of her room, as could have Lord Jeffries. Had Ivor, in some perverted spirit of revenge, set Jesse up as a scapegoat? If only Dulcie had seen fit to fill her in on the details!

"I fancy," remarked the Baroness, disrupting Mignon's train of thought, "that we shall do well enough if the thing does not come too suddenly to a crisis." Her dark eyes rested on her niece. "You look exhausted, child, and so am I. I suggest we all retire early."

Mignon made no demur; this fit in excellently with her own half formed plans. She would take her candle from the sideboard that stood in the hallway and light herself to her chamber; then, when the rest of the household was asleep. . . . She glanced at her aunt, who looked exhausted and weak. Better, perhaps, that she had received no opportunity to burden Dulcie with confidences. If

Miss Montague was in a pickle, it was entirely her own fault.

"Mignon." Lady Bligh laid her hand on her niece's arm. "There's no help for it, child; we do what we must. Try and have a good night's sleep. Things will seem brighter on the morrow, I promise you."

Chapter Twenty-Nine

"So you came," said Jesse, his handsome face aglow. "I had hoped you would. I will never forgive myself for the horrid things I said to you."

Mignon neatly avoided his embrace. "You gave me little enough choice!" she replied bitterly. "I begin to think, Jesse, that you have made a cat's-paw of me."

"Ah, no!" He looked sorrowful. "Can I be blamed if the anguish of separation has driven me to desperate measures? Tell me that you have reconsidered, Mignon."

"I have not." Mignon sat down in a mahogany armchair of graceful proportions, with fine details of grooving and reeding in the arms and back. She drew a deep breath. The journey to Crown Court had proven remarkably free of difficulty; she had encountered only a solitary horseman who was apparently inebriated, judging by his inept handling of the reins. "Jesse, I must talk with you."

"Of course." He lounged upon a lacquered wooden settee with a caned seat, gracefully carved arms, turned legs, and well-designed horizontal splats. "You must know, puss, that you may say anything to me."

Yet, had Mignon spoken her mind, he would probably have dealt her physical violence. She thought with amazement of those happier days when he had loaded her with caresses and sworn eternal devotion, days when his touchy temper had seemed a manly thing. Devotion there had been, Mignon realized, but to her fortune rather than to herself. Unhappily she glanced around the room. This expensive hotel with its honeysuckle-worked pilasters, iron balconies, marble flutings and paterae was hardly typical lodgings for an unknown and penniless actor. Her impulse to warn him of impending trouble died. "I'll pay you nothing," she said abruptly.

"Pay me?" Jesse cocked a brow. "Have I mentioned a word concerning payment? How unfeeling you are, Mignon. I vow I don't know what is to become of you if you persist in this wrongheadedness! Have you no thought for the hours we passed together? Very agreeable they were! I doubt your family would find them so at second hand, were the tale of your indiscretions to be on every tongue." He smiled, rather menacingly. " 'Twould be a wonder that cast the other marvels of the Metropolis into the shade."

Mignon looked at him, her suspicions at last confirmed. A pity that behind that handsome face was a mind so small and mean. "If you ruin me," she said carefully, "you must also do yourself harm. My aunt knows the whole story; she will protect me from your slanders as best she can. It is you who have the most to lose, Jesse. Harm me and my aunt will see to it that you never pursue your career again."

Instead of being taken aback he smiled, and with a chilling confidence. "I have others at my disposal," he said cryptically. "Your aunt will say nothing at all."

Mignon opened her mouth to argue but was distracted by a

slight noise. Before Jesse could move to stop her, she was across the room and wrenching open a door. On the floor of the closet lay Viscount Jeffries, apparently unconscious, bound and gagged.

"What have you done?" cried Mignon, working frantically at the ropes, which were only loosely tied. A pulse beat at Ivor's temple. "Thank God he isn't dead!"

"He will be well enough," said Jesse indifferently. "For all it will avail him! You waste your time, puss. He is not likely to revive under your tender ministrations, having been stretched out stiff as a corpse for the past hour."

"Why have you done this?" wailed Mignon, wrenching away the cruelly tight gag. And then she knew. "Dear God," she whispered, sinking back on her heels. "He *was* in this with you, no doubt the ringleader! Is this how you repay him, by playing him false? What now, Jesse? You will leave him to take the whole blame, I suppose?"

"How protective of him you are!" Inexpertly, Jesse took snuff. "And how indignant in his behalf. It appears you are in love with the man, murderer or no."

"Does it?" Mignon countered. "You must know, Jesse, that I left my aunt a note telling her I'd come here, in case you tried to prevent my return."

"I anticipated no less. You may as well expect a miracle, puss, as expect your aunt to save you." He rose, his stern expression belying his honeyed tones, and Mignon shrank back against the Viscount's inert form. "A pity you would not play along with me, Mignon! We might have had a bright future, you and I. Instead, I have been forced to find other means to support my tastes."

"The robberies," whispered Mignon, through frozen lips. Her wretched tongue was indeed her own worst enemy. "I did not think you so clever, Jesse."

"We have had some small success," he admitted, with a trace of his old daredevil grin. "You served me a bad turn, when at the last minute you developed cold feet. I misjudged you grievously, alas! You were willing enough to flirt with danger, but when it came to the sticking point you turned missish, and rather than eloping with me to Gretna Green confessed all to your brother."

"You guessed that!" Mignon felt as though the ground had been cut out from under her feet. To mask her growing fear, she absently chafed the Viscount's wrists.

"Who else could have told him? Though I suppose I must be grateful you did not divulge my name! It was a terrible blow to my pride—and to my pocketbook." Jesse brushed a lock of black hair from his noble brow. "I confess it pleased me beyond measure to serve you an equal turn, making it look as if you have been my accomplice! You would seem the logical choice to abet me in crime, were my guilt to become known. But Bow Street was slow to take up the gambit, even when we so carefully arranged that the gentlemen at Rundle and Brydges could describe you so carefully."

"We?" echoed Mignon. Surely Ivor was not so heartless that in one moment he embraced her and in the next contrived to put her neck in a noose! So stunned was Miss Montague that she merely blinked when hasty footsteps sounded in the corridor and Mrs. Harrington-Smythe burst into the room.

"What the bloody hell are you doing still here?" she demanded, then espied Mignon, crouched by the Viscount. "Well! I don't know when I've seen a more affecting scene. Jeffries is hardly in the pink of perfection now, is he, miss? I didn't think he'd be overpowered so easily."

"Good God!" gasped Mignon, recognizing that nasal whine. "Charity!" There was scant resemblance between this dark-haired woman, elegant in a traveling outfit of sapphire velvet and fur, and Lady Bligh's homely maid.

"It went well?" Jesse grasped a heavy reticule that dangled from the woman's wrist. "The Baroness?"

"Deep in the sleep of the innocent." Charity wrenched away and moved to a bowfronted mahogany chest with inlaid shell ornaments. She yanked open one of the drawers and emptied into it the contents of her reticule. Mignon saw papers and jewels, among them the note she had penned to Dulcie and a lovely string of pearls. "Which she is not! Even so, I've no stomach for what's planned. I'm getting out while I can."

"It's a little late for that." Jesse watched as Charity extracted a handful of glittering gems from the drawer. "Where the devil did you get those?"

"Where do you think?" Charity stuffed the jewels into her bodice. "From a certain gentleman. As to the Baroness, I've done *my* part. I slipped the drug into her food easily enough."

"He *gave* them to you?" Jesse appeared stunned.

Charity's glance was unfriendly. "Of course not. You may be fool enough to follow instructions and wait patiently for your share. I'm not!" She looked at the Viscount, still motionless and prone. "A pity that Jeffries is fated for so ignoble an end. He was an extraordinarily fine-looking figure of a man."

"You mean to kill Dulcie," said Mignon, not caring to dwell upon Charity's assessment of the Viscount. "Why?"

"She knows enough to hang us all." Charity's voice was cold. "The interfering bitch! They'll prove nothing, now that we have you and Jeffries." Her eyes like ice, she looked at Mignon. "You may blame only yourself, miss, though that will bring you little comfort! If not for you, Jesse would never have come to London, and we would not have fallen into this mess. But no, you had to run scared, and he had to have your fortune. It was a cursed day when you met my cousin."

"Your cousin." Mignon wondered why she had not guessed before. The resemblance was obvious.

"Aye." Charity cast a disgusted glance at him. "My cousin, who wished to marry a fortune. I took the job at Bligh House to keep an eye on you for him, not dreaming where it would lead us." She looked back, maliciously, at Mignon. "It seems fair, doesn't it, since you landed my cousin in the suds, that I should repay you by eloping with your brother?"

"Maurice?" Mignon's voice was faint.

"Maurice." Charity tossed her head. "He's a great deal more credulous than you, miss, having offered marriage. I accepted, naturally. 'Tis a double windfall since, on your death, your fortune will pass to him." Irritably, she moved away. "This is pointless! You must make your own plans, Jesse."

It seemed that Mignon, as her unappreciative mother had often predicted, was indeed destined to come to a bad end. With no hope but to delay the unhappy moment, she played for time. "Since you mean to kill me," she protested, in wretchedly unsteady tones, "you might at least tell me why. It was the two of you who committed the robberies, contriving to make Leda look guilty, who murdered Lord Warwick and Zoe and Mary Elphinstone?"

"It was the three of us," corrected Charity absently. Anxious as she was to leave, she could not bypass the opportunity to gloat. "That, too, is your doing. If not for Jesse's determination to have you, we would not have been drawn into this thing."

"No?" snapped Jesse. "You were already a rich man's mistress, living off the proceeds. And what will *he* say when he finds you've run off with another man? I wouldn't give a brass farthing for your chances then."

Charity shrugged. "Why should he say anything? Maurice is not a healthy man. Doubtless I'll be widowed 'ere long."

"You'd kill Maurice?" whispered Mignon, startled not so much by their callousness as that any woman would choose her brother over the Viscount, for surely it was he of whom they spoke. But why should they be concerned with the opinion of a man who lay trussed up like a chicken on the floor, one who was already slated for death? Mignon suspected that the clarity of her thinking left much to be desired.

"Why not?" asked Jesse, throwing himself sulkily onto the settee. "She's already killed one man."

"Warwick," murmured Charity. "The price I had to pay him for the aid you needed in your pursuit of Miss Montague." And then her voice trailed off as yet another person paused on the threshold.

Charity might have turned into a white-faced statue; Jesse might have frozen in his indolent position on the settee; but Mignon was on her feet in an instant and flying across the room. "Tolly!" she cried and ran into his arms. "Thank God you've come!"

"What the *devil* is all this?" inquired Lord Barrymore, in strained tones which may have been accounted for by the fact that Charity had drawn a deadly little pistol. "Miss Montague, what are you doing here?"

"I had to come!" Mignon babbled against his chest, in an excess of relief. "Jesse was going to blackmail me. Oh, Tolly, they were behind everything, the robberies and the murders! They admitted as much."

"Did they?" He sounded thoughtful, and Mignon peered anxiously into his face.

"They mean to kill Dulcie, too," she added. "Tolly, we must stop them!"

"I see," said Lord Barrymore. "This causes a great upheaval in my plans." He set Mignon gently aside and smiled down at her. "You are very like your aunt, you know, though without her acumen. I believe the Baroness had already determined that Jesse and Charity robbed Rundle and Brydges, that Jesse broke into Lady Coates' home and stole her faro bank, and heaven only knows what else." He looked at Jesse. "You damned bungler! Everything would have gone off perfectly well had you not mixed up those banknotes."

"It was you." Mignon was horrified. "Not Ivor! *You* are the third person, the rich man whose mistress Charity is. Dear God, you cannot be in need of wealth. Why did you do it?" Was it her imagination, or had the Viscount stirred?

If Lord Barrymore noted Miss Montague's tendency to babble, he attributed it to a logical nervousness. "To prove that I could," he replied amiably. "At first it was no more than a pleasant diversion. Then *you* came onto the scene, dear Mignon, and the matter grew more serious. I gained not only accomplices, but an unwitting ally." With a finger, he flicked her cheek. "You were of invaluable assistance in keeping me informed of your aunt's endeavors! Initially, I contrived to make your acquaintance through mere curiosity, to see what manner of female had so enthralled poor Jesse. Then it amused me to take a more active role, thinking that when you overcame your infatuation, as you were bound to do, our Jesse being devilish handsome but not particularly bright, you would turn to me."

Mignon looked at the actor, still sprawled on the settee, his face petulant. "I was a fool," she said somberly. They were all looking at her. What, she thought frantically, was she to do?

"Ah, well," commiserated Tolly, "I was willing to overlook that. A pity, dear Mignon, that you did not allow me to sweep you off your feet."

"It would have mattered little," Charity interrupted waspishly. "Whichever of them you wed, you would not have lived long." Her smile was cruel. "It is not difficult to contrive an unfortunate accident!"

With a little sob, Mignon backed away. Once more she knelt by Ivor, taking comfort from the warmth of his body, the steadiness of his pulse.

"Very touching," remarked Lord Barrymore, as Mignon dabbed at the Viscount's forehead, bloody from a cut. "How much help had you to subdue Jeffries, Jesse? I doubt you could inflict that much damage alone."

Jesse scowled. "They've been paid," he muttered. "They'll keep their tongues still."

"I wonder why I tolerate your ineptitude!" sighed Tolly. "It is due to your cousin, of course." He gazed blandly upon his mistress. "Which reminds me, dear Charity, that you appear dressed for traveling. Planning a midnight flit, my dear? Perhaps to Gretna Green? But you have not even asked about the success of this evening's endeavors!"

Charity's expression was extremely venal. "You got it?"

"I did." Lord Barrymore smiled. "The Bank of England has been relieved of a great deal of bullion, no thanks to your efforts. Your swain must be growing restless, my dear, for you have kept him waiting overlong."

That Charity had turned ashen beneath her makeup, and that Jesse had tensed, went unnoticed by Mignon. She was staring down into Ivor's face, regretting all the harsh words that had passed between them and her own lack of faith in him. Now she would have no chance to apologize. Miss Montague gritted her teeth. How easily she had been brought to a standstill.

"We have wasted too much time," Tolly continued, in different, more authoritative tones. Charity spun around, the pistol once more trained on Ivor. "It will look like poor Mignon killed Jeffries, her partner in crime, and then, guilt-ridden, committed suicide. Not here, of course; but I have the perfect place in mind." He frowned. "A note explaining all, I think, but that can be penned in Bligh House. Come!"

As if on cue, the glass in the French windows shattered with such force that shards and fragments of broken wood and glass exploded into the room. Lady Bligh, looking remarkably unruffled in a fur-trimmed black cloth mantle and an oval-brimmed bonnet tied with a rakish bow beneath her chin, made an entrance as effective as any Shakespearean heroine. In her hand was an extremely efficient-looking pistol. "That wraps it up nicely," said the Baroness. "Jessop, see to the door."

With an agility that belied his battered appearance, Ivor sprang to his feet. He smiled down at Mignon, his brown eyes no longer cold and suspicious, but glowing with a combination of excitement and something less easily defined. "Jessop!" hissed Dulcie, her dark eyes intent on her captives, all of whom showed signs of recovering from their stunned shock. "Do stop making sheep's eyes at my niece and admit our reinforcements. Any effort at escape is useless, Barrymore."

What inspired him to such folly no one could later say, but even as Ivor was admitting Gibbon, Willie and a disheveled Crump, Tolly sprang. Without so much as an eyelid's blink, the Baroness discharged her weapon into his heart.

It was not to be expected that the remaining culprits would allow themselves to be taken calmly off to gaol, but their struggle was brief. Jesse was quickly overpowered by a wild-eyed Gibbon, in league with a frenzied Crump, while Charity went down to defeat when Willie broke a vase over her head. The only further casualty was Lord Jeffries, who received a wound in the arm when Charity's pistol was discharged.

"Poor Mignon!" said Dulcie, apparently no whit disturbed by the fact that a corpse lay at her feet. "It was necessary that we hear the truth from their own lips, but I did not intend you to be placed in danger. If only you had heeded me and stayed safely in bed! Your rebellion caused us a few bad moments and inspired a rapid change of plans." She smiled, a trifle complacently. "It worked out nicely, did it not? All in all, you have done very well, child!"

Miss Montague had no ear for her aunt's accolade, nor eyes even for Tolly's corpse. She stared with horror at the blood that gushed from Ivor's arm. "It's nothing," he murmured. Twittering, Willie fashioned and applied a makeshift tourniquet. "Truly, my darling! May I tell you how very, very sorry I am to have so grievously misjudged you?"

"No more so than I did you," replied Mignon gruffly, unable to drag her eyes away from his gory coat. "You couldn't help but think what you did. I should have told you the truth."

"Mignon," remarked the Baroness, as she callously rifled through Lord Barrymore's coat pockets, "is exceedingly magnanimous. It seems an odd moment for a proposal, Jessop, in front of all these witnesses."

Lord Jeffries ignored this impudent interruption. "I've had a special license burning a hole in my pocket for a week," he murmured, drawing Mignon closer with his good arm. Willie sighed. "My darling, we have got off to a wretched start. Shall we put all that behind us and get to know each other properly, perhaps on a cruise to the Aegean?"

"In case you're wondering," Dulcie remarked, rising to her feet, "it's an honorable alliance he's offering you, Mignon! The man adores you, though he has neglected to say so. Shockingly remiss in you, Jessop, though we must recall that you have been under no small strain."

Mignon roused from her trance to glower at her aunt. "Do you," she whispered, looking at last at Ivor's face, "care for me?"

"No," retorted the Viscount, lips twitching. "It's your freckles, remember? I've a positive obsession and must count them if it is the last thing I do."

It was all too much for Miss Montague. She burst into tears.

"Excellent," said Lady Bligh, dangling an ornate key. "It is not every day that one can solve a series of crimes, dispose of an arch villain, and promote a love match, all in the space of one short hour!"

Chapter Thirty

They occupied the largest room in Bligh House, which was referred to by the Baron as the "Folly," due to the fact that it was impossible to properly heat, and by his more conventional ancestors as the "Great Hall." Great it was, mused Mignon, measuring as it did almost one hundred and fifty feet in length, the walls hung with the first damask made in England, a Spitalfields silk with profuse floral patterns on a rich plum-red ground. The elaborate coved ceiling was patterned with octagons and diamonds, painted with figures by Angelica Kauffmann, picked out in blue and crimson. A deep cornice was decorated with landscapes and portrait panels; circular recesses held vases and busts. The huge doorways were of Italian Renaissance design; the windows were relieved with mirrors and panels in relief, worked in *stucco duro* polished to a marble effect; and the furniture included a set of crimson damask, a pale green and carved gilt set of Louis XIV petit point, and chairs covered in convent-worked needlepoint.

"It all began," said Lady Bligh serenely, "or *our* part of it began, when Barrymore dined with Warwick two days before the murder and unintentionally paid his debt with forged banknotes. He realized the error too late, and when Tolly received a note from Warwick requesting a discussion of a very serious matter, he decided the man had to be silenced, permanently."

"The mix-up over the banknotes was Jesse's fault," offered Miss Montague, who looked extremely fetching in a gown of gossamer satin with festooned trimming, bordered with gold satin *rouleaux*. "And *I* am to blame for Tolly's knowledge of Leda's enmity with Warwick. I'm sorry! Gossip seemed a good way to keep his mind from other things. So they broke into her home and stole the weapon, and Charity shot him."

The Baroness nodded, her lilac plumage gently trembling. She wore an extremely bold gown of lilac and silver, with a petticoat of silver tissue edged with fringe, and her rich copper curls were arranged in an artfully disheveled style. She looked, thought her niece irreverently, like an expensive courtesan.

"Humph!" said Dulcie, with an arch glance at Mignon. "Dressed to look like Leda, Charity shot Warwick. But cold-blooded murder was not among Charity's accomplishments, clever though she may have been. She panicked and fled without the forged notes. They were in quite a tangle when the things disappeared. It is no doubt lucky for Simpkin that no one guessed he'd appropriated them." The Baroness rearranged herself in the chair, leaving no doubt that hers was not a body imprisoned in corsets or swathed with unnecessary garments. Mignon looked hastily away.

"A gratifying turn-out," murmured Lady Bligh, as she, too, gazed at the milling crowd. From the Ballroom issued music. "A pity John refused to attend! I fear he is still angry about what he calls my 'underhandedness.' As if I had not allowed Crump to be in on the kill!"

"Sir John will forgive you, I'm sure." Mignon spoke absently, her attention riveted on a tall figure that made its way through the throng. Surreptitiously, she glanced at her reflection in a circular convex mirror, the hollow molding of the frame filled with gilt balls, the outer edge reeded and topped by a carved eagle.

"Don't fidget, Mignon!" snapped her aunt, then smiled. "Jessop!" She held out an amethyst-encrusted hand. "And Leda. Well, Percy, I'm delighted you could attend."

Though Lord Calvert looked anything but gratified, he executed a formal bow. "I'm told I've a great deal to thank you for," he muttered. "Abominable proceedings, but we must put a good face on it. Protect the family name and all."

"Yes," murmured Lady Bligh. "You have no choice but to acknowledge Leda now."

Mignon observed Lord Calvert with interest—after all, she was to become one of his family. Percy was a portly gentleman, whose high color indicated a tendency to overindulge in food and drink and whose florid features wore an expression of extreme disapproval. Beside him, Leda was an incongruous figure, her customary black enlivened by a striped turban of sheer gauze and velvet trimmed with aigrettes and feathers. At least, reflected Mignon, she would not have to worry about wounding the sensibilities of her mama-in-law.

"So you knew," said Leda to her hostess, "that Barrymore was behind the crimes? Seems to me you let the thing drag out an unconscionable long time."

"Let us say instead," protested the Baroness, rather icily, "that I suspected, and my suspicions were confirmed by Brummell and Trouffant, as well as by my butler. Gibbon had Barrymore's stickpin, you see, and I recognized it from a description I had read some time ago in the Hue and Cry. I might add that various items of interest to the authorities have been discovered in rooms at the Albany which Barrymore had under an assumed name. All the booty was there, including the proceeds of the various robberies, and the things Mignon brought back from Mary Elphinstone's."

"You were aware of Barrymore's nature, yet you let him court your niece." Percy's tone was severe, as was the glance he bestowed upon Mignon.

"Of course," replied Dulcie, unperturbed. "What better way to keep him under my eye? Tolly was extremely enterprising, and more than clever. Had he not utilized less-than-brilliant accomplices, we might never have found him out."

"You knew Charity was his mistress?" asked Mignon, then blushed. Well brought up young ladies should not know of such creatures, let alone speak of them. Lord Calvert frowned.

"I knew," retorted the Baroness, "that she wasn't a maidservant, and that she hadn't been sent round by Fenton's Agency, as she claimed. It was vastly diverting to watch her at her game." She glanced at Leda. "It was Jesse, of course, who paid your way at Newgate, as it was Jesse who, on Tolly's instructions, sent you incriminating notes. Once you were implicated, it was child's play to keep the finger of suspicion pointed at you and away from them."

"And a damned good job of it they did!" growled Lord Calvert, watching with dismay the approach of Crump. Blandly, Lady Bligh performed introductions. "Percy!" said Leda gaily. "I believe you thought I was guilty."

Lord Calvert turned crimson, and Dulcie intervened. "Crump! What of those threads?"

"Found at the scene of the crime at White's," explained the Runner to his bewildered companions. He was in an expansive frame of mind, inspired by a staggering amassment of rewards, and not only from the government. "They matched one of Barrymore's waistcoats right enough. It was he who stole the silver plate." His own waistcoat was a fanciful creation of purple brocade. Crump frowned. "And you were right about Saint-Cyr. He *was* transported, for theft, and had only recently returned to the country before he made the acquaintance of Miss Montague." He glanced at Mignon. "She must have seemed a godsend! I don't know how you figured that, Baroness."

"I have my methods." Lady Bligh waggled a finger. "In the future, it would benefit you to confide in me, Crump." The Runner responded to this promise of continued collaboration with a face of woe.

"It was *you!*" gasped Mignon, stepping forward. "The horseman I saw that night. I thought you were drunk."

"Aye, miss." Crump saw no reason to explain that his appearance had not been due to overindulgence in the grape but to a vast ineptitude with the reins; or that, had not the wretched beast taken the bit between its teeth, he would have arrived much earlier on the scene. "It beats me, Baroness, why you allowed your niece to become so heavily implicated, even letting her risk her neck."

"That is a question," remarked Ivor grimly, "that has also occurred to me. You failed to inform me that Mignon was to be placed in so vile a situation, Lady Bligh, when you put your proposition to me."

"What proposition?" inquired Mignon suspiciously. "Heavens! Did you *let* yourself be taken captive?"

"I did." Ruefully, Ivor regarded his wounded arm, which rested in a sling. "It had to look authentic—although I did not expect that the ruffians would get so carried away. But that is not all, I fear."

"What else?" Mignon demanded, her suspicions growing apace with the sheepish expression that spread across the Viscount's handsome face.

"Calm yourself, Mignon," advised her aunt. "I merely made use of the material at hand. Ironic, isn't it, that only Jessop should have come to question your innocence, as the villains intended? And fortunate that he brought his suspicions to me! Once Jessop had learned the truth of those banknotes from Sir John, I had no choice but to take him into my confidence lest he go roaring about like a bull in a china shop, ruining all my plans."

Miss Montague's freckled features were indicative of mingled indignation and a wrath so profound that it left her speechless. The Baroness leaned forward to pinch her niece's cheek. "Jessop *did* apologize to you for his misinterpretation of your character, albeit a bit later than he wished. After all, you would have been likely to consign your actor to blazes had you known that Ivor knew the truth and did not blame you for it, and that *I* had no intention of allowing the brute to vilify your reputation. Heaven only knows what Jesse would have done then—something damned unpleasant, I'll wager! As to the other, we could hardly take time that night to see you safely home. Our purpose was to catch the villains red-handed, not give them the opportunity to flee."

Mignon closed her lips against angry words. If not for her folly, none of them would have come into contact with Jesse or Charity or Lord Barrymore. "Little did I suspect," mused the Baroness, "what a contretemps would ensue when I had you to Town."

"How did you know of my association with Jesse?" queried Mignon. "At least you might tell me that."

"So I might," said Lady Bligh, "though by now you should have realized. Maurice may be a pompous ass, but he is sincerely concerned with your welfare. He wrote and begged that I should have you come to me, giving me a sketchy outline of the reasons. I suspected your suitor would follow you with all due haste, but it wasn't till I set eyes on Jesse that I realized the suitor could only be he." Delicately, she fiddled with her low-cut bodice. "Speaking of Maurice, I might add that he never seriously meant to elope with his mysterious Mrs. Harrington-Smythe. Your brother knew you were in some sort of difficulty, Mignon, and suspected that his mysterious ladylove might somehow be involved. On the evening of my gala he took the opportunity to follow her home from the theatre and was no little bit surprised when she led him here." The Baroness secured her audience's undivided attention by wriggling in a manner that revealed a tempting expanse of bosom. "Poor Maurice! I fear he had no opportunity to distinguish himself. Lest he thrust his nose into my plans. I switched dinner plates with him. On the fateful night, Maurice only got as far as the stables before the drug took hold. He snored till dawn in a horse stall."

Crump cleared his throat and rocked back on his heels. "If you don't mind, Baroness, there are a couple of things I'd like to know. For one, that handkerchief."

Lady Bligh giggled mischievously. "You must learn, dear Crump, when a clue is not a clue! That item has absolutely no bearing on the matter, belonging to none other than the Regent. Perhaps you might like to return it to him?"

Crump gazed at that stout gentleman, staggering in state attire, and thought he would not. He glanced at Leda. "One other thing," he added, in stern tones. "Just what is the source of those funds of yours?"

"Precisely what I told you." Leda was angelic. "Percy has subsidized me all these years."

"Why?" demanded the Runner. The Viscount looked thoughtful and his uncle, embarrassed.

"Tsk, Crump!" reproved Dulcie. "A lady must retain some secrets, particularly in regard to her indiscretions. It has little bearing on the case."

"An actor." Casting about for diversion, Lord Calvert fixed upon Mignon. "I cannot think, nephew, that your young lady is quite the thing."

"Nephew," stressed the Baroness, before Ivor could voice an indignant retort. "That is the key word, I believe. There is an old adage, Calvert, suggesting that people who live in glass houses should refrain from throwing stones."

Percy's flushed features had turned ashen. He looked accusingly at Leda. "You told her?"

"I told no one," retorted Leda. Ivor looked stunned. "Save Mary Elphinstone, and that was a confession for which I dearly paid. For years the wretch blackmailed me."

"That will teach you," Lady Bligh said severely, "the dangers of drowning one's sorrows." Crump followed the odd conversation with bewilderment. Could it be that Viscount Jeffries was not Lord Calvert's nephew, but his son?

Mignon, who had come to a similar conclusion, took pity on Percy's distress. "So you went to Jesse's apartments," she murmured to Dulcie, "hoping to catch them all with their misgotten gains. I don't understand why they had to kill Mary Elphinstone."

"They didn't *have* to," said Dulcie. "I fancy Barrymore enjoyed murder for its own sake. They had rifled Leda's lodgings, you will recall, and doubtless found among her papers some reference to Mary Elphinstone. It seemed to Tolly a perfect opportunity, I imagine, to have Leda appear guilty of Mary's murder in case she somehow cleared herself of Warwick's death. Consequently, the footprints around the well, made by Leda's shoes, which I imagine Charity wore."

"She did," said Mignon with conviction, remembering the day she'd seen the maidservant limping so noticeably. "I suppose the jewels were left there for Bow Street to find, implicating Leda in the robberies?"

"Yes." The Baroness favored Crump with a severe look. "Bow Street overlooked a great deal! Zoe, of course, was killed because she refused to disprove Ivor's alibis. It was Charity, incidentally, who released the truth of Ivor's relationship with Leda to the newspapers. You will recall, Jessop, that I tried to prevent your untimely confession. Charity made a practice of listening at keyholes."

"It seems to me, Baroness," said Crump testily, "that you could have prevented a great deal of this!"

"Proof, Crump, proof." Lady Bligh looked unaccountably bland. "One cannot proceed on mere conjecture. And Mignon, given the opportunity, displayed considerable spirit."

Leda cackled. "I told you, girl, that your aunt would have plans for you." She squinted at the milling crowd, then raised her voice. "Willie!" Lord Calvert winced.

Willie fluttered up to them and saluted Dulcie's hand. "I have a present for you, Lady Bligh!" He dropped a rather untidy package into her lap. "A token of my appreciation for your enterprise."

"I do adore surprises!" said the Baroness, with an odd glance at the doorway. "I take it you've had a successful interview with Kean?"

"I have." Willie's pale face was blissful. "He has agreed to replace Jesse, though at a staggering price. Alas, that so noble a figure should nevermore tread the boards! Such are the workings of Fate, I suppose."

"A noble figure, indeed," mocked Dulcie, her slender fingers busy untying knots. "Had not Jesse had so great an urge to triumph on the stage, you would have been killed after forging those banknotes. Tolly was not one to leave potentially dangerous tools lying idly around." Her voice was very stern. "Don't you think it time you explained those abraded knuckles of yours?"

Willie looked wounded. "Never had I thought to see so many aspersions cast upon my character!" He spread his hands and flexed his fingers, looking remarkably like a bird preparing for flight. "I suppose it makes no difference now to admit that there were not one but two attempts made on my life." He sighed heavily. "Hired thugs, no doubt. They could not be expected to know that a journalist early learns a certain nimbleness of foot and manual expertise! Though I may be slight of stature, I am not less handy with my fists than with my pen."

Leda snorted. "Does this successful play mean that you will no longer wield that pen in my behalf, Willie? Has the world seen the last of the Bystander?" Mignon watched as her aunt arranged exquisite china figures of actors and actresses—Quinn as Falstaff, Garrick as Tancred, Mrs. Cibber as Vivandiere—on a sidetable.

"Why, Leda!" Willie raised his monocle, this one on a black velvet ribbon and set in gold. "Do you mean to continue with your career? I had thought you might retire from the profession now that your circumstances have so drastically changed."

"Retire?" Leda was offended. "Never! I would never consider such a thing." Lord Calvert uttered a sound remarkably like a moan.

"Pardon," said Ivor, and took Mignon's hand. She gazed up at him dreamily. "Does that mean what I think it does?"

"Yes," replied his mother calmly, "though I quite forgot to tell you in the fuss. Your uncle and I have decided at last to, er, legalize our relationship."

"Better late than never," commented Lady Bligh, and rose gracefully to her feet. "It will save no end of legal fuss." She looked at the Runner. "You will find Gibbon presiding over the refreshments, Crump. I suggest you owe him an apology."

What Crump owed Gibbon was a tongue-lashing, and he was not at all averse to delivering it. Reflecting that Lord Calvert did not appear particularly thrilled at the prospect of matrimony, he wandered into the anteroom.

"In that case," said Willie, fingering his chin, "I believe the Bystander will write an article lauding the detective abilities of Lady Bligh. It will be a masterpiece of pithy acumen, though it will not show the authorities in a particularly favorable light." But he had lost his audience. Willie craned his neck to gawk at the doorway, as had everyone else in the huge room.

The gentleman who paused there was worthy of their fascinated attention; indeed, it was only his just due. He was tall and muscularly fashioned; his dark hair and beard were streaked with gray; his bronzed face was so magnificent of feature that he might have been called beautiful if not for the nose that was harshly aquiline, the lips that were frankly sensuous. If any of the Baron's attributes could be adjudged more remarkable than another, the prize would have to have been awarded to his black eyes. Set beneath strongly marked brows and heavy lids, those mesmeric orbs were irresistibly seductive.

The crowd parted silently as Lord Bligh strolled into the room. Like royalty, thought Mignon, though no prince she'd ever seen had possessed so regal a bearing or moved so confidently. Miss Montague now understood why the bolder of her uncle's exploits had been kept from her ears. The swashbuckling Baron's most exotic explorations had no doubt taken place in the boudoir.

As her aunt might have informed her, Mignon's deductions were correct. Maximilian Bonaventure Bligh was the most profligate of rakehells, an unparalleled voluptuary, steeped in vice and iniquity, lost alike to virtue and shame, a libertine who even in that enlightened age would practice *droit de seigneur;* and there was not a female present who didn't take one look at his compellingly amoral visage and wish that he would make her wicked, for there could surely be no more rapturous fate than to be led by the Baron into sin.

"Maximilian," said the Baroness, and held out a frail hand.

"Not Bat?" he inquired, regarding his wife with a hunger that made Mignon slightly envious. "I conclude that I am in your good graces again."

"You are." Lady Bligh cast a languid glance over his superb physique. He was clad in an elegant blue coat with gilt buttons, a white velvet waistcoat, frilled shirt and lace ruffles, light kersymore smallclothes and a muslin cravat with a huge ruby pin. Another ruby flashed on one bronzed hand. "As I will shortly demonstrate!" Dulcie's voice was husky. "But first I must make you acquainted with your niece. Mignon!"

The Baron turned and Miss Montague was subjected for the first time to the full impact of his gaze. One would have no secrets from Maximilian, she thought, dazed; those piercing eyes stripped one to the soul, exposed every vulnerability. "Charmed!" murmured Lord Bligh, and flashed his niece a smile that left her positively weak-kneed.

So forceful was the Baron's personality that the arrival of yet another guest had gone unremarked. Going unnoticed did not please Lady Montague, although in precedence Lord Bligh outranked her, the widow of a mere knight. With a viselike hand, she urged her son forward. Maurice wondered if Dulcie might help him to persuade his parent to return to Yorkshire while he remained unchaperoned in town.

"There you are!" said Lady Montague. Mignon blanched and clung to Ivor's arm. "I'd like to know just what you've been up to, miss! Your brother has been telling me the most remarkable things."

"Has he?" inquired Lady Bligh, looking a trifle bemused, perhaps due to the fact that Maximilian was blatantly caressing her bare shoulders. "Then you know that Mignon is to marry Lord Jeffries."

"My poor girl!" Lady Montague's faded beauty was not enhanced by the martyred expression that she wore. "It is not necessary. I assure you no one will force you into a marriage that is repugnant to you."

"You misunderstand, Mama," replied Mignon, not at all happy with this scene. "I *want* to marry Ivor."

"Well!" Lady Montague was remarkably displeased at the thought of losing a live-in companion who would fetch her myriad medicines, bathe her aching brow with lavender water, and who furthermore did not require to be paid. "I consider it a shocking negligence that no one has thought to consult me!"

"There was no need," replied Dulcie, leaning back in an unseemly manner against her husband's muscular chest. "Maximilian is the head of the family, and he will give his consent."

Lady Montague, no admirer of the adventurous Baron, glanced at his swarthy face, at the supple fingers which were working havoc with the Baroness's coiffure, to such good effect that Dulcie's eyes were sensually half closed, and she hastily looked away. "What of this Lord Barrymore," she demanded of her son, whose expression was long-suffering, "of whom you wrote in such glowing terms? I thought you said *he* was to marry Mignon."

"He would have liked to," replied Maurice gloomily. "Had not Dulcie shot him dead."

"Dead!" shrieked Lady Montague, staggering back a pace.

"Dulcinea," said the Baron, devils dancing in his eyes. "I congratulate you on your aim."

"Make me no compliments!" murmured Dulcie, tracing with a tantalizing finger the strong line of his jaw. "It is not felicitations that I would have from you, Maximilian, but a certain felicity!"

"I have it!" cried Willie, as the fifth Baron Bligh, to the scandalized gratification of their various guests, swept his wife off her feet and into his arms. "I shall fashion her 'the Baroness of Bow Street'! Egad, how scintillatingly clever of me."